The True Cost of Ignorance
and
False Judgement

by

K.J.Goss

The True Cost of Ignorance and False Judgement
Copyright © 2020 by K.J. Goss
All rights reserved

ISBN Number: 978-0-9997533-4-7

This story is dedicated to a very dear friend, Madison Boyce, who devoted his career to Restorative Justice

Cover design and artwork by Gene Parent, Brookfield, VT.

The True Cost of Ignorance
and
False Judgement

This is the story of one mans indomitable inner strength
against a town who would destroy him.

Chapter 1

Eileen O'Conner always enjoyed her walk up the tree sheltered dirt road to get to Bert's house. That is if you wanted to call it a road. It was more like an overgrown, undersized dirt driveway. Cars had not driven on this for many a year. Five or six to be exact. Not since young Tom Thatcher joined the Marine Corps. The bus dropped her off here Thursday of each week.

Eileen was a silver haired woman in her mid sixties. A warm loving woman, short on stature but big of heart. She was such a sweet tempered lady she never uttered an unkind word about anyone. She had been cleaning old Bert's tiny log home for quite a few years. Bert was eighty three years old and a rather frail eighty three at that. He wasn't always that way but these last few years of being completely alone except for Eileen's weekly visits finally took their toll. He was always a loner but still interacted with a few others. His actions were mostly adversarial in nature where most people just considered him an old crank. No one really knew anything about him, just that he was a bitter old man. The shame of it was no one ever tried to know him. That is except for a young boy. He and the old man were thrown together by circumstances that neither controlled.

Forgive me, I'm letting this story run away from me. Back to sweet Eileen O'Conner.

She didn't mind the walk up the nearly questionable drive. It gave her the exercise she so desperately needed. She looked forward to the solitude of the forest interrupted only by sweet song of birds and wind in the tree tops. She envied old Bert to a degree to be surrounded by natural beauty. The small vegetable garden with its broken fence was showing the signs of the early fall even though it was only early summer. There were now more weeds than vegetables. She knew the deer would soon finish that also.

As she approached the cozy cabin she realized nothing had changed since last week. There were two hand made rockers, one on either side of the center door. She always marveled of how rustic looking they appeared yet were extremely comfortable.

"That's odd." she thought. *"He doesn't usually leave his coffee mug here on the table."* She knew that people considered him a grouchy old crank, but his house was always as neat as could be. Everything had a special place and was never moved for any reason, except when she dusted of course.

Eileen took the two steps onto the rickety front porch, picked up the mug and lightly tapped on the door. She did not hear the usual grumble. She waited a few seconds and knocked again, a wee bit louder. The extra force of her knock pushed the apparently unlocked door open slightly. Before stepping in she called quietly to old Bert. There was no reply. Thinking he might be in the back garden she dared enter the small living room. There was no warm inviting fire that always made the cabin so welcoming. The cast iron pot that held his dinner was cold. She called again only to hear the echo of her own voice. She realized then how eerily cold the cabin felt without the fireplace sharing its warmth.

"A bit unusual." she thought, *"for him not to be home on this, the cleaning day."*

She had grown accustomed to him telling her how to do her job, which she instantly ignored anyway. She knew he meant nothing by it, it was just his nature.

"I'll just go about my business as if he were here grumbling incoherently." she said aloud. As was her habit she headed for the small back bedroom to start. She opened the door which was not usually closed.

"Oh, sorry Bert, I didn't think you were home.

Eileen started to close the door but Bert had not replied or even moved, for that matter. He was sitting upright in the old wooden rocking chair next to the bed. She quietly called his name again. No answer.

"Bert are you alright ?" she asked as she moved closer. It was then she realized old Bert was beyond hearing. He had passed away alone. With a tear in her eye she checked the neck pulse to confirm the obvious.

In his hand was an old newspaper picture of young Tom Thatcher just after he enlisted in the Marine Corps. The article was dated August, two thousand and nine.

Eileen said a blessing prayer for Bert then left the room. The thought that he died alone was really tugging at her heart. There was no telephone at the house so she went out to the garden area that had been cleared of trees to use her small flip phone. She did not possess one of the fancy smart phones but finally relented to her nagging daughter to have this small phone for emergency purposes. In fact this was only the second time she would actually be using it.

~ ~ ~

Twenty minutes later the unused drive had four vehicles parked by the house. Two police cars, one unmarked car and of course the ambulance. There had not been this many people in the small cabin since who knows when.

The sprightly elderly cleaning woman did not appear too shaken by Bert's passing. Being the youngest of a family of eight she had already experienced the loss of loved ones, and handled it rather well.

Everyone who was acquainted with Bert knew it was just a matter. of time with the old man, who had not been in the best of health recently. Of course there would be an autopsy which was a matter of routine anyway because of the circumstances.

Eileen was the closest thing to a friend the old man had, except for Tom Thatcher. Even that was not what most people would call a friendship. Eileen's unfaltering good nature was the perfect counterpart to Bert's grouchy behavior.

The police were satisfied with Mrs. O'Conner's explanation of the situation. She was well known in the community. In fact, probably helped raise half of the local police. She also mentioned that Bert had visited Sam McCort, one of the local lawyers, a few times in the past year.

In just under three hours the house was deserted. The police kindly gave Eileen a ride home under the circumstances.

Chapter 2

As usual with a small town, word of Bert's passing spread quickly. Quite a few townsfolk uttered that they were glad he passed because he was just an old crank who didn't care for anybody. The town would be better off without him. The younger set could not wait to get into the old man's house.

Attorney Sam McCort was aware of the feelings of others and had "No Trespassing" signs posted circling the whole property. He was even able to get the police to patrol the area a few times a day. At least until he could contact the beneficiary of the will.

~ ~ ~ ~ ~ ~

Tom Thatcher arrived back in town, separation papers in hand, a few days after Bert's funeral service which was attended by only three people. Eileen O'Conner and Sam McCort and Martha McClain, Tom's aunt Tom returned to the only family he had. An elderly aunt with a much too large house. Tom barely settled in when he received a call from Attorney McCort. He agreed to meet with Sam nine AM the following morning. All he knew was that Sam said he wanted to discuss something with him. Still holding his military habits he arrived exactly at nine o"clock. After the usual protocol greetings Tom seated himself in front of Sam's desk. On the desk in front of McCort was a sizable folder.

With folded hands the lawyer looked directly at Tom.

"Congratulations on your discharge. Welcome home and my heartfelt thanks for your service."

Tom nodded his head in thanks. He always felt a slight embarrassment with compliments.

"I'm sure by now you have heard of Bert Morrows passing. And I'm also sure that except for Eileen O'Conner, and your aunt, you were probably the only real friend the old man had."

"And I have not been around for the last six years."

"Did you at least stay in touch ?"

"To be honest with you neither one of us was much for letter writing, but yes, we did keep in touch once in a while."

"Did Bert know you were coming home ?"

"Yes, he just didn't know when. Because of my deployment in Afghanistan I wasn't even sure of a date myself."

Sam paused for a moment, took a deep breath and resumed with a more serious manner.

"I know you're staying with your aunt at the moment, but do you have any long range plans ?"

Tom looking puzzled answered;

"It's really to early to tell yet, I'm just getting used to making my own decisions again. Why do you ask ?"

"Before you enlisted the Marines you did share your time with Bert though, didn't you ?"

"Actually, yes. He fascinated me. Believe it or not I learned an awful lot from him. True he could be cantankerous at times, but if you knew him, you could get used to that. I really liked him."

"Apparently he liked you too. He thought a lot of you. He talked about you all the time, when he did talk, that is."

Both men smiled knowing how Bert was.

"He was very proud of you and let people know it too. At least the people who would talk to him."

Again Tom could feel himself glowing a touch of crimson.

"You know of course he did not have any family or even distant relatives of any kind." Sam furthered.

"Yes, Bert mentioned that a few times in a very melancholy way. I think he missed having a family. Down deep inside I believe he had a lot of love to give."

"That's not all he had to give."

Tom appeared confused by Sam's remark.

"Forgive me, I guess I'm talking in riddles. The fact is Tom, he named you his heir in his will. Everything he owned now belongs to you and you alone. The house, its furnishings, the sixty acres, and bank accounts. In his own words Bert had written, *"I know you would love and keep the forest and animals as pristine as I did. Take care of my one last true love."*

Tom felt a numbness overcome him. Was he hearing correctly ? This is either a dream or a joke. He stood and walked over to a window that looked at the main street at the edge of the small town he was now to call home. He remained there staring at nothing, his mind now a blank. Many minutes passed when Sam, somewhat concerned asked,

"Are you alright Tom ? Can I get you some water ?"
Finally breaking the trance of un-believability, Tom turned and reseated himself.

"Could you please repeat what you just said ?" He asked.
Sam McCort smiled.

"You heard correctly Tom. Old Bert left everything to you. And not to worry my fee has already been taken care of."

"I don't know what to say. How do I thank a man who has already passed ?"

"You needn't worry yourself about that. Apparently you already have thanked him. Years ago, many times over with the pleasure of your company. You made the old man happy. I'm sure you were not aware at the time, being so young and all, but from the way he spoke of you, you meant the world to him."

"And he meant the world to me." Tom thought

Reflecting back to when he was younger he realized now that Bert was the closest thing to a dad he ever had. Tom told the attorney he lost his dad in an auto accident when he was very young.

"I know my Mom did the best she could with me but I have to admit I was getting pretty wild. Believe it or not Bert is the one who straightened me out. The Marine Corps did the rest."

Tom sat quiet for a moment, his thoughts again mirroring earlier years. Sam spoke quietly bringing Tom back to the present.

"How about some coffee while we review the rest of the paper work ?"

Tom agreed and even helped himself to a mug of the black liquid. Settled back at the desk he signed some papers and the attorney handed him the house keys. He then gave him separately a lone key explaining;

"This is to a safe deposit box at the bank."

Tom accepted the key curiosity filling his head.

"Lastly he wanted you to have this also." said Sam as he offered another set of keys.

"Downstairs in the back parking lot is a dark green pickup truck. It's not new, I think it's three years old, but it is in tip top shape."

Tom could not contain his emotions any longer and allowed a few tears to roll down his cheeks.

"I'm sorry Mr. McCort, it's just that- - - - ."
Sam cut him short.

"No need for apologies son, I totally understand.

"Oh, one more thing, I almost forgot."

Sam opened his desk drawer and brought out a manilla envelope. It was sealed and taped. He offered it to Tom.

"I was instructed to hand this to you personally."

Tom accepted the beige colored envelope and read the front.

"To: SSGT. Thomas Thatcher" In the bottom corner in bold marker, "Personal and Confidential."

Tom, with a lightly trembling hand, could feel his eyes grow moist again. He was glad for Sam's interruption.

"Tell you what, now that our business is completed, let me buy you some lunch, and I will not take no for an answer."

Tom carefully tucked the envelope into his jacket.

~ ~ ~ ~

The local Country Kitchen, serving breakfast and lunch only was their destination. A short walk of a block and a half found them comfortably seated at a booth near the window. Having placed their order they continued to discuss old Bert Morrow.

The eatery was basically quiet with a few outbursts of noise now and then from a booth full of feeling their oats teen aged boys.

"I'm afraid." apologized Sam, "That they are some of Tylerville's finest youth. In fact it was that bunch and a few others that were constantly giving Bert a hard time. Surprisingly though, he was able to handle them."

Tom smiled.

"It's no surprise to me. I know what he was capable of."

"These kids couldn't wait to get out to Bert's once they heard he died. The police were very cooperative in looking after the place both day and night at my request. Otherwise they would have ransacked and wrecked the place. I tell you this just as a heads up. Just be careful."

"Thanks, I will. I figured on going out there this afternoon, care to join me ?"

"Very tempting but I have a house closing to attend to. But I would like to visit another time."

"It's an open invitation." Tom grinned.

"Just to be on the safe side, I will put the word out that a new owner has moved in."

"Thanks." said a very grateful Tom.

Lunch over they said their good-byes leaving the restaurant to the teens who were growing even louder.

Chapter 3

Tom enjoyed the ride to Bert's house with his new wheels. It had been a little more than six years but the old landmarks seemed not to have changed any. He turned into the overgrown drive thinking to himself how much work he had ahead of him to make the road more acceptable to cars or in his case his truck. He stopped at the top of the dirt drive and sat for a few moments just staring at the small log cabin, that was now his, his mind flooded with memories. And at this point in his life they were all fond and welcome thoughts.

"Get a hold of yourself Tom." he muttered out loud. "You're grown up now and yes, this is real."

He exited the truck and leisurely strolled around the yard. Laughing lightly when he saw the rear garden totally overgrown. Again he remembered how he had worked with Bert on his "Farm" as he called it. Finishing circling the cabin he approached the front door. His hand shook while putting the key in the lock. The door opened easily as he stepped into his happy past. Recalling an old habit, followed by both he and Bert, he stepped out of his shoes on a rubber mat just inside the door. He circled the room with his eyes. Nothing had changed. Everything had its place and was neat and clean.

"I hope I can live up to your standards Bert." he said aloud.

Tom wandered to the small kitchen. It was obvious Bert had still been cooking with the old cast iron wood stove. He touched the stove lovingly recalling how Bert tried to teach him how to cook on it. The refrigerator was from the fifties, but was still working. There was a small pantry off the kitchen well stocked with the necessities as was the fridge.

The bedroom was in the back overlooking the "Farm." Tom smiled to himself again. One wall was all bookshelves filled top to bottom, most of which were non fiction. Historical and true adventure dominated.

There on the corner of the antique oak dresser was Tom's boot camp picture. He had forgotten that he gave one to old Bert. He decided not to go any further with the bedroom right then. Gazing at his watch told him it was already late afternoon and he promised his aunt he would be home for supper. Tom left the special envelope, unopened, on the dresser. *"Tomorrow perhaps, when he had more time."* he thought. Feeling a bit melancholy he locked up and drove to his aunt's home.

~ ~ ~ ~ ~ ~

He discussed his whole day with Aunt Martha who was as surprised as he was.

"I knew you spent a lot of time with the old crank but I had no idea he was so fond of you."

Tom was not upset with her using the term old crank, for he knew she meant it affectionately. Aunt Martha was one of the few people who treated Bert decently realizing he had a difficult life particularly in this town. Why he ever returned here was a mystery to her after the way he had been treated by most of the town's people. She had related a few stories to Tom which barely touched Bert's life story.   He wasn't a bad man as some people thought, he just had bad breaks.

"So you'll be moving in by yourself now that you have your own house. How soon will that be ?"

"Not for a while yet so you will have to put up with me a little longer." Tom smiled.

"Not to worry my dear, I promised your mother you would always have a home and I will keep that promise."

Tom relaxed after dinner although his thoughts kept drifting to the confidential envelope. *"Tomorrow should be an interesting day."*

~ ~ ~ ~

Aunt Martha prepared a hearty breakfast and was off to her sewing club. Tom cleaned up the dishes for his aunt so she could get to her meeting. Once he cleaned up the kitchen and himself he headed for the bank in town before going to the cabin.

At the bank he showed proper ID when asked. Luckily the bank manager recognized Tom from before he went into the service. Sam McCort had already given a heads up about Tom's inheritance.

The safe deposit was retrieved and Tom was shown to a private cubicle. Both nervous and excited, he unlocked the metal container. There was a single legal sized envelope therein, and that's all there was. His name was printed boldly on the envelope.

"What other surprises does Bert have for me." he mumbled under his breath.

Using his pocket knife he carefully and as neatly as possible opened the envelope. He withdrew a life insurance policy with a cover letter attached. The letter was in Bert's own hand.

Tom,
The enclosed insurance policy I purchased for myself naming you as my beneficiary. I know the house and property are going to need repares. This should help ease the burden of repair expenses. Use it wisely as I know you will. Sam McCort will assist you with cashing in the policy.
Good luck my friend. I hope you have a son someday that you can teach what I hope you learned from me. Never forget your roots. I wish you the world.
Love Bert.

Tom opened the policy itself revealing the amount of thirty five thousand dollars.

A tear or two dropped on the letter as Tom tried to keep his hands from trembling. He rested for a few minutes before returning the box and key to the bank manager informing him he no longer needed the safe box.

~ ~ ~ ~

He was admiring his new vehicle and mentally thanked Bert as he drove to the newly acquired home. "That sounds funny. Me having a home of my own and money besides." He was talking to himself again. Something he got in the habit of while serving in Afghanistan.

The drive was about twenty five minutes out of town to the north. As he turned into the drive approaching the cabin he saw a beat up old truck with a few teens just exiting the vehicle. He recognized two from the Country Kitchen yesterday.

"Can I help you boys ?" Tom asked politely.

Shock and surprise registered on the faces of the three young boys. One of them answered in a very smug voice;

"What's it to you, Mac ?"

"Oh, nothing in particular, it's just that this is my house and I thought you wanted something of me."

"This is old Bert's place and we come to check out what he left us."

The three teens laughed together at this.

"Oh so I guess you have a key also. That's funny, the attorney never mentioned another key to me."

Suddenly facial expressions changed.

"So if you boys don't mind removing yourselves I would like to go into my house."

Slowly, grumbling all the time, they reentered their truck. As they drove back to the road they were all screaming four letter epithets along with various hand gestures.

"You have a nice day also." Tom called after them. He laughed as he walked to the door but did caution himself to keep a watchful eye. In fact he decided to stop by the police department on the way to his aunt's that afternoon.

~ ~ ~ ~

As he did the day before he just stood by the door taking in the simple beauty of the log home. There was something soft and warm about the log interior. The warmth was not interrupted by gaudy colored paint. The natural beauty of the wood asked you to come in and enjoy.

The furniture was plain but blended to the overall atmosphere of simplicity. The main fireplace was large. Big enough to handle free swinging cooking irons that would hold iron stew pots or coffee kettles.

Memories came flooding back of winter evenings he spent with Bert being mesmerized by the burning logs. An old six foot long revolutionary era musket hung proudly above the mantle. This was Bert's pride and joy. The five volume set of the history of George Washington and the revolutionary war by Washington Irving stood neatly on one side of the mantle. The other side was balanced by an antique pewter candelabra holding three bees wax candles of different size.

A simple braided rug had its place of honor in front of the hearth. He recalled Bert saying it had belonged to his mother. It was about the only possession that remained as a memory of her. To Bert it meant the world.

Tom vowed then and there that he would always treasure it as his friend did.

The loud cry of a raven from the surrounding forest nudged Tom back to the present. He stepped all the way into the house and closed the door. As he took off his shoes he was thinking that it was hard to believe that this was now his home. He truly loved Bert, as so often happens it was now too late to tell or show him. He felt bad that he had missed him by only days. Perhaps he could have made a difference. He knew, down deep, this was just wishful thinking.

"Remember the good things Tom." he told himself to pull out of the down funk he was in.

He would eventually settle in here but there was no immediate rush. He still had his aunt to consider and look for a job. The employment could wait for a few weeks. He would allow himself a break after six years in the Corps. Which included three deployments in Iraq and Afghanistan. Remembering the envelope from yesterday he went to the bedroom and retrieved it from the dresser. He sat on the edge of the bed studying the rather thick packet memories flooding his mind again. After sitting idle for a time he finally broke the seal and opened the flap. There were quite a few paper clipped groups of pages. When he removed the papers he noticed a key fell out from among them. Peering inside there were three other keys. They were all dumped out onto the bed. There were four groups of paper work, each with a number tag attached.

"**T**ypical of Bert, always organized." Tom said aloud.

He examined the keys, each, as the papers, had a number inked on it. Tom figured the numbers were there for a reason, so he reached for the papers marked ONE. Removing the blank cover page revealed Bert's hand script, neat and legible.

Tom,

Please read carefully and pay strict attention. As you have seen by now there are four keys, each has a purpose. Read all the paperwork first before you attempt to figure out the keys.

Tom smiled recalling Bert always spoke as if teaching, which is what it actually was. Thinking back he did learn a lot from Bert, not even realizing it at the time.

"You have surmised by now, I'm sure, that you are the recipient of my life. It was not all for naught as most people think. Perhaps even you. You were the closest thing to family I ever had. I truly thought of you as my son. You made me especially proud when you joined my beloved Marine Corps."

Tom put the paper down staring across the room at nothing. "His Corps ?" I never knew he was a marine. Smiling again, "I guess it stands to reason, the way his whole life was structured. At least the life I know of." Tom was once more speaking out loud to no one. He continued reading.

"That brings me to key # 1. Upstairs in the loft you will

find, among many other things, a large metal trunk, locked of course. In it are assorted journals that I have been keeping over the years. You may read them if you wish. They are nothing but my rambling's about my disconnected life. When you are finished with them, whether you read them or not, please burn them. I would not want them to fall into the wrong hands to allow further ridicule by people who do not take the time to learn of others misfortune or future."

Tom again put the paper down reflecting on what he just read. He felt a sense of sorrow for the old man. He actually hurt for him. Before he got too carried away with his feelings he read on.

"If you choose to read them, remember this is only one mans opinion of his own life. The journals are numbered so that you may follow my story that I did not have time to relate to you. I would have liked very much to have shared them with you in person."

Tom could sense his emotions welling up. Laying the paper down, he made his way to the kitchen and prepared some coffee. Mug in hand he went to the porch to his favorite rocker. He took a deep breath and concentrated on the sounds of the surrounding forest. His thoughts drifted to the earlier days and his time with Bert. At times even he thought Bert to be grouchy but all in all he enjoyed those days and a few evenings. He was glad his aunt did not object.

Tom refilled his coffee and returned to the confidential envelope. He neatly put number one back in the envelope and reached for the second.

"With this note also goes a key, naturally labeled # 2. This is the key to the safe deposit box at Tylerville National Bank. They never liked to see me in their establishment but they had no choice. Sometimes I would go there just to watch the reactions."

Tom smiled again picturing the scene in his mind.

"When you decide to retrieve what is in the box take Attorney Sam McCort with you. There are two reasons for this request. First the bank will then not give you a hard time.

Secondly, it will be up to Sam to follow up on my instructions with your oversight of course. You may trust Sam implicitly."

He returned this second note to the larger envelope. Tom Thatcher wanted to rest his eyes and decided to walk outside for a bit. *"I wonder what other surprises are in store for me."* Bert himself was turning out to be his biggest surprise.

~ ~ ~ ~

He truly welcomed the break, his thoughts going to spring when he would plant the garden. Fresh veggie's would also be welcomed by his aunt.

He decided he could take care of the fence repair this fall to be ready for the Spring. Making his way to the pond he noticed the beavers had been busy. He watched as one lone beaver was still at work.

"Don't get too carried away there young fellow, we still need the creek to flow." Tom said quietly.

The beaver stared at him for a second or two then proceeded to resume his building.

Tom laughed answering with; "Thanks for your interest."

He wandered further into the woods enjoying the serenity.

"Far cry from Afghanistan." he thought.

Walking quietly which he learned to do so well in combat, he surprised a doe and her fawn feeding on the rich greens by the creek edge. Mama deer, startled at first sensed she was in no danger and went about her grazing. Tom, sensitive to her feelings, faded away in the opposite direction.

"The old man made the right decision on choosing to live here. You couldn't ask for more privacy and yet be relatively close to a town. Remembering a promise to his aunt to take her shopping this afternoon he headed back to the log cabin, secured the papers and locked up. His aunt was waiting when he returned.

~ ~ ~ ~ ~ ~

The next day Tom spent helping his aunt around the house. After all there was no particular hurry to get to the cabin. He cleaned up after lunch, kissed his aunt goodbye and drove to his new home. The day was warm with bright sunshine so he carried the envelope out side to the handmade rocking chair.

Paper number three, and of course, a matching key.

This group of instructions is again different. It also pertains to a safe deposit box. The location of which is, I'm afraid, a bit of a distance. It is with Chase Manhattan Bank in New York City."

"There's a bit of sophistication." thought Tom smiling .

"This box contains very important information pertaining to others. If necessary you may consult Sam McCort. I repeat to you that he can be trusted with anything you may want to share with him. You will understand more after you read the contents. From then on everything will become your own decision."

"What other surprises do you have in store for me Bert ?" Tom laughed again as he returned Number three to the large envelope. *"It's still early, so I may as well go on to number four.*

"This next and last key I entrust to you and you alone. There is a second and smaller box in the loft, locked of course. The contents would only mean something to you and me. I'm sure no one else would be interested. Do with it what you feel is necessary. I trust your judgement. I always did. I am proud of you and always have been. This, I guess, will be our last contact.
I love you son."

Tears this time did overwhelm Tom and he cried openly into the crushed paper in his hand. He sobbed uncontrollably for many minutes. A curious squirrel chattering at his feet finally caught his attention. With a shaky voice Tom spoke to his furry friend.

"You understand, don't you pal ?"

The squirrel answered with a twitch. Tom knew automatically that he did. He sat there rocking for another hour not even paying attention that dusk was enveloping the cabin.

He drove back to his aunt's yet feeling down. He knew she would be able to cheer him up because of her always positive attitude. He looked forward to her company.

Chapter 4

Tom was up early and in the kitchen long before his aunt stirred. He needed his morning coffee. His night was a restless one, he was not able to tune out his thoughts and memories. Right now everything appeared to play on emotions. As he sipped his coffee he thought of the four keys and four sets of instructions. He was positive he wanted to pursue all four, but which to do first.

*"**P**erhaps I should stick to Bert's order."* he thought. *"I wonder how many journals he's talking about. Probably just a few note papers with scribbles on them. I guess I will start with number one."*

Aunt Martha entered the kitchen just as Tom was refilling his coffee.

"**M**y, you're up bright and early." she commented.

"**I** hope I wasn't making too much noise to awaken you."

"**N**o need to worry about that my dear. My internal alarm has been going off at the same time for years." she smiled. "What are your plans for today Tom ? Back to your own house to do some more straightening up ?"

"**T**here's really not much to take care of Aunt Martha. Bert was super neat. Would you like to come with me to see the place ?"

"**I**'d love to dear, but not today. Our garden club meets today to plan for our fall festival. Some other day perhaps."

"**W**ell have fun with your garden group. I probably will go out there again. There are a few more things I want to look into."

"**O**h, by the way, I almost forgot. Sam McCort called yesterday afternoon. If you get a chance today drop by his office. He didn't mention why but did say there was no immediate hurry."

"**T**hanks, maybe I'll drop in before I go to the cabin."

Tom helped his aunt clean up after breakfast and wished her a good day as she left for the garden club. After cleaning himself up he headed for the attorneys office.

He was there just before ten AM.

"**T**om I see you got my message. Good to see you again. All is well I hope ?"

"Everything is fine Mr. McCort."

"Sam, if you please. I have an idea we are going to be seeing a lot of each other for a while."

Smiling, Tom agreed with him.

"Why did you want to see me today ?"

"There is another insurance policy that old Bert had taken out naming Eileen O'Conner as beneficiary. I thought perhaps under the circumstances that you would like to give it to her. As you know she had been with Bert for a number of years."

"Yes, I also remember her from when I was a teen. She really is a sweet lady. I would love to bring a little cheer to her life."

Laughing a little Sam said;

"That's not hard to do. She appears to be happy all the time."

Tom laughed along.

Driving to Eileen's Tom was trying to recall how long it had been since he had last seen Mrs. O'Conner. He had no problem remembering where her old farm house was. It was obvious that she still grew a variety of vegetables and of course her flowers were always picture perfect.

Pulling into the driveway he noticed a car with out of state plates. He hesitated for a moment not wanting to disturb Eileen if she had visitors. Just dropping the paper off would be okay he decided. He rang the bell and waited admiring the full blooms around the front porch.

The door was answered by a strikingly beautiful dark haired woman with sparkling blue green eyes. Tom was so taken aback by the vision before him he was speechless for a time. Finally stuttering a hello he introduced himself then asked for Mrs. O'Conner. Eileen, from deeper in the house knew the voice.

"Tommy, my lad, come in, come in. I heard you were back."

Now face to face she threw her arms around him in her usual motherly bear hug.

"My, you're quite a picture of a man now. Don't you think so Arlene ?"

Both Tom and Arlene were slightly embarrassed by Eileens straight forward remark. With her eyes staring directly at Tom's, Arlene confirmed her aunt's opinion.

"Yes, that grand he is."

Tom could detect a slight Irish lilt in her voice.

"It's good to have you home my boy. My condolences on Bert's passing. I know you meant much to each other. He really was a good man no matter what other people said. Come in dear, come on and sit."

Tom followed Eileen and Arlene to the living room never taking his eyes from Arlene.

"Oh, forgive my manners Tommy, this cute little thing is my niece. She's just over from the old country. Maybe you would be kind enough to show her around, not that there's much to see in this town."

Again a faint blush could be seen on both young faces.

"That would not be a hardship at all, Mrs. O'Conner." Tom answered his eyes still on Arlene.

"So what is it you came to see me about ?"

Not wanting to, but turning to Eileen he answered;

"Oh, I almost forgot. I guess you know by now Bert left me his house and a few other things."

"And no one deserves it more than you my boy. You were Bert's whole world. That tough old bird stuff was just an act. He was really a pussy cat."

Removing an envelope from inside his jacket Tom offered it to Mrs. O'Conner.

"This Bert entrusted to you."

Eileen accepted the envelope her curiosity showing.

"What's he up to now. Probably a note telling me how to clean his house." she laughed as she opened the seal.

She extracted a group of papers with a cover letter written by Bert.

"My dear Mrs. O'Conner,

You have truly been a very precious lady and dear friend. If it had not been for you and that rascal Tom, I would have really been grouchy as most people thought of me. You brightened my day every time you came. I know I paid you for your labors, but not nearly enough for the joy you brought to my life. Enclosed is just a little something to show my true appreciation. Look after Tom for me.

Your friend, I hope, Bert.

P.S. You forgot to dust the mantle."

"See, didn't I tell you he would complain." Eileen laughed along with a tear in her eye.

Putting the letter aside, she opened the tri folded paper.

"Oh, glory be." she exclaimed out loud looking suddenly flushed.

She fell into the chair that was luckily behind her.

"Saints preserve us, will you look at this."

She was staring at a bank check made out to her in the amount of twenty five thousand dollars. Arlene rushed to her side.

"Are you alright Auntie ?"

"Yes my dear, just a wee bit shocked at the moment." Eileen answered after a few more tears rolled down her reddened cheeks.

"Did you know about this Tommy ?"

"I know what Bert is capable of but I knew nothing of whatever it is you're looking at."

Eileen handed the check to Arlene. "Show this to that handsome young thing over there." She said with a big grin. Yet again Arlene and Tom blushed a light pink at Eileen's forward remarks.

After viewing the bank check, Tom smiled at Mrs. O'Conner.

"And what's wrong with a little extra pocket money ?"

"Pocket money !" Eileen cried out. "I've never seen that much money in a lump sum in my whole life."

"Leave it to Bert." Tom thought. *"And people thought him mean."*

"I don't even know what to do with all that money." commented Eileen.

"How about a visit back to the old country." suggested Arlene. "In your letters you said you would like to see Roundwood again.

You could see the sparkle in Eileen's eyes as she thought of her niece's suggestion.

"You can't give it back." quipped Tom.

Wiping the tears away, Eileen showed an even bigger smile. Finally standing and tucking the check and papers into her apron pocket Mrs. O'Conner stated that she would make some tea for the three of them.

"Tommy, you stay here and talk to this pretty thing. I think she likes you."

"Aunt Eileen !!." the young girl protested as Eileen headed for the kitchen.

In order to ease the tension Tom started the conversation.

"She has never been shy with her comments. Just enjoy her, she's a wonderful mother to all."

"Aunt Eileen welcomed you home. I take it you were away for a while."

Tom, without too much detail, quickly outlined his six years in the Marine Corps. Arlene's interest was genuine urging a more detailed story from him.

Eileen re-appeared with the tea tray and some small pastries.

"I hope you two were getting acquainted while I was gone. You make such a grand couple. If he asks you out my dear, it's okay, you already have my permission."

"**I** guess you have been reading my mind Mrs. O'Conner." Tom remarked smiling. The sparkle in Arlene's eyes showed her agreement with the idea.

The conversation during tea was naturally focused on Bert. By the time Tom was ready to leave Eileen had accepted the fact that she was twenty five thousand dollars wealthier than two hours earlier. Eileen busied herself cleaning away the tea dishes leaving Tom and Arlene alone.

"**I** already have plans for today but I would like to call you tomorrow if I may."

Arlene answered without hesitation, "I would like that very much."

Mrs. O'Conner reappeared to give Tom a goodbye hug, "Say hello to your aunt for me."

Chapter 5

Tom felt quite happy on his drive to the log cabin and yet still anxious to delve into Bert's secrets. As he approached his driveway from the main road he saw the same broken down truck starting to turn into his drive. Obviously seeing Tom approaching they quickly turned out to the road again and sped away. Tom recognized one of the teens from the other day.

"I guess I will have to address them directly. I will make a point of it. But not today."

He checked the house inside and out upon arrival. Everything appeared to be in order with the door still securely locked.

~ ~ ~ ~

The envelope with the keys was still on top of the dresser. While reaching for key number one he thought it best from now on to take the envelope with him when he left. He moved to the loft pull down ladder and remembering old Bert using the fire place poker, he copied his actions and managed to lower the steps. Sure enough in the far corner of the loft he spotted the large metal trunk. He hesitated a moment before unlocking the lid. Surprised again, the books inside were true journals. There were seven, nine by twelve, canvas bound books, each about an inch thick.

Stunned by what he was seeing Tom paused to look again. He thought perhaps he was seeing things. Collecting himself, he realized this was yet another surprise.

"Did he really write in all these journals ?"

He reached for the top book, in doing so he noticed the number one in the upper right corner.

Smiling, he said aloud, "Ever organized."

He closed the trunk and made himself comfortable on the lid, carefully opening the journal. Just inside the cover was a hand written note.

"Tom,

As I mentioned in the other paper, if you chose not to read this then please burn them. I don't need any more ridicule now that I have passed.

    Your friend forever,

      Bert."

Putting the note down Tom could feel the hurt the old man was carrying. He held back the tears as best he could but his cheeks dampened anyway. It was about ten minutes of no movement at all before he remembered the book on his lap.

Answering Bert silently; *"You will always be my friend and my other Dad."*

Tom turned the first page:

"I was born in 1932 on the third of June. I couldn't have asked for a better life as a child. I had parents who loved and protected me and actually shared their own love with me. Unfortunately all that changed with the outbreak of world war two.

Dad joined the navy in 1941. Of course I was proud of him and would go around bragging to my friends. At least as proud as a nine year old could be.

My happiness was not to last. Dad was crewed on a destroyer in the South Pacific. The ship was torpedoed by a Japanese submarine. All were lost.

This was something that Tom was unaware of. He continued reading.

Mom remarried when I was twelve and a half. That's

about when my life changed, and not for the better. The man she married definitely did not like me. When my mom was around he would use a few pleasant words. When we were alone I thought his only vocabulary was four letter words. I owned a dog then who was my only real friend. It was only a mutt but I trained him well. We were inseparable. That is until my new step Dad deemed he was bad and shot him. I cried the whole day as I buried him in the woods.

Then came the hitting. I tried to stay away from him but I think he sought me out on purpose. If I did something wrong, at least in his eyes, he would force me outside and beat me with his belt. I did not tell my mother because I did not want to hurt or upset her. I tried to stay away from him as much as I could. This worked for a while until I saw him hit my mother, more than once.

That's when I attacked him and wrestled him to the ground. I was only 14 at th time and not as strong as he was. I was over powered and severely beaten.

Two days later a few men came and took me away to a home for wayward teens. Try as I did no one would listen to my side of the story. Even my mom was helpless because of his threats. I received word in a round about way that my mother was ill. I had been in the correctional facility about two months. I was finally allowed, under supervision of course, to visit her. Her husband had already bugged out taking anything *of value she had, including the car. Mom finally convinced the authorities of my innocence and I was free to go home. I took care of my mother as best I could but her weakness overtook her and she passed away. The county buried her in a paupers grave.*

A foster home was my fate but I was considered trouble by the whole town. Yes, this town of Tylerville. The option I then chose was to run away.

Tom was feeling angry, mainly at the towns people. He now understood why. He felt himself becoming more upset in the face of the ignorance of the towns folk, believing rumors rather than trying to ascertain the truth. Instead Bert was isolated and ostracized by his own kind.

"Some how I will make this right Bert. That's a solemn promise." Tom swore aloud.

Tom put a marker in the book and put it aside. He needed to calm down. He randomly picked book number three. Skimming through this journal showed anecdotes of the Korean War. Tom knew this was going to be interesting reading for him. He next chose number five again just skimming. He noted articles of different cities and states. Obviously he was well traveled but no one knew about that. He did recall now, there were times when Bert would be gone from his beloved "farm" for extended periods.

"That's when I took care of the garden for him." he remembered.

Tom never knew where he went and being young he didn't care. That left him in the woods alone which he liked.

Tom sat back, his mind drifting to the first time he met Bert.

"His mother passed away and he was living with his aunt Martha. Not having his mother to keep him on the straight and narrow, not that his aunt didn't try, he developed a single minded independence that would sometimes lead him into trouble. Such as when one of the local gangs started to pick on some innocent young girl, teasing her beyond tolerance. He went after the leader only to find out he was greatly outnumbered by the rest of the gang. They took great pleasure in punching and kicking him. The girl, in the meantime, managed to run away. While down on the ground they dragged him into an ally to teach

him a lesson. That's when old Bert came by. It was amazing to watch the seventy one year old man take on five supposedly tough teens. They eventually ran with their pride dragging on the ground. Bert lifted me and carried me to his truck and drove me to his cabin. I tried to say something but Bert shushed me. He cleaned and dressed my wounds all the while speaking softly but friendly to me. He told me he knew of my mother and that she was a good woman. When she remarried he said he feared for her safety because of the man she married. Bert made me promise that when ever I felt a troubled situation about to occur, just walk away. Do not pay attention to what others say or how they ridicule. Your opinion of yourself was all that mattered. He drove me to my aunt and explained the day to her. She was most gratified and promised Bert not to be to hard on me. He explained to her I was protecting a young girl and doing the right thing. He made arrangements with her that he would like to see me a few times a week. To learn more about being a man. In the beginning Bert would pick me up and take me home. After a while I would ride my bike. I looked forward to going there, even though I knew Bert would be cranky and lose his patience with me".

Bringing himself back to the present, Tom checked his watch and decided it was time to go. He did not want to keep Aunt Martha and dinner waiting.

He returned the books to the chest and locked it keeping number one for reading at home.

~ ~ ~ ~

He willingly discussed his day with his aunt even highlighting his meeting of Arlene. She smiled happily at this trying not to make it a big deal.

"**I** knew Eileen mentioned a visitor but I did not know when." she commented. "I'm afraid I'm going to leave you alone tonight." she added.

"**T**his is our monthly Bridge Club night."

"**N**ot to worry Aunt Martha, I have more then enough to keep me occupied." Actually Tom was thankful to be alone. He wanted to read more of Bert's journal. Tom said he would take care of the dishes so Aunt Martha would not have to rush.

By seven thirty he was settled in the recliner with a glass of wine and Bert's first journal. Removing the book marker he continued the story.

I didn't stay away for long though. After hiding in someone's barn for a few days I chose to come back. I had decided not to let the people of this town rule me only because they didn't like me. I turned myself in. It took a while for them to place me in a foster home. When they did find one I promised the people I would behave. After all I had to have a place to sleep and eat. I kept my word although at times it was very difficult Just about all in town disliked me and for no reason other then rumors about how bad I was.

I kept to myself whenever possible and grew both in stature and physical strength. At the age of eighteen I was legally emancipated. The year was 1950 and the Korean War was upon us. I joined the Marine Corps. I spent two and a half years in Korea. And was honorably discharged in 1954.

I returned to Tylerville. I must admit I was not exactly welcomed. No one cared that I served in Korea. The only thing I heard on the streets was that trouble was back.

I didn't care though. This is where my mother was buried. This was my home. I had fond memories of both my father and mother. I had enough back pay from my time in Korea which I used to buy this sixty acre parcel. I was determined to make my life here.

"**B**oy, talk about stubborn." Tom thought. "Yet in a way I can see his point."

Here there was an obvious interruption in the journal entry. Tom accepted this pause willingly. He could feel himself getting up tight once more. He put the book aside and reached for the telephone.

Tom spoke with Arlene at length and made arrangements to take her to lunch. Before his luncheon date he would check on Sam McCort's availability to go to the bank with him to see the contents of this other safe deposit box. He could not plan any further until he knew.

Tom's spirits perked up after his chat with Arlene. He went to bed looking forward to lunch.

Chapter 6

Tom had a light breakfast and called the attorney at eight thirty. Sam answered directly mentioning he had a light schedule that morning and would meet him at the bank just after nine.

Both Tom and Sam arrived at the bank at the same time. With Sam McCort there was no questioning the access to the safe deposit box. The medium sized box was handed over to Tom and they were ushered to a private room. Tom was curious of its contents because of the weight of the metal container. The pair now alone, Tom unlocked the box yet again amazed by the contents. A stack of typed pages almost two inches thick held secure by cardboard and a heavy rubber band. Tom lifted the heavy bundle from its storage and noticed a note on top just under the rubber band.

Tom,

Because of my previous instructions I assume you have Sam McCort with you. I'll let him fill you in on the boring details. That bundle before you is a completed manuscript. It has not been edited yet. You can do it, if you feel up to it, or you can have it done. Again see Sam for details. He can also give you the scoop on getting it published. But as I have indicated previously it is now your decision as to what to do.

Thanks for being my other arm.

Bert.

Tom had read the note out loud and now looked at Sam with questions. Sam picked up the bundle of papers and smiled at Tom's expression.

"I gather from the look on your face you know nothing of Bert's writing abilities.."

"You're right, I know of no such thing. Will a publisher accept such a manuscript out if the blue like this. I would hate to see Bert's dreams dashed to pieces. I wouldn't even know where to begin."

Sam still grinning answered quietly.

"**I** don't think the publisher of Bert's last five novels will have any problem accepting another book from Bert's hand."

Tom was literally in shock right now. He stuttered a few seconds before finding his tongue to speak coherently.

"**W**hat other five books ? I didn't know Bert could write. He never said a word."

"**T**hat's true." Sam commented. "Nor did he plan to until you were home safely. He wanted you to be proud of him. This was his legacy to you."

Embarrassed now Tom hesitated before speaking again.

"**E**ven with the success of five novels the town did not accept him ?"

"**T**hat's correct Tom. They did not accept his success because they did not know about it."

"**H**ow would you not know of a person who wrote five books ?"

"**T**hey did not know because he wrote under a pseudonym."

"**W**hy did he do that ? He must have had a reason ?"

"**H**e had a number of them. The main reason was you."

"**M**E ! Why me ?"

Sam sat back and turned serious now.

"**M**ainly, and these are his words, he loved you. He originally did not expect the success he had. But once it came he wanted whatever financial results there were to be put aside for you so that you would not have to struggle through life as he did."

Tom was quiet, memories of Bert rushing through his head. After a very long break Tom asked in an almost whisper.

"**A**nd were there any financial rewards ?"

Sam answered as softly.

"**Y**es Tom there were. All five novels were on the New York Times best seller list for very extended periods."

Tom remained quiet. A faint memory pushed its way into his head.

When I was about fourteen or so I remember Bert at the writing table with various papers, but when I would approach him he would cover everything up. Because I was so young I didn't think much of it. He was probably writing then.

Focusing back to Sam he asked;

"**H**ave you seen any of these books ?"

"**I**'ve read them all and someday I will most likely read them a second time. I believe there are copies in the small library at the cabin."

A little more relaxed now Tom commented,

"Will this man ever cease to amaze me ?"

He checked the box one more time. It had contained just the one manuscript.

"Well Tom, it's your call. What do you want to do with this?"

"I wouldn't want to disappoint ole Bert, so I guess we go ahead and publish it."

Sam was all smiles now. "I knew you would see it his way."

"May I suggest though that you take it until such time that we actually send it, or take it to the publisher."

Looking a bit puzzled Sam asked why.

Tom explained about his run- in with the local teens. Sam instantly took on a concerned look. Noticing this Tom remarked;

"Not to worry, I can handle anything they want to throw. Remember I was raised by Bert."

"And the Corps." added Sam with a grin.

"I have been to the local police just to keep them informed. I don't really expect them to do anything yet."

"If you need help motivating them, let me know." volunteered Sam.

"Thanks, but so far I'm okay. I guess that about wraps it up for now. Give me another few days, then perhaps we can get together about the book."

"That will be fine Tom. Remember Bert's words, from now on everything is your call."

They returned the box and learned the rental fees had been taken care of in advance. In fact he was due a refund. Tom said to keep it as a courtesy for taking care of things for Bert. As they parted Sam reassured Tom that the manuscript would be kept in his safe.

~ ~ ~ ~

Tom, pleased with learning more of Bert's life was also looking forward to lunch with Arlene. Eileen answered the door with her always happy face.

"Come in dear. Arlene is just finishing dressing. She wanted to look her best for you."

Tom could feel a bit of a flush come over him. Within minutes Arlene appeared. As yesterday Tom was mesmerized by her.

"You two make such a lovely couple. I just know your mother is going to be so pleased."

"**A**untie stop that, you're embarrassing the poor man. We're just going to lunch."

In order to change the subject Tom asked;

"**W**ould you like to come to lunch with us Mrs. O'Conner ?"

"**T**hat's very kind of you my dear, but, oh my no. You two young things go and enjoy yourselves. Just don't keep her out too late." Eileen said this all the time smiling.

"**A**untie, you're impossible." scolded Arlene jokingly.

By now all three were laughing.

In the truck driving to town Arlene apologized for her aunt.

"**N**o need." Tom explained that he knew Eileen for a long time and that's just the way she was. "Actually I find it rather refreshing. I wouldn't want her any other way. That's probably why she got along with Bert so well."

"**Y**ou'll have to tell me more about this Bert. It sounds like he was a very loving man."

"**T**hat he was, but within this town you would never know it. They have carried a prejudice against him for seventy years for something he never did. I hope to right that wrong."

Arlene detected the seriousness in his voice. Instead of becoming afraid of him, she admired his determination for the truth about his friend. Tom caught himself getting emotional with the subject.

"**I**'m sorry, I apologize for my behavior."

Arlene gently touched his arm.

"**I** completely understand and I respect and admire your devotion to your friend. You need not worry. If I can help in any way please allow me."

Tom gently smiling within told himself, *"You already have."*

Arriving in town proper Tom parked in the only parking lot and they walked the short block and a half to the Country Kitchen. Being that it was lunch hour they were fairly busy. The couple found a small booth for two in the anteroom off the main dining area. Tom was pleased with the booth away from the main flow. He found it a bit more intimate. He politely apologized to Arlene for the diner but did say the food was great, beside the fact it was the only place in town.

"**P**erhaps you would allow me the honor of escorting you to a proper dinner some evening. There is a wonderful steakhouse just outside of town."

"**I** would like that very much Tom." Arlene answered with a soft blush crossing her face.

They each ordered the soup and sandwich combo accompanied by tea for her and coffee for him. As the server left Arlene picked up the conversation with a glowing smile.

"Now I want to hear more of this Bert of yours."

"I wouldn't want to bore you with my past life."

"Nonsense, I want to know more about both of you. Aunt Eileen only highlighted a few things which only made me more curious.." Looking directly into his eyes she added the sweetest "Please" he ever heard.

It was now his turn to feel a flush come over him.

"Who could refuse a plea like that ?"

This answer only made the green of her eyes glow even more.

Tom started with his first meeting with Bert when he was being beaten by a teen gang. An instant sadness filled Arlene's eyes but soon vanished with her smile as she commented.

"From the looks of you now I don't think that would happen any more."

Tom just smiled. He recalled some of his early years with Bert and how the fact that, in hind sight, it was later in life he realized how much he learned from Bert. Not just tangible things such as gardening and carpentry and such but the more realistic aspects of life and fulfillment. Proper behavior showing respect for others without ill judgement. The things that truly carry you through life. The things that give and show you happiness.

" Bert was like the father or grandfather I never really had. My own Dad was killed in an auto accident when I was quite young."

Arlene smiled and hung on his every word. Returning an equally pleasant smile Tom inquired:

"Okay, enough of me for now, I would like to know something of you."

Suddenly, not shy, Arlene gladly opened up her life and all with a large smile.

"I am twenty three years old and I was raised in a small village just south of Dublin with a truly loving family which included Aunt Eileen. I graduated from Trinity College in Dublin as an art major. Aunt Eileen begged me to stay with her for a while until I settled on a job."

"Remind me to thank your Aunt Eileen."

Arlene's eyes sparkled even more as they held each other's gaze, the mood only broken with the delivery of their lunch. They continued to trade stories during lunch, each becoming more comfortable with the other. The hour plus long lunch finally over Tom suggested a ride to Bert's, now his log home, which Arlene eagerly accepted.

"But first a quick trip to the powder room." she said as she stood.

By the sounds of some comments and whistles Tom knew she had reached the rest room area.. Obviously that group of teens were feeling their oats again. He waited patiently for her return. As he downed the last sip of coffee he heard stirring again along with the waitress saying let her pass which only brought more laughter. Tom raised his six foot one inch two hundred ten pound frame from the booth and slowly walked to the laughter. Arlene smiled and the server stepped aside. In a pleasant but serious voice Tom spoke directly to the group of overactive teens.

"Excuse me gentlemen, but I believe you are blocking the lady's path."

Arlene smiled again and nodded to Tom as the young men parted to make a path. She did not look back but proceeded to the booth.

"In the future gentlemen I would strongly suggest that you show some respect towards women. Not just to this particular lady because she is with me, but to all women no matter the age. In doing so you will find your life will actually be more fulfilling. If you feel you do not know how to show proper respect I will always be available to give courtesy lessons, free of charge I might add. You may call on me anytime, I do believe you know where I live. You may go back to enjoying your quiet lunch now gentlemen, and remember there are other patrons here looking forward to their own quiet lunches. Thank you in advance for your cooperation."

Tom turned to the server as one by one the teens quietly sat down,

"I'll take the check now Brenda, thank you."

Tom returned to Arlene smiling.

"I knew you would be a formidable presence. Thank you kind sir."

"The pleasure was all mine." Tom returned.

Brenda showed with the check and with a grateful sigh said "Thank you, Tom, I really think that will help for the future."

Arlene sat quietly beaming with pride.

While Arlene waited by the door Tom walked to the register to pay the check with a sizable tip. There was no eye contact with the teens nor was there any comments from them. As Tom turned to the door he nodded to the youngsters saying, "Good day gentlemen."

He and Arlene exited while she hooked her arm in his as they walked to the truck. They remained silent until they reached the truck. Once belted in and on their way to Bert's cabin Arlene softly spoke.

"Now I know why Aunt Eileen thinks so highly of you."

Tom felt good with her comment but also was aware of the flush he felt.

To change the subject he asked Arlene about her future plans.

"I don't really know yet." she answered vaguely.

To be more direct he asked if she planned on staying here in the states or going back to Ireland.

"That's an unfair question right now. There are a number of new options I have to consider." she said with a shy smile.

Tom turned into his drive noticing Arlene's excitement.

"Is your house on this road ?"

"Well, sort of." Tom laughed. "This is my driveway."

"Wow, you really are back in the woods."

Her eyes never stopped moving taking in the beauty of the forest and then the house appeared.

"What a beautiful home Tom. I guess Bert really knew how to live." she giggled.

She was jumping out of the truck before he was even at a full stop. She ran around like a school girl yelling back to Tom.

"I want to see everything."

She disappeared around the back of the cabin before Tom was out of the truck. He enjoyed the childlike excitement she was not afraid to show. He met her coming around the far corner of the cabin.

"I just love this place, you are so lucky Tom. Can I see the inside, please."

She grabbed his hand pulling him toward the front door. He was laughing so much he had trouble fitting the key in the lock. Finally opening the door he stepped aside for Arlene. Once inside she froze in place.

"Tom." she marveled, "This place is perfect. It is so cozy. You must love living here."

She was all bubbly with excitement. May I look around ?"

"Of course, go anywhere you want."

The next ten minutes she spent Oooing and Aaahing at everything while Tom made himself comfortable reaching for the journal he brought along. She finally sat across from him politely asking;

"May I ask if I could listen to Bert's story ?"

Tom looked surprised returning the question.

"Are you sure ?"

"Yes Tom, I would love to be part of what your life is or was. It's apparent he meant a lot to you. Please." she added sweetly.

"I think that would be nice but, if you think it's getting too rough, please let me know."

"I promise." she smiled.

Tom opened the journal to his marker and continued to read of Bert's life.

My next battle with the town wasn't too bad because I had the law on my side. Although many hurdles were put up. Probably to discourage me. I was stubborn enough not to let that stop me.

I purchased a plot in the local cemetery and had my mother re-buried with proper attention to detail. I ordered a head stone and finally was satisfied my mother had her proper place in this town.

Of course this process took nearly six months because of the road blocks they threw at me.

"That poor man. It just doesn't seem fair the way they treated him. Why would they do this ?"

"Ignorance and prejudice." Tom muttered. "In order to give you a better background you should probably read from the beginning."

"I think I would like that if it's alright with you."

"Tell you what, let me continue from where we are now and then you can have the journal for the night."

"You would allow me to do that ?"

"Of course, then I have a good excuse to see you again."

Arlene again showed her all captivating smile.

"By the way , just to warn you ahead of time, there are five of these journals spanning some sixty years."

Smiling in return, Arlene stated;

"I guess we're going to be spending a lot of time together." which drew a smile from Tom also.

Tom returned to reading.

In spite of the odds I found the girl of my dreams. I was twenty five at the time, she was twenty three. After one year I proposed and she happily accepted. I was the happiest man in the world.

I was away for a few days on a job and when I returned I was arrested. It was then I learned my fiance' had been raped and murdered and that I was the guilty person. The trial was a farce. The jury was fixed and none of my witnesses were allowed to testify. The whole trial took only an hour and a half. I was sentenced to twenty years to life.

I served seven months at the state prison and was suddenly released. The truth finally came out. The neighborhood bully knew I was away and took advantage of the situation.

The town had to accept the decision of the State court but that did not change their opinion of me. In their eyes I was still no good. Even though there was proof and the punk finally admitted the crime, the local people found it hard to believe. After all he was the son of one of the towns upright citizens.

Call me thickheaded or whatever but I stayed here in my home town. Life then became even more difficult for me. The wonderful townspeople even tried spreading erroneous rumors about me to the surrounding towns. I ended up having to drive an hour plus to buy food and the other necessities of life.

It wasn't too long after that when I met you Tom. You changed my whole life. You renewed my purpose in life. Your mother was a beautiful soul, not judgmental at all. She allowed

Tom could not read any further. He was overcome with feelings he had no idea he possessed. His chest heaved lightly as tears rolled down his cheeks. He turned away from Arlene. She also was red eyed for both he and Bert. She moved to where Tom was sitting and pulled his head to her shoulder, hugging him with shaking arms. Tom absorbed himself in the comfort of her warmth. They remained that way for uncounted minutes. Eventually Tom book marked the tear stained page and closed the journal. He tried to apologize to Arlene but she shushed him, kissed his forehead and pulled his head back to her shoulder.

"I feel for the man also and I never knew him. But I would truly like to know him through you. Please allow that to happen."

Tom slowly pulled away, stood with her enfolding her in a comforting hug whispering;

"I would love to share him with you."

Arlene allowed a true contentment to fill her being. She snuggled closer putting her arms around him. They held each other, not moving until a ravens cry broke the silence outside. Tom, ever the gentleman, pulled away reluctantly, softly smiling,

"Thank you." he whispered.

She smiled gently wiping a tear from the corner of her eye.

I think I have some lemonade in the fridge. How about a cool drink and a walk outside ?"

"That sounds great." she agreed.

Tom took her on a quick tour of the property, barn, pond, garden, and woods. His whole private world as he called it.

"Believe it or not this reminds me of my home in Roundwood. We don't have forests like this but the peace and quiet and privacy is the same. I don't know how people could live in the concrete jungles of a city. I even thought Dublin was too big."

They strolled the woods following different trails and creeks now and then. Checking his watch Tom realized it was just after four.

"We better head on back before Eileen sends the police out for us." he quipped.

"Do we have to ? We still have time before dinner and I do so want to hear more from the journal.'

Tom, looking surprised asked;

"Are you sure you want to do that ? It's not exactly an enjoyable comedy."

"Very much so. I want to know more of both of you. *"PLEASE."* If you want I can read for a while."

He could tell by the glistening eyes that she was genuine in her request.

"Okay you win, but not for too long. I have to get back to my aunt for dinner also."

Arlene was delighted with Tom's answer and squeezed his hand in thanks.

Back in the cozy living room sipping another lemonade Tom handed the journal to Arlene. She gladly accepted with an ear to ear smile.

"Thank you for your trust."

She opened to the marked page and sat back comfortably.

You may not remember Tom, but there was the time you wanted to join the Boy Scouts but your membership application was turned down. You were quite upset at the time. I discussed it at length with your aunt and we both agreed it was most likely because of your association with me. I was yet again being punished by the beloved townsfolk. Only this time it spilled over to you and your Aunt as it had done earlier to your Mother. Your Aunt, being the strong woman that she was, was not going to deny you what other young boys had. She agreed with me that I could take on the role of your own personal Scout Master. We managed to get hold of the necessary scouting manuals from another town. Of course you didn't receive the actual badges to wear but you learned all the skills that merited them. I never made a comparison but I would be willing to bet you did better than any other boys your age. We probably had more fun too. At least I did when I wasn't grouching at you. Your aunt was so proud of you as your Mother would have been. Of course being friends with me did not go easy on her. She was not as ostracized as I was but was also not accepted by all. But you can be proud of her. She stuck to her principals and values. She was really a great and remarkable lady.

Arlene looked over to Tom to see his soft smile, his thoughts obviously lost in the past years she had just covered. She closed the book returning it to the table and silently waited for him to return from memory lane. She smiled within and was very content to be with him.

Sheepishly Tom looked at Arlene, smiled and said;

"We better be on our way."

She returned his smile lovingly as he handed her the journal.

"I will take very good care of this, I promise."

Driving home Arlene commented.

"You said there were five of these journals ? Bert must have written about his whole life."

"That's not all." Tom volunteered. "I just learned this morning from Sam McCort, the attorney, that he successfully wrote six novels. Five of which were best sellers. The sixth I now have and will get it to the publisher as soon as practical. Even I had no idea he was such a prolific writer."

"You must be very proud of him. He was obviously proud of you."

The rest of the ride home was quiet, Tom still reflecting on some memories. Arlene understood and respected his private thoughts. Arriving at Eileen's he escorted Arlene to the door which was opened immediately by a smiling Mrs. O'Conner.

"You two look happy. I hope you had a good day."

"The day was perfect." exclaimed Arlene.

"Can you stay for dinner Tommy ?" inquired Eileen.

"Thanks but no Mrs. O'Conner, my aunt will be waiting dinner for me. Perhaps another time. May I call you again Arlene ?"

"Remember you have to, I've got your journal." she smiled in answer.

Tom returned to the truck with Arlene following with her eyes a bit disappointed that she didn't get a kiss.

Dinner with Aunt Martha was great as usual. He told her of his day and the trouble with the teens informing her that he would be sleeping at the log cabin for the night to be on the safe side. She understood and supplied him with a large chunk of apple pie.

Tom was tucked safely in the cabin just after nine PM. His thoughts, of course, went right to Arlene and how good it felt to be with her. He poured a glass of milk to go with the pie as he grabbed journal number two making himself comfortable at the kitchen table. He turned to the first page.

Another routine incident of my garden being trampled. I was away for a few days. Not long enough to have you, Tom, to look after the house. Though in hindsight I guess I should have. No matter, the damage wasn't too bad. I guess who ever did it did not have a sufficient amount of time to do a thorough job.

I was thinking of getting a dog but I talked myself out of it. I didn't want to endanger an innocent animal because of the town jerks. That was just before the weekend your aunt was visiting out of state and you stayed with me for three days.

Do you remember Tom ? We both worked our butts off in the garden then. That's when I allowed you to burn the steak and potato's on the grill and we ended up eating cereal. You apologized about fifty times that night, but you did learn. I may have been rough on you that night but I thoroughly enjoyed those three days.

Tom paused in his reading outwardly smiling, recalling how embarrassed he was and how sorry he felt for wasting all that good food. He rinsed the dishes, grabbed the journal and made himself comfy in the living room with another day's entry.

I had some business at the bank today only to find four flat tires on my truck when I returned to the parking lot. That's when I found out what a true friend Sam McCort was. Luckily the tires had only been deflated and not destroyed. I never did find out who the culprit was. Most likely some of the upright teens of the community who seemed to have raised others to be just like them. I'm proving to be more stubborn then they are.

I'm slowly recruiting true friends which means a lot to me. There was your mother and of course your wonderful Aunt Martha and dear sweet Mrs. O'Conner and recently Sam McCort. There are those in town who do not like that idea but they can't attack all of us. It's nice to see there are a few non judgmental people left in this world.

Tom put the journal aside allowing himself to drift to the past again.

"I wish I had been more aware of Bert's troubles when I was younger but I know now he was shielding me from any more hardships than I already had."

Chapter 7

     Arlene helped her aunt clean up after supper and chose to stay home with the journal while Eileen went to a book club meeting. Settled on the couch with feet up she opened the journal with a smile. She read from the beginning the part that Tom was upset about. She too was moved by Bert's plight as a youngster.

     Her aunt was not home yet so she made herself a cup of tea and returned to the couch advancing past the part she read earlier with Tom. She started to read hoping it would be less heart tugging.

It seems all I have been writing about lately is the hard times I had growing up. But after meeting you, Tom, my life changed. Oh it wasn't all peaches and cream from then on but I saw some of my own youth in you. Losing both a mother and father at an early age would be a hardship for any young person. That personal guidance from loving parents is a gift of gold all should share in and cherish, but not all of us can through no fault of our own. True, you had a loving Aunt Martha who tried to be a mother, but that does not replace the genuine thing. I learned a lot from growing up alone. Yes, I had some foster homes and I'm not faulting them. What I observed in others my age was something I was missing and wanted. I made up my mind to overcome the obstacles put in my way because of ignorance and lack of compassion for others.

Meeting you gave me the opportunity to share the better things I learned. I don't mean skills or academic education either. It was to help you understand life, love, respect, tolerance, inclusiveness and understanding. I have often silently thanked your Aunt Martha for sharing you with me. What you became as you grew made us both very proud. Seeing and helping you mature fulfilled a need in me that was missing in my own growth. I'm thankful I had the opportunity to instill in you the principals of life that were denied me by ignorance of others.

Arlene placed the book on her lap and reached for a tissue to pat her eyes. She wished she could have personally known this man who moved her so emotionally.

Hearing her aunt Eileen at the door she marked her place in the journal and put it aside.

Eileen in her usual bubbly excitement spoke of her book club meeting. Before actually turning in for the evening Arlene asked if she had any pictures of Bert. Not considering the request as odd she thought a bit then answered;

"I believe I do my dear. Why do you ask ?"

Without going into too much detail Arlene told her she was thinking of making a sketch of Bert for Tom.

"Oh, that would be lovely dear. I'm sure he would like that."

Eileen immediately went to an old bureau and rummaged through a couple of drawers.

"Here we are love. It's a few years back, about four I think. Tommy had wanted it when he was stationed in Afghanistan. It's not a very good one, actually there are a few different ones."

She handed them over to her niece. Arlene studied them carefully smiling to herself.

"These will do just fine Auntie. I believe I can work well with them. May I have them for a while ?"

"Of course my dear, anything you want. That's wonderful thing you'll be doing. I know Tommy will just love it."

"I want this to be a secret Auntie. I want to surprise Tom with it."

"I totally understand love." Eileen put her hand to her lips in a motion of zipping it closed. "Mums the word."

Laughing now they both got ready for bed. Arlene took the journal with her to her room. Making herself comfy with a few pillows she continued to read.

I'm sure by now Tom, that you have discovered I tried my hand at writing. If not talk to Sam McCort. He can fill you in with details.

I spent such a long time in Korea, some two and a half years, I was witness to many things. That wartime life became second nature to me, so much so that is what I based my first book on. Amazed by its acceptance I eventually compiled my stories into a second book. Perhaps Tom, you will get a chance to read them. You can then make comparisons with your own experiences in Afghanistan. I just hope I can be around to do those comparisons with you in person. If not, Oh well, enjoy anyway.

Enough nostalgia.

I'm at the point now of not being persecuted too much. Far from being accepted but I think my thickheadedness out lasted their persistence. They sort of gave up the harassment. A few young teens still try things now and then but I have no trouble handling them. They almost add some humor to my day.

Arlene laughed softly at Bert's self deprecating humor. She knew it was time for lights out and ever so reluctantly put aside the journal. Her last thoughts, of course, were of Tom.

~ ~ ~ ~

After a quiet night Tom was up early thinking of too many things at once. *"Slow down boy, there's no hurry in life anymore. Learn to relax."* Tom scolded himself. Then talking out loud he said; "If I'm going to stay here I should get a telephone installed. I guess I could go the cell phone route but the idea of that sort of turns me off."

He fixed a quick breakfast, hopped in the truck and headed for Sam McCort's office.

Sam smiled a welcome asking what the reason for the visit was.

"New York City." was Tom's answer.

Sam turned a bit more serious.

"What do you need to know ?"

"To start with, will I have any problem accessing the safe box ?"

"You shouldn't, but if it will make you feel better I can call with a heads up. When are you planning to go ?"

"I thought perhaps in a few days. I was wondering if you would join me ?"

"That would not be necessary Tom. I believe it would be better if you went alone. There is much to know about the contents and the arrangements there of. I will give you the names of two gentlemen that Bert has been working with. You will need to talk at length with both of them if you are to understand Bert's wishes."

"Sounds ominous." Tom said looking serious.

"Not really but I would rather not say any more. I believe you should discover everything for yourself. Trust me, you will be pleased. There is no need to be concerned."

Sam wrote two names on a note paper and handed it to Tom

"Remember, let me know the exact day you will be going and I will call ahead. Plan on a good four hours. I would love to meet again when you get back."

Tom left McCort's office, curiosity playing with his mind. He knew Sam was not purposely being secretive and concluded this was going to be a good thing.

It was now ten thirty and Tom aimed the truck for the O'Conner residence. Arlene answered the door with the excitement of a child on a birthday.

"I was hoping I would see you today."

"Why, what's so special about today." Tom teased.

A voice rang out from inside the house.

"Come in Tommy love, come in. You did come to see me didn't you ?"

"Of course Mrs. O"Conner, why else would I be here."

Tom stepped past Arlene and gave Eileen a gentle hug. They both looked at Arlene who was sporting a bewildered expression.

"Hello, I 'm here too you know." she said with a put on pout.

"Of course you are my dear, and perhaps you can make some tea for my guest and I."

"No milk in mine, please." Added Tom straight faced.

As she walked past the pair heading for the kitchen with a real pout on her face both Eileen and Tom grabbed her and pulled her into a three way hug. Arlene took advantage of this and snuggled deep into Tom's arm.

"How could anyone forget you my pretty little thing." voiced Eileen.

Arlene beamed again. Mrs. O'Conner pulled away saying.

"I'll leave you two for now I have my laundry to do."

As Eileen disappeared Tom asked;

""Care to go to the woods again ?"

"That sounds like a wonderful idea. Will I be safe ?"

"Most definitely." Tom pledged.

"That's too bad." Arlene joked back. "Let me get the journal." she added.

"Are you finished with it ?"

"Not quite but I did read a lot."

"Keep it till you're finished. I already started another at the cabin."

Arlene smiled in answer and squeezed Tom's hand.

"Let me just tell Auntie."

On the drive to the cabin Tom inquired;

"How much longer will you be in the States ?"

"I'm not exactly sure. Why do you ask ?"

"Nothing special, I was just thinking of having a lunch or dinner for both our aunts some day at my cabin. You and I can do all the cooking and serving. Just sort of a thanks for all they have done for Bert, and for me for that matter."

Arlene was instantly animated. "That's a wonderful idea. You are so sweet to want to do that. We can invite the whole town to help celebrate Bert's life."

Tom snapped his head around to look at her. Then she was laughing.

"Seriously though, that would be a great idea. You even cook too. What a catch." her eyes twinkled.

They strolled around the outside before entering the house. Tom poured each a glass of lemonade before they settled on the couch. He reached for the journal looking at Arlene.

"Do you mind ?"

"Not at all. I'm looking forward to hearing all they contain."

Deep inside Tom was pleased.

I had some business in New York City and knew I would be gone for a week or so. I had you to care for the farm but being away for so long I didn't know what might happen. Thanks to my friend, Sam McCort, now your friend I hope, there was someone to check on the place at night. When he couldn't do it himself he had some friends with the State Police who made known patrols of the area. This made me feel so much better while I was in the big city. I know this may not be big news but I like keeping the journal. It was these journals which pushed me into writing novels. Naturally I started with the Korean War which I was most familiar with.

Tom paused here looking at Arlene.

" Bert mentioning New York City brought to mind something I have to discuss with you."

"Okay, I'm your captive audience."

Tom went on to tell her the story of the letters and the four keys and how important they all were. Important to him anyway.

"And to anticipate the next part of your story you have to go to New York City. I will miss you."

Tom surprised by her insight, smiled.

"I thought about asking you to go along but after talking to Sam this morning I realized it would not exactly be interesting for you."

"Not to worry Tom. You do what you have to do. I will still be here when you get back. In fact it will give me a chance to take care of some other personal business that I have neglected."

"I hope I will still be able to see you when I return."

"You had better or I will really cause you some trouble." She laughed in answer.

"Is that a threat young lady ?"

"You bet it is, Now quit the delay and get back to reading."

"Yes Mam." Tom quietly answered.

Another incident I almost forgot about. I was about fifteen, just finishing my second year of high school.

A bicycle was stolen and when word spread it was said that I did it. Naturally word travels fast in a small town school. Without warning, a small vigilante posse of my class mates surrounded me. I was told my kind were not welcome in their school and that I would have to be taught a lesson. All seven attacked me at the same tome. I remember getting in a few good licks but the odds were just too great for me at the time. I was being punched and kicked all at once. I was a "Hurtin Puppy" as the expression goes. A couple of teachers finally broke up the lynch mob and I was taken to the principal's office, who called the police. I was to be dealt with in a proper fashion . It was more than an hour before I was *allowed to go to the nurse.*

Just as the police were about to take me away, a young new teacher who obviously did not know the politics of the town yet, came and told them I did not steal the bike. She saw the whole thing but did not realize at the time it did not belong to the boy who took it. It turned out the same boy who took it was also the leader of the vigilante group. It was just another way to get at me.

I was released and taken to the hospital for my wounds. And yes you guessed it. Nothing, absolutely nothing happened to the young outstanding citizen who was the guilty party. As an added note, for some unknown reason the young female teacher was let go three weeks later. And to put salt on the wound the foster home I was with returned me to the State. It was almost three months before they found another to take this troublesome young boy.

Epilogue: And look at me now. I beat them all.

Arlene smiled at Bert's ending comment. Smiled through tear dampened eyes. Tom closed the book obviously shaken by Bert's story.

"I never knew any of these things were happening when I was with Bert." Tom mumbled.

"Obviously Bert was keeping you shielded from the not so nice side of people. Besides, there was nothing you could have done."

Tom appreciated Arlene's interest and understanding.

"There was not anything I could have done then but perhaps I can do something now."

Looking a bit confused Arlene asked.

"What can you possibly do now, that was years ago ?"

"Years ago yes, but the stigma still exists. Those teens for example were just prolonging their parents ignorance."

Seeing how Tom was getting himself overwrought Arlene tried to lighten the mood.

"Maybe showing examples of the good side of Bert could help change the old image. You know, how he treated you and your mother. Even both our aunts. Things like that."

Tom warmly smiled at Arlene. He realized his fondness for her was growing and it was her concern such as this that was making it happen. He reached out and gently squeezed her hand in thanks. Her eyes sparkled which only added to this vision of his Irish angel. He shyly removed his hand from hers knowing now how good she was for him, but not knowing how to say it.

Detecting his uncomfortable state Arlene enthusiastically suggested they read more of the journal then head home because she would love to meet his aunt. Showing her contagious smile she gently took the book from Tom's hands softly saying,

"Let me read for a while."

Tom made no attempt to stop her.

The new foster family I ended up with was no joy either. The man of the house was very strict. Although I must say to his credit he was fair. They had two children of their own, the girl was a year older and the boy a year younger but all three of us were treated exactly the same. We were all equal in his eyes. As I said he was very strict but fair.

The girl was being harassed on the way home from school one afternoon. What I, at the time, considered unusually cruel with sexual overtones. I already had the reputation of being a trouble maker yet I could not let this go on. She was really a very nice and good girl. Naturally I took up her defense and was soon in a physical tangle with three of my school mates. No one was seriously hurt but my fighting skills were getting better all the time. Let's just say I had a lot of practice. A few teachers broke up our little rumble. Out of the four of us I was the one who got suspended.

My foster Dad was of course very upset until he received a full explanation from his daughter. Being the honorable man he was he went right to the principal with me in tow. I was subsequently taken off suspension.

My foster sister and I had a mutual "Thank You" party over a dish of ice cream. At least I wasn't thrown out of another Foster home.

As Arlene closed the journal she smiled again.

"**N**o wonder you love old Bert. He was quite a man. Both old and young."

Before leaving the house they went to the small library/ writing room. Tom was looking for Bert's novels. He never did ask Sam what the "non de plume" was. Scanning the small room he noticed a row of neatly standing six books. Reading the titles he realized these were Bert's novels because the first two were Korean war stories. They bore the same name. "William McClain". Tom stared with pride at the six books not touching them. He would leave that for a later date. Arlene read his mood and remained silent.

Tom would learn later from Sam the pseudonym was a combination of Bert's fathers first name and his mothers maiden name. Arlene again instinctively understood this and did not push Tom.

The drive back to town was quiet but Tom did feel content. He was looking forward to showing off Arlene to Aunt Martha.

Martha fussed over Arlene as if she was her own niece. She had prepared fresh lemonade and a cookie tray. Tom excused himself to change clothes which gave the two women the chance to chat.

"**I** must say young lady I think you are a good thing for my young

Tom. I only hope he sees it."

Smiling Arlene returned;

"I too hope he sees me, but I feel his devotion to Bert is keeping him away from any other feelings."

"Do not give up on him my dear. With all his strengths of character and determination, they seem to be overshadowed by his shyness with women. Your aunt and myself are the exceptions but then again we are also the mother figure and he adored his mother. Have patience, I do believe he likes you."

"Truth be known, I like him too, and I want to help him with this Bert dilemma."

"Then stick to it my dear, we all want to help with that."

"And what have you two been gossiping about." interrupted Tom returning from upstairs.

"If you didn't trust us alone you shouldn't have left us. Our gossip is our secret. Right my dear ?" replied Aunt Martha.

"Absolutely Aunt Martha, and our secrets will remain our secrets." stated a grinning Arlene.

In order to go along with the charade Tom joined with,

"Okay, I know when I'm not wanted. I guess I'll go back to my humble cabin by myself."

He turned and started for the door.

"Hey, what about me." yelled Arlene. "How do I get home ?"

Tom turned back half smiling.

"I suppose I could take time to drop you off on the way."

Arlene looked to Martha.

"Don't look to me for help, I'm already home."

Arlene put on a pouting expression.

"Fine, I'll just walk home if some one will tell me the way."

"You will do no such thing young lady. I may not be a lot of things, but I'm still a gentleman."

A smiling Martha now took Arlene into a motherly hug.

"I'm so glad to have met you love. Remember, have patience my love."

Tom kissed his aunt goodbye telling her he would spend the night at his own home again tonight. Taking Arlene's hand firmly into his own he walked her to the door.

"Good night Aunt Martha." Arlene echoed his words with a wink.

"Will I see you tomorrow ?" inquired Arlene as they neared

Eileen's house.

"I would like that." replied Tom. "I decided on New York City for the day after."

"I wish you luck." whispered Arlene. "Remember, anyway I can help with your Bert thing please don't hesitate."

"I didn't forget, and it really pleases me that you want to help."

"And that pleases me." she thought to herself. "Do you want to say hello to my aunt ?" Arlene asked as they pulled into the driveway.

"Not tonight, it's late and we both need our sleep."

Tom walked her to the door politely saying good night. He would call for her the next afternoon. He started to leave when she pulled him back, stood on her tip toes and quickly kissed him. "Good night Tom." and without further delay entered the house. Tom remained standing alone for a time surprised yet smiling.

He drove all the way home thinking of her kiss.

As tired as he was when he arrived at the cabin Tom brought one of the journals to bed with him. This was again journal number three. He randomly opened the book towards the middle. As he remembered it was one of Bert's anecdotes of the Korean War. He read for a while intrigued by the tale of frozen, bloodied feet. They suffered below zero temperatures for weeks at a time without proper winter clothing. Tom thought of the great contrast to his serving in Afghanistan in severe heat. They both served their country under harsh conditions the people at home were totally unaware of. Some did not even care. Life for them went on as usual.

Tom finally dozed off, book in hand.

Breakfast was simple and Tom spent the morning preparing for the New York City trip, making sure he had proper ID and a two day change of clothes. He could feel the excitement building and wasn't quite sure if it was his planned trip or getting to see Arlene again. Probably a bit of both he decided.

A light lunch and he was on his way to Sam McCort's office for whatever last minute details he may have.

At one thirty Tom was lightly tapping on Mrs. O'Conner's door. Arlene opened the door looking like the perfect advertisement of a young colleen from Ireland. He almost expected a commercial to begin.

Tom trying to be serious inquired;

"Excuse me miss, I did not expect such a beautiful vision to answer the door. Is Arlene Treherne at home ?"

Catching on and playing along Arlene answered.

"I believe she is at home, whom shall I say is calling ?"

"No one special, just a longtime admirer."

"Won't you come in sir and I will announce you."

Tom entered suddenly feeling shy in her presence.

"My aunt is not home so you'll have to put up with me for now."

With a courage he did not usually have with women, Tom answered;

"You my dear would fill any man's dream."

He felt himself go red. Smiling like a child she answered instantly.

"I only want to be your dream."

Knowing he was really flush now Tom took her in his arms and held her tight.

"I want that also."

Not wanting to cause Tom any further embarrassment Arlene, against her own wishes slowly pulled away and changed the subject.

"I finished reading the journal last night."

Surprised, Tom gazed at her.

"I really admire Bert for keeping such a good attitude and clear head under such stress. I don't understand how people can treat a fellow being that way."

Knowing her concern was genuine Tom replied.

"It only takes a few ignorant minds to poison a community. It hurts me to think that people don't think for themselves. Instead of looking for the real truth they blindly believe others propaganda. I plan on making this right for Bert."

Tom gazed into Arlene's sincere eyes and reworded his last remark.

"We will put this right for Bert."

Arlene broke into a huge grin and again standing on tip toe kissed Tom's cheek.

"Thank you " she whispered.

Both feeling good now Tom asked,

"How about a home cooked lunch at a lovely cabin in the woods ?"

"I think that is a perfect idea. We can discuss and plan for the dinner for our aunts."

"I see you're one step ahead of me as usual." Tom smiled.

On the ride to the cabin Arlene shyly inquired about reading the second journal.

"By all means. You can have it while I'm away in the big bad city.

I started on the one of his experiences in the Korean war."

"I just may skip that one." smiled Arlene "That's obviously more up your alley."

Nearing his driveway Tom thought he recognized the beat up truck of the teens rushing in the opposite direction. He would have to check the house and grounds carefully. He would not alarm Arlene about this either.

While lunch was cooking Tom made a quick survey of the outside and luckily found no disturbance but he did retain an uncomfortable feeling.

It was a relaxed and enjoyable afternoon for both. The lack of stress was welcomed. Arlene was home early evening with a good night kiss witnessed by Eileen's happy face.

Chapter 8

The three block walk from the parking garage to the Chase Manhattan offices reminded Tom just how much he did not miss New York City with its wall to wall people. At last locating the right building he entered, identified himself and was directed to the office of Richard Zancle. Mr. Zancle was one of the two names Sam had supplied.

"Good to meet you, Tom. Sam called and provided your whole story to date. I know now there are a lot of missing pieces to Bert's life that we will be able to fill in for you."

Tom felt at ease instantly looking forward to whatever information he could glean to help better understand his beloved benefactor.

"Before we go into any details we should retrieve the safe deposit box. Did you bring your key ?"

Tom reached into his pocket returning with the key in hand.

"Good, then follow me. I have the other key."

"The other key ?" Tom questioned.

"Yes. A service we offer that Bert insisted on. It's a double method for added security."

Tom retained a confused look.

"I'll explain in more detail when we return to my office.

Tom was more than surprised when he saw the size of the safe box. He guessed it to be fifteen by twenty inches by ten inches deep and quite heavy. A small rolling cart was provided to carry it to the office.

Rather than the office they entered a small conference room adjacent. They were soon followed by another gentleman. A Howard Martin. The other name on the list from Sam. After introductions they all seated at the table. Tom was a bit uneasy, not worried or uncomfortable, just anxious of the unknown.

Richard opened the discussion.

"I can see you are a bit confused by all of this and I know Sam McCort did not fill you in on all the details. He thought it better if we outlined the intricate program Bert set up."

Tom could not wait for the explanation.

"As you know by now Bert turned out to be a very successful author."

"An extremely successful author." added Howard.

"Once he realized how fortunate he was he wanted to share it. Not just with anyone but with the town that almost destroyed him."

Tom gave out a soft snicker.

"That sure sounds like Bert."

Howard picked up the story.

"Right from the beginning Bert set up this account with us. This account was strictly for the royalties from his success. Because he wrote under a pseudonym the local bank at Tylerville was none the wiser. As you can surmise these royalties grew rather fast. Of course he did withdraw a few dollars to live on but in actuality it was a pittance. After his third book we formulated a self sustaining account that would allow regular yearly withdrawals to be used as charitable donations , most of which were for the people of Tylerville."

Tom was now completely dumbfounded. He sat back in his chair overcome with bewilderment of the words he was hearing. Richard and Howard both smiled knowing what Tom was going through.

After the pause to let the news sink in Richard continued the story.

"Bert had us set up a foundation to give out these donations. This completely left his name out of it."

Howard resumed his part.

"In addition to these donations he set up a method of capital investing in small business's. Start up financing and the like. He almost single handedly put the town on its feet financially."

Howard moved his hand up to the safe box.

"This box holds all the records and names of those transactions. Any questions up to this point ?"

"I'm still trying to soak up the first thing you mentioned." Tom replied with a smile.

"Tell you what." suggested Richard, "We'll open the box and leave you alone for an hour or so for you to familiarize yourself with the files and process. There's a fresh pot of coffee in the corner. Buzz me if you need us, if not we'll see you later."

Richard unlocked his side of the box and the two bank people departed.

Tom was thankful for the coffee and the privacy. He used his key and slowly lifted the lid. He viewed stacks of folders, each labeled. As he began to inspect them individually he realized there were many more than he anticipated. Noticing a pad and pencil on the conference table he started his own list of names and annual amounts. He couldn't believe the amount of organizations or people Bert supported. He then started on the business investments. Over a ten year period there were twenty two start ups or bailouts, all in the town of Tylerville.

Starting to return the folders to the safe container, Tom spotted a legal sized envelope with his name on it. It was sealed. He sat down and carefully opened it. It was dated about a month before Bert passed away.

Tom, my friend, my son, my everything.

Obviously with your reading this you are into my secret # three. It shows that the towns people did not defeat me, so don't let them beat you down. I kept all these proceedings as my own secret, but as all my other instructions, from here on out everything is your decision. I would, however, ask you to keep the donation foundation going. It is self sustaining so you should have no financial worry's in the future. If something does come up the two gentlemen you are dealing with at Chase can assist in any thing you want to arrange.

I had my own personal reasons for doing this but as I mentioned earlier from here on it is all your call.

Good Luck,

Bert.

P.S. Find yourself a good woman and treat her like gold. You will find that more rewarding than money.

Tom laughed inwardly immediately thinking of Arlene.

Mr.'s Zancle and Martin rejoined Tom.

"Well, what do you think of old Bert now ?" asked Howard.

"I always found him to be amazing and unpredictable but this is a total surprise.

"There is yet one more surprise." proclaimed Richard. "You should probably sit for this. Bert had briefly outlined both of your early lives and struggles you endured. His writing obviously freed him from that and wanted you to be free from worry also."

With that he handed Tom a savings deposit register book. Tom

Accepted the book and opened it. He read it and closed it with almost no reaction. This appeared odd to Richard and Howard, so Howard asked.

"Did you read it ?"

"Well, yeah. I am slowly finding out how generous Bert is. He already left me his home."

"What did the statement book say ?" Howard pursued further.

Tom looked at him in a funny way.

"It said seventy eight hundred dollars."

Smiling, Richard directed him to read it again. Tom opened the register and starred at it. He didn't move. He just starred.

"Does this say what I think it says ?" he inquired.

"Yes Tom, it does. It's seven hundred and eighty thousand dollars. Bert has been doing this for many years. He started it long before you joined the Marines. The success of his books and his investments was beyond belief. Even his publisher was astounded."

"And I still have another at home yet to be published."

"He mentioned another but that was quite a while ago. He was saving it for you."

"I have already discovered it with Sam and yes I will follow up and get it to the publisher. Are you sure this is the right amount in the register ?"

"Quite sure Tom, Bert was a very wealthy man."

"And yet he chose to live like an average man." Harold added more unknown facts. "He chose to live that way because he wanted the town of Tylerville to accept him as a person and not because he was wealthy."

Smiling again Tom replied that was typical of Bert. "And as you know even that didn't work. They still treated him like the scourge of the town all based on things that occurred years ago. They really knew nothing about the man nor did they try to find out. They prolonged a grudge against a young boy who, as it turned out was not guilty of anything except protecting his mother. But I guess that's what happens when you're not part of the "IN" group. Bert was a proud man. Some might say thick headed or stubborn but he never quit."

At this point Tom turned serious. "I hope to correct all of that. I don't know how yet but I will get back the decency he deserved. The respect he deserved."

Shaking the seriousness out of his head Tom apologized to the two gentlemen and changed the subject some what.

"Are there any other surprises I should know about." he asked smiling.

Richard answered with a matching smile,

"I don't recall any other secrets, at least right now"

"This is more than enough for now. Bert out did himself. I never expected anything like this. And since Bert chose to set up these systems of trusts and donations I will not go against his wishes, as long as the money allows."

"Unless there are drastic changes in the country's finances this should be able to maintain itself for quite sometime." added Howard. "Bert said that would be your decision, I guess you two knew each other well."

Tom smiled proudly.

"The notes I made for myself are all I need for now, I will leave everything as is for now. I'm assuming I can continue maintaining this safe box and you will continue to handle the foundation dynamics.

The Chase people were pleased to hear Tom's decision.

"Not to worry Tom, this is all yours now and we will fulfill all your wishes."

"This is all new to me so I will heed and probably need your advice on some matters."

"You will have our undivided attention when ever needed." Howard answered.

"Thank you gentlemen, Bert mentioned that very thing in one of his notes."

"Will you be heading home now ?" inquired Richard.

"No, it's been a long day already. I made hotel reservations for the night, I'll make the drive home tomorrow when I'm more rested."

The usual pleasantries were exchanged and Tom found his way to his night's lodgings.

Chapter 9

An early room service dinner and Tom was asleep by eight PM. In spite of the days surprises and shocks it was a restful night without a single dream. The next morning after a full breakfast Tom paid the ransom for the return of the car. Another reason to remember not to drive to New York City. Trying not to be too belligerent he told the parking attendant he did not want to buy the garage he only wanted to park overnight. He paid the exorbitant fee and drove north out of the city.

The drive home took the regular five hours. It just appeared shorter because his mind was non-stop with yesterdays enlightening session.

~ ~ ~

Tom turned into his driveway only to find three cars already there. He recognized Sam McCort's and the teens wreck of a truck. The third car was a state police vehicle. Having learned a long time ago not to panic he approached the two men standing outside the house.

Just in time Tom." voiced Sam. "Apparently your favorite teens decided to help with your gardening. No, they did not get into the house."

Turning to the uniformed man Sam made the introductions.

"Sgt. Adams this is Tom Thatcher, the owner of the property."

Extending his hand the trooper said "Semper Fi" along with a strong hand shake. Tom welcomed the hand and returned the warmth in kind.

The Sgt. readily volunteered;

"I got out in ninety two after the Gulf War. I understand Afghanistan was a bit rougher. At least you're home safe."

Tom looked at both men questions in his eyes. Sam spoke up first.

Don here." pointing to the Trooper just happened to make a stop here as our enterprising teens were in the middle of serious garden modifications."

There was a slight smile on his face.

Looking at the policeman Tom replied.

"I can see that. I'm glad you came when you did. Thank you."

"Don't thank me, thank Sam here. But I'm also glad I happened by, I caught them in the act. They had no excuse and actually didn't even try. They were all arrested and taken to the Constable station at Tylerville awaiting your decision."

Sam joined in. "I mentioned earlier the house wasn't touched but you might want to check it anyway while Sgt Adams is still here.

Tom reached for his house keys while all three walked toward the cabin. Inside all was well. Who knows what they would have done had they gained access.

"Okay, what's the next step." asked Tom.

Sgt Adams in an official manner stated;

"That's up to you. You will have to go to town and press charges or not. That's strictly up to you. I would imagine though this incident should stop the harassment for a while anyway."

"I want to thank you Don, for your vigilance. It's good to have a friend like Sam to keep my back covered."

Sgt. Adams finished up his paper work and said his good byes.

Tom prepared a pot of coffee and he and Sam made themselves at home at the kitchen table.

"So, Tom what are your plans for your unwanted guests ?"

"Well, I don't want them to get away with this, that will just lead to more serious antics. But I do want them to realize they can't do things like this because they want to."

"I think I know of just the thing." Sam suggested. "There is a program slowly taking hold which appears to be having some success."

"And what would that be ?" Tom asked.

"It's called Restorative Justice. They go before a judge or a board of citizens. Their misdeeds and consequences are openly discussed and appropriate judgements are metered out. A record is kept but it is not a police record and there is no permanent black mark that they would carry for life. The recidivism or the success rate is well above eighty percent. It has been particularly successful with the younger generation. It give them a second chance without something hanging over their heads for the rest of their lives."

"And what sort of judgements or punishments are given ?" Tom inquired.

"That, of course, depends on the judge or panel of inquiry. It is usually some type of community service or reparation to the offended party."

Tom was now sporting a quiet smile. Sam noticed this stating;

"It looks like you already have something in mind."

"I think I do. Tell me, just out of curiosity, are any of these boys related to the ones who persecuted Bert for so long ?"

"As a matter of fact I know two of them are and a third may be. The fourth probably went along for the ride. Why do you ask ?"

"Well, just between you and I this may just fit in with a plan I've been thinking about for some time now. A plan to right the wrongs that were perpetrated against Bert."

Looking slightly alarmed Sam spoke abruptly.

"You're not planning to get yourself into trouble with some kind of revenge, are you?"

"Thanks for your concern Sam, but not to worry. I'm planning just the opposite of trouble. Particularly now that I've learned what I did from the people at Chase Manhattan."

Sam took on a small grin.

"I take it you had a successful visit yesterday."

"Beyond my wildest dreams." Tom commented.

"I thought you might like what they had to say. That's why I left it up to them."

"I haven't worked out all the details yet, but when I do I would like you to be part of it as well. I know Arlene has already volunteered, especially after reading some of Bert's journals. Never mind that for now, back to the present dilemma.

As you know Bert kept me on the straight and narrow and probably kept me from being like these teens. It's my turn now to pay Bert back by perhaps teaching these same lessons to the next generation. How do we go about setting up this Restorative Justice program."

With a big smile Sam commented.

"You certainly are Bert's son. Let's go to town right now then and get things started."

~ ~ ~

Seeing Tom from the holding cell was not a comfortable thing for the young teens. They were trying to act indifferent but their uneasiness showed.

Without paying much attention to them Tom completed the necessary paper work and left the Constable's office.

Much to their surprise the four teens were released to their parents custody pending a hearing in one week in front of a judge. The parents all pledged to be there, with lawyers in tow of course. Sam McCort kept Tom appraised of the arrangements assuring him Judge McCallister was a fair and decent man, always open to new ideas. This week gave Tom the time necessary to prepare his thoughts and presentation.

~ ~ ~ ~

By the time Tom left Sam and the constable's office it was dinner time. He was very tempted to drop in on Arlene but finally decided to go straight home. He still needed time to process the last two days events. Another night apart wouldn't hurt either one of them.

At home and secure in his own world he fixed a quick dinner then relaxed with a glass of wine and one of Bert's journals. Tom never realized the intricacies of the Korean war. Bert's first person, on the spot, reports were most enlightening. He was now really looking forward to reading Bert's two war novels.

He found he could not concentrate on the reading. Thoughts of Bert's past and the garden attack he just suffered kept creeping into the battles of Korea. He put the journal aside, his mind drifting to the teens and the Restorative Justice idea.

"This will fit in perfectly with my rebuilding Bert's image plan." he thought. Tom then poured a second glass of wine feeling better about everything. "If I'm going to stay here I will have to get that phone installed. Things to do tomorrow." he said aloud. "I will wait until next week for the garden repair which will leave me free tomorrow to spend time with Arlene."

Tom was all smiles as he prepared for bed.

~ ~ ~ ~

Not wanting to call too early Tom waited until ten o'clock. Arlene answered on the first ring.

"I was hoping it was you." she whispered. "Are you still in New York City ?"

"Actually I'm a few streets away right now. Are you busy today ?"

"By the time I get to the front door and open it you had better be here." she laughed in answer and hung up.

-66-

As Tom entered Eileen's driveway Arlene was at the door waiting. She ran down the steps and threw herself into his arms.

"**W**hat took you so long ?" she scolded with a smile. Pulling him by the hand towards the house she said, "Tell me all about your trip to the big bad city.

Within a few minutes Eileen joined them. "I just put on a fresh pot of coffee and the tea is steeping. I have a meeting to go to, I'll see you two this afternoon. Think about staying for dinner Tommy love, I'm sure you two have a lot to catch up on. Bye for now."

She was out the door before either could answer.

Tom outlined the results of his New York visit including the three quarter million dollar account at the same time urging secrecy about that.

"**W**hy of course Tom, you didn't even have to ask. I'm not interested in your money Tom. It's you I care about, not your money."

Tom then mentioned the teens garden party visit. Arlene appeared a bit alarmed and instantly inquired. "Are you alright ?" Tom went into detail of the afternoons events and even described the Restorative Justice option.

"**I**f these young teens are related in any way to those who mistreated Bert, this program could be useful to rebuild Bert's reputation."

Tom was smiling now as he spoke,

"**Y**ou're always in step with my thinking. I plan to do just that."

"**A**nd of course you will let me help. I'm beginning to love that old man as much as you. I don't know if you finished reading the second journal as I did while you were gone. Some of those stories are a must read for all the people in this town."

"**T**here is a lot of reading I have to catch up on and eventually I'll get to it along with other plans."

"**N**ot to worry Tom, we'll get to everything and together we'll set everything right. But for now you have to read this one particular memo of his. I believe it will help with this present dilemma."

She handed the journal to Tom, a page marker indicating the story of interest.

"**Y**ou read, I'll get the coffee and tea.."

Tom, you were too young to remember this and I purposely kept this little incident from you at the time.

It seemed that one of the town's very upstanding citizens, who was a bit of a lush, was so out of it because of the booze that he had fallen behind one of the old factory buildings. Unfortunately for him there was a lot of broken bottles in the area where he fell. He was pretty badly cut and bleeding. I tried to help him as best I could to get him the first aid he needed.

When he recognized it was me helping him he began yelling help and the half empty bottle he was clutching suddenly came flying at me. It broke on my belt buckle and sprayed the cheap liquor all over me. I smelled as bad as he did. But even through his struggle I did my best to assist him. Eventually, with the noise of all the ruckus others came to assist me. At least so I thought.

It wasn't me they came to assist. My explanation was ignored but Mr. Important citizen was taken as bible. How I attacked him in a rage of revenge. Mr. Good Guy was taken to the hospital while I was arrested for assault and battery.

In jail, as you can imagine, I was treated like scum. Forever the no good. I was no good since I was young. After all I attacked my stepfather in the same violent way.

After two days I was released and charges were dropped. An unknown witness had come forward. Lucky for me she went to the state police. She was an out of towner. The State Police could not establish any damaging evidence against me, hence my release. As you can imagine, a renewed effort of harassment began. They soon tired when it was realized I was not about to cower to their will. The sad part of the whole story is that Mr. Drunk Good Guy went on to become mayor for four years. How's that for town control.

Lesson learned: If you know you are in the right, don't give in.

Arlene had already returned with the coffee though he was unaware of her presence. Tom set the book aside with mixed emotions; uplifted by Bert's outlook on life and upset and saddened by the treatment he received from the town folk. Arlene sat quietly sipping her tea staring with admiration at her new found hero.

"I'm sorry." Tom apologized, "I guess I got lost in my thoughts."

Her winning Irish smile told him all was okay.

"May I go with you when you go to court. For moral support if nothing else ?" She asked.

"I guess it would be okay though you might find it boring.

You are anything but boring Tom. Besides I enjoy being with you in case you hadn't noticed."

"How about lunch ?" he asked to change the subject.

"Only if you let me prepare it. I want to show you I'm not completely useless."

Tom just smiled. "Can I help ?"

"Nooo, let me spoil you for a change."

Chapter 10

Finally getting a telephone installed he received his first call from attorney McCort notifying him of the court date on the following Tuesday.

"May I suggest." said Sam, "That you wear your uniform. The more points in your favor the better for you."

Tom did not like to be a show off but Sam coaxed him into finally consenting.

The next few days were spent enjoying Arlene's company and preparing his presentation for a Restorative Justice remedy interspersed with visits to his aunt and Eileen.

During that time his mind kept recalling the last journal entry he read. Something about this particular passage kept nagging at him. He pushed it aside so as not to ignore Arlene.

Two days passed and once home alone after a refreshing day with Arlene he had time to concentrate on the upcoming hearing. Bert's journal came to the forefront again. It was like an itch exploding. Smiling to himself he now fully accepted Sam's idea of wearing his uniform. He even decided that it would be the dress blues with full medals. He sat down and wrote notes with Bert's journal writing in mind along with his own few experiences he had with the locals. Satisfied with his notes and thoughts of his presentation he happily went to bed and slept comfortably through the night.

The next day being Friday he and Arlene planned and partially prepared Saturday nights dinner for both their aunts as promised. The dinner party was a great success. Martha and Eileen drove out to the cabin together mid afternoon and did not leave till almost eleven PM. Arlene rode home with them leaving a relaxed and satisfied Tom alone with Bert's journals.

Sunday was a short visit with Arlene in the afternoon. It was agreed he would not see her on Monday to allow him the time necessary to finish preparations for court on Tuesday.

~ ~ ~ ~

Eight thirty Tuesday morning Tom, in full dress uniform, was ringing Eileen's door bell. It was Eileen herself who answered the door with her usual warm greeting.

"Come in Tommy, My don't you look sharp."

Tom was just entering the living room as Arlene descended the stairs. Half way down she stopped, frozen in place. She starred, eyes wide open along with her mouth. She stood, not moving close to a minute. Tom with a half smile commented.

"Well, you could at least say hello."

Her trance broken she blurted out.

"My God, you look beautiful."

"I've been called many things before but never beautiful." he returned.

"I have never seen a Marine in full dress uniform before." she said as she at last approached him.

"Am I allowed to kiss such perfection ?" she smiled.

"You are allowed and required to do so."

"You two are just perfect together." Remarked Eileen who then wished Tom good luck.

They arrived at the court house at a few minutes past nine. Court was to convene at nine thirty. Sam McCort met them in the parking lot. Tom exited the truck with Sam commenting.

"Looking sharp kid. The enemy is already inside; four teens, eight parents and two lawyers. I'll be with you for legal support but from here on the show is all yours." Sam, looking at Arlene added: "I see you brought along reenforcements."

Arlene beamed her smile; "Lead me to them, I'm ready for anything."

"I'll bet you are my dear. I think Bert would approve."

She blushed but remained quiet.

The trio entered the courtroom quietly walking to the front left. Tom and Sam took their place at the table while Arlene quickly seated herself a few benches back.

You could hear a pin drop in the silence of the room. All four teens sat dumbfounded as they stared in disbelief. Apparently the uniform was having the desired affect. The parents were equally struck. Sgt. Donald Adams of the State Police silently entered the room and almost unnoticed sat one row behind Arlene.

Judge McCallister made his entry to the customary respect tradition. Looking over the room his eyes returning to Tom slowly and seriously remarked;

"This court does not look favorably on theatrical dramatics. Staff Sergeant. Thatcher. I hope you have a good reason for the uniform."

The two opposing lawyers were smirking at the judge's remark.

" I believe I do Your Honor and with the courts indulgence I would like to address that reason before the proceedings begin."

The judge was silent for a few moments then addressing the attorneys for the teens.

"If the opposition agrees I will allow it."

The two men still wearing sly smiles agreed thinking this would be in their favor.

"You may proceed Staff Sergeant."

Judge McCallister sat back not taking his eyes from Tom.

"Thank you Your Honor." Tom took a deep breath thinking of Bert, feeling his presence.

"I have only been home for a few weeks or so Your Honor. I chose to wear this uniform today for what I think is a very good reason. You see Sir, to me this uniform represents freedom. My uniform and thousands of others like me, both men and women are present throughout the world. We are there voluntarily. We believe we are there to protect freedom. Not just ours in this country, but every ones. Especially these young teens before you. To keep them free to get an education. Free to participate in the career of their choice. Free to live where they choose. Free to respect others.

When I was younger than they are now my mother passed away. My aunt was thrown into the job of trying to raise me, which I'm sure was not easy for her. I could have ended up as unruly as they are today had it not been for a gentleman, not unfamiliar to most of you. He took me under his wing. He mentored me on how to be a good person, to respect others, particularly others we may not agree with. The value of honesty was always fore most in his teachings. How to accept failure as part of our learning experiences. How to be true and honest to yourself. This is a must before you can be true to others. These are the principals I learned to live by, and with no regrets I might add. This man taught me these things because he wanted to save me from myself. I can never thank this man enough for putting me on the straight and narrow. It has served me well both in uniform and out. I would like to thank him by living these same principals.

These four young men before you committed an act of destruction of another's property. Yes there should be consequences. But Your Honor I do not think it should be through the court process. This could lead to a permanent black mark on their future. I personally do not want that to happen. A few misguided deeds of youth should not ruin the rest of their lives. There are other ways to show them there are consequences for misguided actions.

I am here to ask the courts indulgence that they not be prosecuted in a court environment."

During this whole short speech Tom was continually engaging other eyes. Parents, teens and lawyers. He now refocused back on Judge McCallister.

"Those are very persuasive words Staff Sergeant. What exactly did you have in mind."

"Your Honor." Interrupted one of the youth's attorneys. "May I have a word ?"

The judge raised his hand to stop him.

"You will have your turn counselor. I'm anxious to hear what this Marine has to say. Proceed Staff Sergeant.

"Thank you Your Honor. I'm sure you are aware of the program called Restorative Justice."

"I am aware of such a thing."

"That is my proposal Your Honor. To impress upon these young gentlemen that there are consequences for their actions, now and throughout the rest of their lives. I feel a punishment should be metered out for their misdeeds but not to put a blot on the rest of their lives."

"And what do you feel is a just punishment ?"

"Something along the lines of community service. Say about thirty hours each. The start of which should be the restoration of my property that they destroyed, under my supervision or a court appointed supervisor."

"I do have a few reservations regarding your idea, Staff Sergeant. First, this community does not have such a program as of yet. We need approval from the State Department of Corrections. That only comes if there is funding. Second, I realize they damaged your property but I can't believe four young men need thirty hours each to repair the damage done. After yours and my satisfaction of your damage what do they do with the rest of the hours still to serve."

"We could than turn to the town itself. Parks, hospital, Senior housing. I'm sure there is plenty of work that goes undone for lack of funding.

"You make a good point young man. As you just mentioned

yourself, lack of funding is a key issue. Supervision being another."

"**I** believe I can answer that also Your Honor. I will personally volunteer as a supervisor until a permanent program can be established."

"**A**nd funding ?" asked McCallister.

"**I** am prepared to take on that challenge also. I will personally fund such a program until outside funding becomes available."

Tom stood quietly while the judge pondered his offer. After two minutes Judge McCallister turned to the interrupting attorney.

"**N**ow counselor, you had something to say ?"

"**I** withdraw my question Your Honor, I believe I received my answer."

"**V**ery well then, there will be a fifteen minute recess. We will continue this hearing when I return."

"**A**ll rise." called out the bailiff.

~ ~ ~ ~ ~ ~

The judge returned wearing a poker face that no one could read. He sat quietly shuffling papers before he spoke. Finally scanning the whole court room he stated calmly.

"**N**ow then, I have considered Mr. Thatcher's overly generous proposal and am not in disagreement with it. But in order to keep everything fair opposing council may now have its say."

Attorney Albert Johnson stood to represent the four teens.

"**Y**our Honor, during the recess we met with the young men and more importantly their respective parents. We all unanimously concur with Mr. Thatcher's more than generous offer. We would, though like the courts assurance that no permanent record will be held against these young men ."

With a satisfactory inward smile, Judge McCallister personally gave that guarantee. Turning back to Tom and smiling again he quipped.

"**S**taff Sergeant, are you sure you're not a lawyer."

Before an answer could be given the judge continued.

"**I**t is the ruling of this court that community service be fulfilled in the amount of thirty hours each. If during that time period there are any other infractions committed against the public at large they will be seriously dealt with in a regular court. The ramifications of which, I'm sure you young gentlemen do not want to deal with. Council for both parties will meet in my chambers tomorrow morning at ten o'clock. Court is adjourned."

Arlene was alight with pride but remained seated while Tom and Sam McCort huddled in a quiet conference. They were joined by Sgt. Adams who congratulated Tom.

"That was a good thing you did for those kids. Let's hope they learn from it."

The court room slowly cleared out with Tom and Sam being the last to leave.

Arlene walked to Tom and blushing threw her arms around him and kissed him. As she broke the kiss she whispered,

"I think I love you."

Tom not knowing what to say squeezed her hand and in the same whisper replied.

"And I you."

Jokingly Sam interrupted;

"Break it up you two, they're trying to clear the court."

Once outside Sam went straight for his car while two women hesitantly approached Tom.

"Mr. Thatcher may we speak with you for a moment."

The other politely, while looking at Arlene, apologized for the interruption. Tom recognized them as two of the mothers.

"Why yes, of course. How can I help you."

"You already have Mr. Thatcher. We wanted to thank you for your more than generous treatment of our sons. Not pursuing prosecution under the law was a very gracious consideration, and for that, as mothers we are thankful. Our husbands don't exactly agree with us but I'm sure, in the end, will come around. We wish you luck with this program and we both feel certain that you can make a difference in our sons."

Looking over her shoulder to very impatiently waiting husbands, the second woman added,

"If we can help in any way please let us know. We are anxious for your plan to work."

"Thank you again." the first woman finished as both turned and rushed away.

Arlene followed with her eyes with a proud smile.

"See, I'm not the only one who admires you. Now Mr. Wonderful you may take me to your beautiful log cabin where I will make lunch for both of us."

She hooked her arm in his asking;

"Is this allowed with a Marine in uniform ?"

Tom just smiled as the two strolled to the truck.

On the ride home Arlene mentioned; "Did you see the look on the four teens faces. They were quite taken with you."

"Just the uniform." Tom replied brushing it off.

"No, I think not. The change that came over them when they realized you were not going to prosecute was amazing. It wasn't just a look of relief. I think I detected a hint of contrition in their eyes. And admiration for you, I might add."

Tom felt a flush at her words. He was not accustomed to being singled out for praise of any kind. He changed the subject to the perfect weather today. Arlene caught on and silently smiled and agreed about the weather.

Pulling into the drive was the first time Arlene saw the yard and garden damage. She was actually shocked and dismayed that they could have done this. Right away she thought of Bert's journal.

"What a terrible thing, to carry on a taught hatred for so many years." She thought. *"They weren't even born when their parents and grandparents started this hateful prejudice."*

She could feel tears building for both Bert and Tom.

Tom parked the truck and opened the door for Arlene who again threw her arms around his neck to hide the tears while repeating; "I love you, I truly love you, my darling."

This little act made her feel better and was able to subdue the tears.

~ ~ ~ ~

After lunch they walked the garden area deciding what to do and how to redo the whole yard. Arlene was very content. So much so that she started hinting at the surprise she had for him back at Eileen's house. She enjoyed teasing Tom about it the rest of the day.

It was nine o'clock and both agreed Arlene should go home. As they entered Eileen's house they announced that they were back.

"You can show me the surprise now." Tom suggested.

"Oh no, it's much too late tonight. You have to get home to rest. I'm sure you will be having a busy day tomorrow, with meeting Sam after his session with the judge and the other lawyers."

Of course she said this while smiling continuing her tease.

Tom knew it was time to give up and she was right about the next day being busy. After a lingering proper good night he headed home.

Relaxing in the rocking chair with a cold beer he returned to Bert's war journals.

Chapter 11

Tom's meeting with Sam McCort the next day proved to be anticlimactic. He was pretty much given Carte Blanche with the young men and their community service. Their were absolutely no objections from any of the parties. He and Sam worked out a schedule of Tuesday, Wednesday and Thursday from ten AM to two PM As an added feature Tom would give them lunch when they were working at his house. This schedule would take effect the following week. Sam would follow up with arrangements for all concerned.

Tom then began thinking ahead for other jobs after they finished at his place. He would wait and discuss this part with his aunt and Eileen. They would be more in touch with the needs of the community. Satisfied with the days results he returned home choosing not to see Arlene. He did , however, call her on the phone.

After a quick lunch he decided he would attack Bert's last remaining mystery. The last key. Retrieving it from its safe place he went right to the loft. There in the far corner was an old metal box about two feet square and eighteen inches high hosting an old steel padlock. Tom thought of taking it downstairs, but he hesitated. He seemed to enjoy the secretive air about the whole thing and changed his mind. Up here in the loft it was just between he and Bert. He liked this idea or at least until the contents were known. Taking the key from his pocket he unlocked the container. Ever so slowly he raised the lid. He laughed to himself for purposely drawing out the suspense.

The first thing his eyes caught sight of was a legal sized envelope with his name printed on the front. He smiled knowing it was another personal note from Bert. Tom liked this connection to Bert that he missed so much. He held the envelope for a time while his mind wandered to past times with his mentor. Thinking only of the fun times he eventually brought himself back to the present, envelope still in hand. Undoing the clasp he exposed the contents. As he anticipated there were several pages of letter sized notes. He focused on the first page.

Tom,

You are now at the last and final key. I do hope I haven't upset you with all my mysteriousness. Bare with me, I felt it brought me closer to you while doing this.

I mentioned in an earlier note that the contents of this box would mean something only to you and I. Again I say do with these things what you will. I share this with you because of who you are and what you mean to me.

Enjoy your life as I did mine. I may have had a few bumps in my road but I lived life my way and am happy and proud of the way it worked out. It enabled me to meet you. I hope you find a good woman to share your life with.

Well son, this is my final contact with you. Remember, your life is only what _you_ make it.

Love you, my son,

Bert.

PS.- My military dress sword is hidden in this loft. I forgot where I put it.

~ ~ ~ ~

Tom sat there staring at nothing for the longest time, his mind wandering from Bert to his mother and back again, memories of his youth running rampant. The envelope fell from his lap breaking his nostalgia. He laughed at himself as he put Bert's letter aside.

Turning his attention to the box he removed a cardboard covering the top. A well folded winter dress uniform showed. As he removed it he noticed Staff Sergeant stripes. Tom knew that from the Korean War era achieving such rank was difficult, more difficult than his era. He was impressed but not surprised.

Setting the uniform aside there were more papers. His discharge and other separation papers. At the bottom of the pile was a listing of awards and achievements. Tom was stunned as he began reading. It read like a catalogue describing all the ribbons and medals ever issued. Without reading word for word he put the list aside choosing to reach for the boxes containing the various awards. He touched each one as if he were in contact with Bert himself. The two purple hearts caught his attention. He could not recall seeing Bert with any type of infirmity. He carefully opened each medal case exposing Bert's battle prowess.

The Bronze Star, Silver Star, (two awards), Navy Cross, Purple Heart (two awards), Republic of Korea Presidential Unit citation, Good Conduct Medal (two awards), Navy and Marine Corps Medal, U.S. Presidential Citation. United Nations Service Medal, United Nations Medal, Korean Defense Medal, National Defense, Korean Service, Marine Corps Expeditionary Medal, and misc. ribbons not connected with actual combat.

Bert's biggest secret of all at the very bottom of the box wrapped in a red velvet cloth was the medal of honor. Tom had no idea at all. Bert was apparently more than just a hero, he was a one man army.

Tom could feel the tears welling up in his eyes as he held the medal of honor. He rummaged through the awards papers finally locating the citation. He read it through tear strained eyes. It seems he single handedly held off a company of Red Chinese regulars receiving his second Purple Heart, all the time helping his fellow wounded Marines to safety. He alone saved countless lives while taking a heavy toll on the enemy. He was still fighting hand to hand as friendly reenforcement arrived. He continued in charge until the enemy was totally subdued. Even then he had to be physically carried from the conflict area under protest.

~ ~ ~ ~

Tom, filled with an uncontrollable pride in his friend vowed then and there that this would no longer be kept secret. As of yet he had no idea of what he would do but he knew it would come to him eventually. Still in awe of the distinguished awards he turned his attention back to the box. Miscellaneous articles and news reports interspersed with a few pictures of Korea, obviously his fellow Marines, made up the rest of the contents. Another envelope appeared, eight and a half by eleven in size. It too was sealed. Tom broke the seal to reveal a picture of the Medal of Honor award ceremony with President Eisenhower placing the ribboned medal around Bert's neck. Standing next to the President was the then Commandant of the Marine Corps, General Shoup.

Tom smiled proudly gazing at the picture, his mind returning to the idea of unveiling Bert's secret. The people if this town should know who Bert really was. He carefully returned the medals and papers to the metal safety container knowing he would see them again soon. Leaving the box where it was for now he returned downstairs.

Content with himself he went outside to the small barn to ensure he had the tools necessary for the garden repair. He thought of the input he received from Arlene and along with his own designs drew a few sketches for the boys to follow. Tom was actually looking forward to working with the young men. Recalling Arlene's comments about the teens admiration for him he thought perhaps he could put that to good use and get the youngsters to straighten themselves out.

"This would be a perfect job for Bert." he laughed to himself.

~ ~ ~ ~

Having a few days before the errant teens were to arrive, Tom took advantage of the time to work around the cabin both inside and out, taking breaks now and then to further read from Bert's war journals. "I thought I had it rough in Afghanistan, but Korea was no picnic either. It was probably even worse because of the winters." he murmured aloud.

He did, however, find time for Arlene and both their Aunts. Their preplanned second dinner for them was also a great success. Since both Aunts knew each other rather well he and Arlene were open targets for their teasing, especially along romantic lines. Their early embarrassment easily turned into a return game of one upmanship against the older pair.

Arlene renewed her taunting of Tom about her special surprise. Eileen and Martha soon joined in knowing of the gift. Tom soon realized he was out numbered and gave up on forcing the issue. He knew eventually he would be privy to the "Big Secret".

The evenings of these last few days Tom spent with his favorite girl from Ireland. Either long hand in hand walks in the woods surrounding the cabin or quiet strolls in downtown Tylerville. To Tom's surprise the town folk passer byes actually acknowledged them with smiles and polite civil greetings. This, of course further fueled Arlene's pride in her special man. Without comment or complaint she accepted Tom's slow pace of romance. She wanted him to be as comfortable as she was already.

Chapter 12

The long awaited day arrived with clear skies, sunshine and moderate temperatures, quite suitable for some physical garden work. At ten minutes of ten some driveway dust announced the arrival of Tom's new work crew. The beat up truck carrying three was followed by a car with two others. The car was driven by one of the mothers who addressed him outside the courthouse. Tom exited the cabin to meet the young men. He nodded with a smile at the woman who returned a quick wave and smile but left again without verbal contact.

"Good morning gentlemen. Being on time is a good sign for both of us. We obviously did not get off to a good start on our first couple of meetings. Let us hope, for both our sakes, that can be forgotten and perhaps we can become friends."

His words went unanswered but Tom could see in their eyes their acceptance.

"My name is Tom." he said extending his hand welcomeingly. "And yours are ?"

Each in turn stated their name and accepted his hand shake. There was Bill, Fred, who seemed to be the leader, Steve and Josh.

Tom looking at the fifth young man stated with a smile "I see you brought along reenforcements."

"My name is Mark and I hope you don't mind that I joined my friends."

"Not at all Mark. Glad to have you. You will just be taking some fun away from the rest of them."

They all smiled at his remark.

Tom, then with a soft smile and warm eyes replied.

"Now that didn't hurt a bit , did it ?"

The younger set answered with a chuckle and an apparent sigh of relief.

"**O**kay then, let's get to work, follow me." Tom suggested as he headed for the barn.

Tom recognized Mark as one of the ones at the cabin the first time he came upon them. *"He was probably just as guilty, just didn't get caught."*he mused. *"I'm glad to see he is willing to do his share to right the wrong."*Tom decided that the best thing to do now was to let it go by.

We'll grab some tools and decide where to start. The usual assortment of garden implements were waiting; shovels, rakes, hoes, pitch forks etc. Walking back to Bert's "Farm" area Tom outlined his rough idea of what he wanted done. "But" he said, "By no means are these plans written in stone. If any of you has what you think is a better idea, please feel free to speak up. All suggestions will be greatly appreciated and discussed by us all."

This remark had Tom's planned reaction. All five boys exchanged glances of surprise that someone would actually ask for their advice.

"**M**y lady friend has already volunteered her suggestions."

Now looking directly at the teens Tom continued.

"**I** do believe you already met at the Country Kitchen."

All five boys suddenly avoided Tom's gaze looking down at the ground.

"**N**o matter you will meet her again soon I'm sure."

Ignoring their reactions Tom kept walking as if he didn't see.

"**O**kay you guy's wait here, I'll get my preliminary diagrams for your perusal."

Tom purposely took a few minutes before returning. To his surprise, but not really, the boys started weeding and raking on their own.

"**O**kay guys gather round. This was my original plan which of course you obviously disagreed with when you decided to redesign my garden."

The young ones all sheepishly looked away, their guilt easily showing on their faces. Tom on the other hand was smiling not harboring any ill thoughts. He was delighted to see a genuine reaction. He could work with them from here on.

With a serious voice for a moment he carefully spoke.

"**W**hat is past is past gentlemen. Let's all work on a better future from here on."

Not waiting for any comments Tom quickly slid right onto his rough garden design.

"**N**ow, I want you all to seriously review my sketches for the yard and garden, then physically look around at all available space. I am genuinely open to all ideas."

Still amazed that someone would ask for their input the sketches and notes were passed around. They eventually spread out each looking at different areas of the property.

Josh spoke first.

"Mr. Thatcher, I don't really know anything about gardening but remembering things my Mother does in our back yard I have a question about this area you have marked as tomato's"

"Go ahead Josh, I'm listening."

"Well Sir, it seems there are an awful lot of shade trees here. Mom always talks about how the tomato's need lots of sunshine. This doesn't look like a very good place for sunshine."

"Great observation Josh. Obviously I don't know that much about gardening either. Let's look for a more open spot."

Tom's acceptance of Josh's idea broke the ice. The boys, with a much changed attitude, one by one made suggestions. Tom finally called a meeting at the picnic table allowing each individual to add or subtract his idea to the pre sketched plans. The pros and cons of each idea were openly discussed and voted on before being made a permanent change to Tom's original plan. Proud of what had just transpired Tom suggested a break. Arlene was kind enough to supply a huge amount of lemonade.

"What say we refresh ourselves before we get into any physical labor."

Tom retrieved a two gallon jug and some plastic cups from the house.

"Help yourself guys. After you have rested give yourself an assignment and we can turn to." I will redraw these updates to the plan tonight."

Being treated with respect by an adult appeared new to the youngsters. They almost did not know how to respond. Each chose a job for themselves asking Tom for his okay which he willingly gave.

"Any questions, don't hesitate to ask."

Soon all were spread out doing what they thought was best for a particular area. All was quiet for a while yet slowly, joking with each other started. Tom was warmed at seeing this comradery. It reminded him of his recent days in the Corps.

Lunch was provided which the crew enjoyed and did not abuse the time. Each returned to his chosen task without prompting. Joking persisted throughout the early afternoon.

"Sorry guys." Tom apologized. "Time is up , it's already ten past two. Stack you tools over here and you can head out. Have a safe ride home and thanks a lot."

Each boy said their own thank you to Sir or Mr. Thatcher.

The yard was suddenly quiet. Tom sat alone for awhile thinking of years gone by and the good times with just he and Bert.

~ ~ ~ ~

Tom felt good about the day's results. Not so much the progress made on the garden but the youngsters reaction to doing the community service. He sensed a definite change in their attitude. He wasn't sure of the reason for the change. It could have been any number of things; the court threat, their parents counseling or perhaps his own words got to them. No matter, as long as the change is for the better. The benefits are all theirs and soon, perhaps not yet, they will realize it. After clean up and a shower he headed out to see Arlene.

~ ~ ~ ~

Chapter 13

Both Arlene and her aunt hung on every word as Tom outlined the days activities. Arlene appeared even more pleased than Tom upon hearing the days results.

"**I** would like to meet them while working. Do you think that's possible? That is if you agree."

"**I** would encourage it." Tom responded. "But not just yet. Give me one more day with them alone. Let's plan on Thursday. I'll pick you up early so we can be back to the cabin before ten."

"**I'**m already excited." bubbled Arlene.

"**Y**ou'll be staying for dinner Tommy love, and I'll not take no for an answer." exclaimed Eileen. "The two of us have been planning this all afternoon.   After dinner I'll leave this pretty young thing all to you alone. I have a meeting to go to."

Dinner was more than filling and Tom and Arlene volunteered to clean up to allow Eileen to go out. Time passed quickly as the young couple discussed the house and garden plans. Tom mentioned the teens input for the garden which again pleased Arlene. She knew deep inside this Tom Thatcher was the man for her.

Tom was leaving just as Eileen returned.

"**H**ave a good night Tommy love." she called after him as he drove away.

~ ~ ~ ~

The work crew was early by fifteen minutes with all raring to go. The day passed as the previous one with progress faster than expected. At the end of the second day a bond was obviously developing. Not just between the teens but with Tom also.

At the rate they were working Tom would be losing them soon. He suddenly realized he had better line up some additional job sites. Both Eileen and his Aunt Martha would need to advise him. He would pursue that tonight hoping to get both Aunts together again.

His Aunt Martha planned dinner for four that very night. When the teens departed Tom picked up Arlene and her Aunt for the short ride to his Aunt's welcoming arms. They were no sooner settled in the house when the teasing began. Tom was outnumbered again and was the brunt of all the verbal barbs being thrown. Dinner, however, was most pleasant, the conversation concentrating on community work for the young nere-do - wells.

Tom and Arlene volunteered for table cleanup and dish duty allowing the two seniors time to put their thoughts together. With the dishes finished but before rejoining the aunts Tom and Arlene took a casual after dinner stroll holding hands like two school children. Few words were spoken. They took comfort with each others company. Returning to the house they discovered they were not even missed with Eileen and Martha were so enmeshed in their topic and a second glass of wine. Before Tom could ask about any progress he noticed a number of papers with assorted scribbles.

"Tommy, my lad." Eileen started, "We think we have a number of suggestions that you may or may not like. We also thought we could go to our various women's clubs and gather more ideas."

"No need for that yet, I'm sure you two ladies have some great ideas."

With both Aunts now smiling Martha suggested we sit down and they could review their scattered notes. Tom made himself comfortable on the sofa while Arlene snuggled up close not letting go of his hand. Eileen caught her act instantly and quipped,

"Leave the poor lad some room to breathe Arlene, you're going to suffocate him. At least wait until you're married for that."

Martha joined with a big grin as Tom and Arlene went crimson. Arlene self consciously moved away somewhat and unclasped her hand from his. Tom looked at her and retrieved the hand, naturally to her pleasure, her eyes glistening like stars. Ignoring what just happened the two Aunts began their presentation.

"To start with Tommy love," Eileen began, "The local library, which does not have a very large budget, sells used books from donations a few days a week. They do this from an old barn on the site beside the library itself. The barn is in bad need of repair and a good paint job. We both know you have the skills necessary for such a task and your teens would be of great assistance.

Tom's answering smile could not get any bigger. Arlene picked up on this and joined in. Martha jumped into the conversation with another suggestion.

"The downstairs of our little church that we use for small dinners and meetings could really use a facelift. Even if it is just some paint."

As she handed that particular paper to Tom Eileen spoke again.

"The town has not really kept up with repair on the young children's playground and I'm sure they would accept any volunteer labor they could get."

"The senior center could also use some garden updates." added Martha."

Continuing the alternating presentation Eileen took her turn.

"More importantly than even that is the fact that there are a number of house bound seniors who have no means of keeping up with the necessary maintenance of their own houses. The poor dears want to stay with their own memories. There are a number of us who volunteer whatever time we have to help out but that still leaves a lot of physical work we are not capable of."

Eileen paused for a few seconds allowing Tom an opening.

"Whoa, slow down ladies. This is already beyond my expectations. I think you two and probably some of your friends should be the ones running town hall." he joked.

"We were just trying to help as you asked Tommy love." replied Eileen.

"All joking aside, this is really wonderful. I will get together with Sam McCort and make a presentation to Judge McCallister. As I said this is more than enough for now and the hour is getting late. Tell you what. These four things are a great start, but you can keep working on your list for future projects. Thank you ladies."

Tom stood and walked to each of the aunts and gave a kiss on the cheek.

Tom drove Eileen and Arlene home then returned to the cabin thinking how wonderful the whole world could be sometimes.

~ ~ ~ ~

The beat up old truck dusted up the driveway at nine forty five. Tom had already picked up Arlene and both waited by the cabin door as the young men disembarked from the vehicle. A sudden stillness and seriousness overcame the boys when they spotted Arlene. They approached cautiously. You could tell they were uncomfortable. Fred, their apparent leader assumed his position. In a soft voice but with his eyes to the ground he politely stated,

"**I** apologize Mam, for myself and my friends for our unjust actions at our first meeting. We meant no harm or offense."

Arlene, with her winning smile extended her hand to Fred's face, lifting his chin so her eyes could meet his.

"**A**pology accepted and no offense taken. The incident is now forgotten. Can we be friends now ?"

She moved her hand from his face to take his hand. He gently shook her hand a grin slowly building on his face. After that each boy introduced himself and softly shook her hand. The group was now one large smile. Tom was happy for the boys and proud of Arlene for the way she handled what could have been a touchy situation. With his own smile Tom asked,

"**A**re we going to party all day or are we here to work ?"

This took the younger men by surprise until they saw the smile on Tom's face. Tom continued with,

"**Y**ou can look at how pretty she is later, right now we have a garden to build."

The teens gladly retrieved their chosen garden tools and dispersed to their preferred areas. Arlene was all bubbly again and told Tom she would go prepare lunch for everyone.

Arlene set a wonderful lunch table, cold salads and luncheon meats for sandwiches along with plenty of milk. The boys treated it like a party but could not take their eyes from the beautiful Irish lass. Arlene enjoyed the attention yet maintained a proper demeanor in her interaction with the teens.

At two PM Tom gathered the boys around making sure Arlene was in the cabin first.

"**Y**ou men did a great job with this yard. I am very proud of what you accomplished and in such a short amount of time. I would guess next Tuesdays session will definitely finish it. We can then move to another project. You can be proud of yourselves and I will speak to the Judge accordingly. Have a safe trip home and enjoy your weekend. See you next Tuesday."

Tom turned to go noticing the boys were hesitating as if not wanting to leave. This time Josh spoke up.

"**A**h– Uh–Excuse us Sir, but we sort of wanted to thank Miss Arlene and say goodbye,"

Tom smiled at their request while replying,

"I think that would be very nice, I'll call her."

He turned to the house, the boys following.

"Sir !" Fred took the lead again.

"We were wondering if we could ask a few questions about your time in the Marines ?"

"I guess that would be okay if you think you can take the time."

"We have no place to go." joined Steve.

The anxious look on their faces convinced Tom they were sincere.

Arlene joined the group at the picnic table to many praises and thank you's for the lunch. She glowed again with the attention but soon reentered the house.

Tom turned his full attention to the boys.

"Now, what is it you want to know about the Marine Corps."

"Well Sir," Fred started, "We wondered if it was really as tough as the stories we've heard."

With a slight grin Tom replied.

"That depends how you approach it. What kind of an attitude you bring with you. After watching you boys for the last three days I believe you could handle it."

Tom's statement caused many happy expressions. Bill, the obvious shy one found his voice asking,

"Mr. Thatcher, those medals you were wearing in court, do they stand for anything special ?"

Tom felt a twinge of embarrassment, not liking to talk about himself.

"Yes Bill, they all have their own reference."

Tom hoped to let it go at that but Bill persisted.

"Could you tell us about them ? I did recognize the purple heart. My uncle had that from Korea. Were you wounded also ?"

Tom felt self conscious but knew he had to answer the young inquiring mind.

"I don't usually like to talk about this but since you asked I will try to explain. Just promise not to make a big deal of it."

The younger men caught on and understood Tom's uncomfortable feeling.

"We were on a small six man patrol through a road filled with IED's. By passing the road led us in to an ambush. We were outnumbered about three to one. Thank goodness the Isis forces were not very good marksmen. All six of us sustained wounds but nothing serious. Mine was in the upper thigh. It sort of knocked me on my ass but because of the situation there was no time to dwell on self pity. We did win the day and managed to obtain the information we set out to get.

Thank goodness for corpsmen. They work miracles with nothing. We all had light duty for a week or so but stayed on the front so as not to lose our foot hold."

The teens were all wide eyed with open mouths.

"One more thing gentlemen, please, not a word of this to Arlene."

"Not a problem Sir, we understand." Josh offered.

"If you are actually interested," Tom volunteered, "We can speak more of this but not today. Tell you what, we will make next Tuesday a short day, then we can spend more time getting to know more about each other. And don't worry, it will still count as your time."

Of course the young group was pleased to hear this, though they were beginning to adjust to working for a common good. Saying their polite good byes they piled into the old truck and set out for home.

Tom returned to the cabin and Arlene.

"I think you have won them over." she smiled.

"And so have you with your perfect handling of their meeting you. You were wonderful."

Arlene tip toed again and placed a kiss on Tom's cheek.

"Thank you, I had a good teacher." she replied.

Tom outlined next Tuesday's plans and before he could finish she interrupted.

"You will want to do that alone and I thoroughly understand. It's a man thing. Not to worry, I will spend my time helping Aunt Eileen."

To show she was not at all upset she immediately changed the subject.

"They did a wonderful job on the garden. The whole yard for that matter. The place is starting to look special. I just love it here."

The rest of the day the two spent attending to little touches here and there around the yard. Tom suggested a pizza and beer supper was in order before returning to her Aunt's home.

~ ~ ~ ~

Friday found Tom at Attorney McCorts office discussing the work suggestions he received from the two aunts. Sam's agreement with the ideas came easily and he instantly put a call in to Judge McCallister. All was in their favor today with an appointment being made for ten Monday morning.

Tom was feeling jubilant that everything was coming together so nicely. This now left him free to spend the weekend with Arlene. He and Sam had an early lunch at the Country Kitchen. As usual some of the teens were there but this time without the noise. A few even went out of their way to say hello to Tom addressing him in their new found Sir or Mr. Thatcher. Sam, almost in shock asked,

"What have you done to these kids. If I didn't see it for myself I wouldn't have believed it."

Tom replied in a smiling voice,

"Let's just say we came to a mutual agreement and let it go at that."

"You truly are Bert's prodigy." Sam commented in a half smile.

Tom was humbled by this statement.

When Brenda brought the check to the table she thanked Tom with pretty much the same surprise as Sam.

"Whatever magic you performed on these youngsters is much appreciated. I'm not the only one who has noticed the drastic difference either. Thank you again."

As she finished speaking she reached her hand out to softly touch Tom's. Tom could feel himself getting flush again yet politely smiled a thanks.

"Don't worry pal I won't tell Arlene." Sam chided.

Chapter 14

Arlene could hardly wait before pounding Tom with questions about his meeting with the attorney. She was as elated as he was and not afraid to show her emotions by throwing her arms around his neck along with a big kiss. Taken by surprise Tom almost lost his balance which set Arlene to laughing. After leaving his arms and curtailing her laughter she decided it was time for his surprise.

"Since you have been such a good boy about everything I think you deserve a reward and I have something special for you. Wait here." She added as she left the room.

She was away for about two minutes returning with the words:

"Please turn to the wall and no peeking."

Not wanting to spoil her fun he did as he was asked. Tom heard what sounded like moving chairs or something similar but did not peek.

"Okay you may turn around now but close your eyes."

A little confused he smiled and followed her wishes. He felt her presence close to him, her soft perfume filled his senses as she lightly kissed his cheek.

"This is for you my darling because I love you. You can open your eyes now."

Tom's eyes were opened wide, his mouth followed suit. He remained speechless as he viewed a life sized oil painting of his friend Bert. The head and shoulders portrait contained all that he remembered of Bert, the mischievous eyes and forever half smile. To Tom this was so real he thought he even heard Bert's voice. He remained frozen, taking in every detail until his eyes blurred with tears. Arlene remained close her hand holding his. Regaining control of his emotions, yet not moving his eyes from the painting he struggled to find his voice.

How ??? When ??? He is so real."

"Auntie had some old pictures. That along with the journals and your stories of him I feel I grew to know him. I wanted so much to please you. I could feel in my heart your love and admiration for Bert which seemed to flow into my heart and wanted to be released through my hands. The best and only gift I can give you is my art. I hope I was able to please you."

Tears, now free flowing, Tom gathered Arlene into his arms and with a shaking voice spoke softly.

"You have more than pleased me which makes me love you even more. I'm sure Bert would have loved you a well."

Now the pair were sobbing openly with tears of joy. Tom slowly moved away to be able to look into her eyes.

"Thank you my love. You have renewed my strength to fight for Bert. You have showed me love I didn't know even existed." He paused a few seconds. "Please, don't ever leave me. I need you with me. With you at my side I can take on the world."

Arlene had never experienced this kind of joy and happiness before and hoped it would never end. They remained silent for a while, still in each others arms staring at the portrait. Eventually Tom composed himself.

"This is the greatest gift you could have given me. You truly are an artist. You not only captured his image but you captured his soul."

Tom's words brought on the flush Arlene felt growing in her cheeks.

Eileen arrived home her always cheerful self.

"I see you two were getting mushy over the painting. She really did capture the old goat pretty well, didn't she, Tommy love."

Tom was not offended by her old goat reference knowing of her true feelings for Bert.

"That bare piece of wall to the right of the fire place would be the perfect place to hang the old Geezer." said Eileen, all the while smiling.

Tom and Arlene instantly agreed. Eileen, ignoring their comments continued;

"There's an excellent frame shop over in Cedarville you might want to consider."

Looking directly at Tom and Arlene with a knowing smile Eileen finished with;

"You two might want to dry up them tears. You look like two silly school children."

She moved to the couple and kissed each on the cheek.

"I'll go make us all some lunch."

During lunch Tom seated himself so that he could still view Arlene's magnificent painting. One might say he was totally preoccupied with the image. Arlene and her aunt sat quietly smiling to each other knowing this was a special moment and a good thing for Tom. Realizing his selfishness he apologized to the women and joined in enjoying the lunch and their company.

The weekend was nondescriptive with Tom and his true love occupying themselves with the mundane tasks around the cabin and garden with some additional help from their respective aunts. The young couple were content with their lives with each other.

-95-

Chapter 15

Ten o'clock Monday morning Judge McCallister arrived at his office to find Sam McCort and Tom Thatcher already there. He did, however, anticipate this and was all smiles as they shook hands. Once the three were settled around the desk the judge opened the dialog.

"Some of your success precedes you Mr. Thatcher. I have already heard rumblings of the change in attitude of some of the boys. What kind of a magic pill are you using ?"

Tom, smiling bashfully, answered.

"Nothing special Sir. I'm just treating them as equals and showing respect."

"Part of your Marine Corps training I suppose." the judge commented.

"Some, I guess Sir, but most is from old Bert Morrow. This is the way he taught me."

"Interesting, too bad the town is not aware of this."

"I'm working on that, Sir." Tom replied quickly and firmly.

"I'll bet you are Staff Sgt.." McCallister sort of mumbled. Now to the business at hand. I understand you have some suggested projects for these youngsters."

"Yes, Sir, I do. I just wanted your approval before I instituted anything."

Tom then outlined the two senior aunts suggestions with obvious enthusiasm.

"Again I'm impressed Mr. Thatcher. You obviously did your homework. The most impressive part of the whole thing is that you are going out of your way to save kids who, with malice of heart tried to destroy something near and dear to you.

Without hesitation Tom replied with emotion.

"I could have been one of them Sir, had it not been for Bert Morrow. He set me straight without me knowing it. I owe this to Bert. I owe this to myself and I feel I owe this to these kids. Well, they are not really kids, but this town's future, this country's future. I believe in what I'm doing and I think I can get these teens to believe in themselves also. As you said yourself you have already heard of some changes. Trust me , there will be many more."

Tom seated himself deeper into his chair while Sam just quietly smiled knowing Tom was probably correct. The judge sat back in his large leather swivel chair and softly replied.

"Remind me, Staff Sgt. Never to argue a court case against you."

After a half smile half chuckle Judge McCallister continued.

"You have my full backing Tom. May I call you Tom?"

Tom cheerfully nodded his approval.

"I'll leave all planning and decisions to you. Should you need any of the courts assistance please do not hesitate. And just to keep you in the loop I am pursuing the Restorative Justice Program with the State. Actually I'm excited. I wish I had more people with your interest and enthusiasm."

McCallister stood extending his hand which Tom received gratefully noticing the hand shake was firm and warm indicating his sincerity.

Back on the street Sam commented,

"I wish Bert was here to witness this. I'm sure he would be quite proud, as I am, by the way."

Tom speaking somewhat seriously without looking at Sam answered.

"Trust me, Bert is here alright. I would not be able to accomplish any of this if he were not looking over my shoulder. After you see the miracle Arlene performed, you will agree with me Bert is here."

The attorney looked a bit confused with Tom's statement. Tom, now proudly smiling, looked directly at Sam.

"This is something you have got to see in person. How about you and your wife joining us all for dinner some evening. You will understand then."

"You have now piqued my curiosity and I would love to come to dinner. That will also give me a chance to see your rebuilt garden. Tonight is out, so how about Thursday ?"

"Thursday it is my friend." returned Tom. "I know Arlene will be thrilled to have you."

With this they parted company with Tom anxious to tell Arlene of the day's results and to plan Thursday's dinner with Sam. He wanted to include both aunts also.

Chapter 16

The former wayward teens presented themselves at nine thirty rearing to go. They already selected their favorite tools and were busy at their chosen garden patch before Tom even exited the cabin. He joined them, smiling, proud of their initiative, deciding to let them know of his feelings.

"I must admit guys I am very pleased and proud of what you have done with this place. The results of your good work and even better attitudes, as promised, has been expressed to the court. I have personally met with Judge McCallister on your behalf."

The teens all were bashfully grinning at Tom's words. Tom enjoyed their reaction. Not to linger on this Tom moved on to another topic.

"I don't know how you guys feel about the grounds now but I do believe we're finished. At least I'm more than satisfied."

Again the young faces lit up. Fred, obviously concerned questioned.

"But today will only make sixteen hours. We still have fourteen hours to go. What do we do now ?"

"I'm glad you brought that up. I have another assignment planned which has already been approved by Judge McCallister. I think we will enjoy doing this together."

Curiosity took over the yard. Tom allowed it to become a pregnant pause. Finally ending the suspense Tom asked if they knew of the old yellow barn by the town library.

"Who doesn't ?" was the unified answer. Then individual remarks followed.

"That's a dump." "It should be torn down." "What an eyesore." "I heard the library still uses it."

"That's true guys. They sell used books to raise money."

"Money for what ?" Josh asked.

"To fund activities for the elderly and less fortunate so they can enjoy the library and new books."

"That sounds like a pretty nice thing." commented Fred.

Tom took instant note of this being impressed by the remark. *"There is hope for them yet."* he thought.

"So why did you mention the barn Sir ?"

"Because guys that is our next project. Some badly needed, overdue repairs and a paint job."

"But it's so old and broken down." was the next comment.

"That's the beauty of it Steve. It's not as bad as it appears. A little TLC will go a long way. Those old structures should be preserved and I believe, together we can do that."

A hush came over the yard as the youngsters looked at each other. The two minutes of silence was finally broken when Josh asked.

"Do you really think we can Sir ?"

"Yes I do Josh. Because of the way I have observed you men work, I know we can do it. I have a lot of faith in you men and I think we can show this town just what you are capable of."

Again looks were exchanged. Tom could tell that his use of the word men caught their attention. One by one each stated they were up to the challenge.

"Great!" Tom cried. "Now that we're finished here, let's get some lunch, then as agreed upon, we can get to know each other better."

The cleanup went fast while Tom supplied the makings for a cold lunch with milk a plenty.

Lunch was relaxed along with the usual fun and jokes so common with youngsters not quite adults. Tom joined in but still kept an air of friendly authority. All joined in the cleanup of lunch leaving everything at the end of the picnic table.

Bill picked up the conversation from where he left off the previous Thursday.

"Sir, I did some research over the weekend remembering the medals you wore. If I'm not mistaken one of them was the Bronze Star. Isn't that for valor of some sort ? Could you tell us about that ?"

Tom, his usual shyness showing again tried to skirt the issue but the others joined in urging him on. Not wanting to dampen the teens curiosity he went into a watered down version of the incident that garnered him the award. The young men soaked up every detail interspersed with questions of the dangers faced by Tom. When he finished his shortened story the table was quiet as the group stared in awe at their now hero.

Tom silently convinced himself this would be a good time to pursue the topic of why he was, or more so Bert, being targeted.

"Enough about me guys. I'd like to know more about each of you. You know, how school is going, what you do for hobbies or what you would like to do. What may be your career choices when you get older."

The table became quiet until Bill spoke up.

"School is such a drag right now. The mandatory subjects we must take leave a lot to be desired. They are down right boring."

The other lads readily agreed.

"What subjects are you referring to ?"

"All of them." Josh quipped.

To keep in line with the boys Tom let himself laugh at the remark.

"To be more exact." Bill continued, "These advanced math classes. Why do we have to go through that? We already know how to add and subtract."

Tom was shocked to hear this kind of remark. Keeping his feelings to himself he further inquired.

"Do they offer a physics course ?"

"Yeah." answered Steve. "But that's even worse. Very few of us understand anything."

"You can ask questions, can't you ?"

"Some of us do but the only answer we get is read the book."

Tom suddenly became aware that there was a serious problem here and not all just the kids fault. Trying to turn the subject mood around he enthusiastically volunteered that both math and physics were two of his favorite subjects.

"And by the way the skills of math and physics will come into play on our yellow barn project."

Confused looks circled the table. Tom knew he had their interest.

"The work we are going to do on the barn is going to be more than just slopping on some paint to cover up faults. We are going to be doing some reconstruction and structural reenforcement to make sure that the whole thing doesn't fall down on some unsuspecting old lady."

This remark drew some laughs along with interested looks.

"And believe it or not the basics of all of that is both math and physics."

Tom was positive he had them hooked now.

"Is that something you can teach us Mr. Thatcher ?" Steve asked.

"It would be my pleasure and privilege to do so. I'm hoping by the time you return to school you will be well versed and more than willing to return to both math and physics classes."

Questionable grins showed on their young faces but their renewed enthusiasm prevailed.

"Can we start on the barn this afternoon ?" Fred asked.

"No, it's too late for that now but I'll see you all there bright and early tomorrow. Just make sure you wear old clothes. We are going to be tackling some pretty dirty work. We still have some time left so let me ask you a question. Why did you target me for your garden redesigning? Actually why any destruction at all ?"

The mood of the whole yard changed. Some shame and guilt could be detected on the young faces. Fred took the initiative stating,

"Our time is up, we should be going now."

Tom answered smiling.

"Actually you still have about forty five minutes to go. Look fellows, I'm not trying to put you on the spot. I thought that now that we were friends some explanation would be in order. I will not force you into anything and I am not trying to embarrass you. I just thought we could become even closer friends if we cleared the air. And that goes both ways. The more honest we are with each other the stronger our friendship can become, and that is something I would really like."

Tom could see the nervous glances and fidgeting taking place.

"Okay guys. If you really want to leave then go ahead. I'll meet you all tomorrow at the barn. Remember what I said, old clothes. Have a good afternoon."

Hiding a slight disappointment Tom turned to the dirty dishes to return them to the cabin. The boys moved slowly to their old truck with obvious second thoughts. Tom kept his back to the group as he purposely re-stacked the lunch dishes. He heard the truck door open and his spirits dipped some what.

"Oh well," Tom thought, *"I'll have to try a different approach to get the boys to open up."*

He lifted the tray and aimed for the cabin, his thoughts filled with disappointment. As Tom neared the door there was a quiet voice, almost a whisper.

"Mr. Thatcher ?"

He recognized Fred's voice even from the whisper. He turned to see all five young men looking at him sheepishly.

"We would like to talk to you, that is if you have the time."

Filled with hope again Tom answered.

"I'll always have time for you men."

Tom set the dishes on the step by the door and returned to the picnic table followed by the teens. Once all were seated again Tom inquired,

"What's on your mind guys ?" knowing full well what the topic would be.

"To start with I have a confession to make." stated Mark quietly.

The other four boys looked at Mark, encouragement in their eyes.

Tom waited silently not wanting to further the uncomfortable feeling he knew Mark was going through.

"Well Sir, I - - - I - - -I was with the guys when we- - - we- - - messed up your garden. I just happened to leave before the police came. In all good conscious I wanted to share in their punishment, if you will. I'm sorry."

With that Mark lowered his head and eyes. With a warm half smile and soft voice Tom replied.

"I figured as much because I remember you from your other unwanted visits,"

Looking dismayed Mark asked.

"If you knew Sir, why didn't you say something ?"

"I didn't feel it was my responsibility and now I'm very glad I didn't bring it up."

All five pair of eyes were now staring at Tom with confusion. Tom's smile was warm and almost contagious.

"Why I didn't bring it up is because of what you just did. You, Mark, just performed a difficult and most honorable deed." Tom paused here a few seconds. "You admitted and took responsibility for a mistake you made. A mistake that affected others. You were willing to make amends by joining your friends in the negative consequences of that collective mistake. To me Mark, that shows strength of character, not just yourself but all five of you. That alone, in my eyes, makes it worth while to consider you as friends. I hope the feeling will be mutual for the present and for long term."

Four young men looked at Mark and one by one started smiling. Fred then turned to Tom;

"Mr. Thatcher, I think we would like to answer your question now.'

Tom was inwardly pleased but maintained an air of aloofness.

"In the spirit of friendship I hope." he commented.

"Yes Sir, I think we would all like that." Fred replied and then continued with, "It wasn't you we were targeting. It was old Bert."

"But why him ? What did he do to you ?" Tom inquired calmly and as softly as he could.

There was no immediate answer as the boys looked at each other bewildered not knowing what to say. Josh finally found some nerve saying;

"He was an old grouch and not very friendly."

"How do you know that. Did you ever try to talk to him ?"

Silence reigned again as the youths exchanged glances.

"**W**ell everybody knew he was an old crank." Steve finally answered. "He was a nasty old man and was not well liked by the town for years and years."

"**B**ut what did he personally do to you ?" Tom pushed calmly. "Did he hurt you in any way ?"

"**W**ell- - - no, but others said he was not to be trusted. He lived here in this dump and wouldn't talk to anyone."

"**H**e was an old recluse." joined Bill.

Yet maintaining his calm Tom asked;

"**D**id you ever try to talk to him ? Did anyone ever try to talk to him ?

"**W**hy ?" inquired Steve. He was crazy and possibly dangerous."

"**D**o you know for sure he was dangerous ?" Tom replied.

Again silence.

"**E**verybody said he was." Josh answered.

"**B**ased on what and who is everybody ?" Tom furthered.

He could read the uncomfortable tension he was causing and rather then lose the teens he changed tactics. He so wanted to show who Bert really was.

"**T**ell you what guys. I don't want to turn your friendship away nor do I want to make you upset or angry, so I'd like to show you something. Come with me."

Tom headed for the house, the group following again, their curiosity building. They always wanted to see the inside of the log cabin and how Bert lived. Just before opening the door Tom, smiling to himself, said;

"**Y**ou'll have to excuse the mess inside. I haven't had a chance to clean or dust since I moved in. The place is just as Bert left it."

Smug grins appeared on the five young faces knowing how messy Bert's place was going to be. Pushing the door wide Tom echoed his previous invitation.

"**C**ome in, please. Make yourselves comfortable, I believe ther are enough seats."

Maintaining his inward smile Tom enjoyed the surprised expressions overtaking the youngsters. This was not what they were expecting. Pretending not to notice their facial changes Tom seated himself as central as possible to the group.

"**I**f you don't mind." he smiled, I'd like to tell you a little about old Bert."

Tom hesitated a few seconds making sure he had every ones attention.

"Bert Morrow helped to raise me since I was about ten or twelve years old. My mother passed away when I was very young and I went to live with my Aunt Martha. I'm sure most of you guys either know her or know of her. I was becoming a handful for her as I got older, That's when Bert stepped in."

Tom went on to relate the story of their first meeting when he got beat up.

"From then on Bert took me under his wing. He was the one who made me what I am today. He taught me both honesty and honor, acceptance not ridicule, to help others, not ignore, pride not cockiness. He was the driving force in my life of learning fairness.."

Wonderment covered the boys faces. This was a whole new picture of Bert they were not aware of. They all seemed to be stumbling to find words. Bill was the first.

"I apologize Sir. For all of us. We had no idea that you were close to Bert."

"Bert was like the father I never had. But my relationship with Bert has nothing to do with the present situation. Your misdeeds were uncalled for under any circumstances."

"We know that now Sir." Fred interrupted. "And I can assure you that deeds, or misdeeds as the case may be, like this will never take place again. By any of us, here or anyplace else."

One by one the crew verbalized their agreement.

"I think I knew that before you did." Tom answered with a warm understanding smile. "By the way, now that the air is somewhat cleared I would like to state once again that my name is Tom. I appreciate your respect and in turn respect you for it. Now that we can agree to be friends I would like to share a little more of Bert with you. Things no one ever attempted to inquire about. Please allow me to read a few things."

Tom retrieved a few books from the small library.

"These my young friends, are journals that Bert kept most of his life. There are a few passages I would like to read to you that may answer some unasked questions."

The five teens indicated their sincere interest which Tom instantly took advantage of. He read the passage of when Bert attacked his step father and the resultant punishment. He paused to let the words sink in while gauging the facial expressions he was now seeing. As if Tom was not present they all agreed they each would have done the same thing given the same circumstances. They also could not understand the injustice of the punishment. Why ? They asked. He did nothing wrong. Their intimate remarks went on for a few minutes until Josh finally looked over to Tom apologetically stating;

"We had no idea."

All the group nodded in agreement.

"There's more if you want to hear it ?" Tom suggested.

Fred, softly and politely answered, "Yes Tom, I think we would all like that."

The room became quiet with all eyes on Tom.

Rather than reading from Bert's journal Tom went into additional detail of his own first meeting with Bert. How the old man saved him from the bullies. And how he then, along with his Aunt Martha, started his initiation into manhood concentrating on respect for others no matter what. The teens sat spellbound.

Tom gazed at his watch reading five minutes past four. Closing the journal he stated;

"Okay guys it's getting late. Your folks will think I kidnapped you."

They all protested instantly, pleading to hear more.

"I'm more than willing to read more but not today. You're already two hours past your time to go home. Tell you what, after work tomorrow I'll read some additional passages if that's what you want."

"That would be great Tom." exclaimed Steve, "We really do want to hear more of Bert."

Reluctantly they all stood to leave letting their eyes drift around the cabin. Eventually making it to the door saying their farewells, each in turn reminded Tom not to forget the journal tomorrow. It was not until four thirty that the foot dragging young men finally left in the beat up old truck. Tom's eyes followed the dust cloud down the drive feeling extremely satisfied with today's results. He could not wait to tell Arlene.

Chapter 17

Up with the sun and birds Tom was still floating on the high of the day before. He arrived at the yellow barn at nine forty only to find his anxious crew waiting for him. Tom happily accepted the ribbing he received from the boys for being the last one there. Once comfortably parked he opened the trucks tailgate taking a seat with his mug of black coffee. He smiled inwardly after observing the teens' attire. They were truly dressed for dirty work.

"Okay guys gather round."

Before he could finish his sentence questions flew. All with the same curiosity.

"Yes, I did bring the journals." He answered laughing but inwardly pleased.

"But work before pleasure. The first thing we all must do is to closely examine this place, bottom to top and back again, to assess what we think needs to be done. I am going to give each of you an area of responsibility."

This of course perked up the boys spirits. An adult was again trusting them with their input. Each boy in turn stood a little taller.

"You are to inspect your area in detail and record all that you feel could or should get attention."

Tom proceeded to hand out pad and pencil.

"When you are finished report back here with your detailed list. I will give you further instructions after you complete this task."

Tom's crew hurriedly accepted their assigned area and separated in all directions. Within twenty minutes the five teens were smiling at Tom, pages of notes in hand.

"Good job." Tom commented, "We'll check notes later. Now each of you switch and do the same thing. Keep changing until all have inspected the five locations."

Smiling eagerly they disappeared from view.

"**T**his alone is going to eat up the four hour day." Tom said aloud to himself. "That only leaves me twelve hours over three days. I guess I'll have to finish the job myself.

The always friendly Eileen O'Conner startled Tom.

"**W**hat world are you on Tommy love ?"

He turned smiling at the sound of the familiar voice. His smile turned even brighter when he spotted Arlene behind her aunt.

"**W**e brought lunch for the crew." she offered. And if you are a good boy we may allow you to have some also."

"**D**on't listen to her love, you can have whatever you want. The library ladies think this is a wonderful thing you are doing. I'm afraid though they may have a few additional suggestions of their own." Eileen added apologetically. Tom kissed Arlene lightly while taking the lunch cooler from her his mind hanging on Eileen's last remark.

"**H**ello ! I'm still here." chuckled Arlene touching Tom's shoulder.

Tom slightly embarrassed looked into her eyes.

"**I**'m sorry, I was just thinking ahead."

Taking Tom's hand in both of hers she spoke softly;

"**I**t's quite obvious you like what you're doing, and we all think you're doing a great job."

The young lads started returning and were all smiles to see Miss Arlene. Each, almost overly polite, greeted her warmly. They also, to Tom's pride, respectfully addressed Eileen O'Conner.

"**O**kay guys, leave me your lists and you may follow these two lovely ladies who were kind enough to supply lunch. I want to see you all in forty minutes."

Arlene snapped to attention, saluted and said "Aye, aye Sir." much to the delight of the five young men. Tom, now laughing followed with

"**G**et out of here." as he turned to sit on the tailgate of his truck.

Once the food was set up for the boys and Eileen to play mother, Arlene joined Tom with a specially made sandwich and lemonade. They chatted quietly as Tom continued to review the work crews list. Exactly forty minutes later the boys were at the truck staring more at Arlene than Tom.

"**I**'ll pick up you and Eileen for dinner at my aunts' tonight." Smiling she bid goodbye to the crew and helped Eileen cleanup.

"**O**kay gentlemen, it's time to get serious again." Tom said with a smile. "Your lists are even better than I expected. Let's review them together and make plans accordingly. Then I would like each of you to choose a section based on what you think you would like to work on. This should also be based, not only on what you would like to do, but what knowledge you think you can bring to that given area."

The fact that, again, they had a say in planning the project boosted the group's morale tremendously. Serious and enlightening discussion filled the next two hours resulting in a base plan that all agreed would work. Areas of responsibility were then assigned, each teen knowing they would also be helping the others.

It was now a few minutes after two and Tom could see his crew was anxiously awaiting the journal reading.

"**O**ne last bit of important business to discuss before Bert's journals." Tom stated to five serious faces. "It seems the ladies committee of the library may have additional requests or projects. They would like a short meeting with us as to the feasability of their ideas. I don't think all of us should appear as a group. I feel that would be overwhelming to these gentle elderly ladies. I think two of you should represent us. I'll let you decide which two would be the better spokesperson for the group."

The teens eyed each other with concerned smiles. Tom then added;

"**I** will not be attending that meeting but I know whoever you choose who will represent our group in a professional and gentlemanly way.

This really took the teens by surprise. You could see all their thoughts in their eyes and their expressions turning to serious smiles.

"**Y**ou can give me your decision as to who the representatives are tomorrow."

Not allowing for any more questions or comments Tom immediately reached for Bert's journals. The question buzz of the teens faded and all attention was now on Tom and Bert's stories. Tom chose Bert's narrative of the time he was arrested for the murder of his fiance. He read it slow and deliberately letting each sentence register fully with his captive audience. Even though he had read this passage before it took all the control he could muster to keep his emotional composure intact. The silence of the young men told Tom he held their complete attention. He finished the passage and looked at his silent audience, their eyes self consciously averted from his. Tom decided not to interrupt their silence. After a long spell of quietude Tom slowly closed the journal planning on putting it aside. Bill, almost in a whisper spoke.

"**W**e still have time Sir, aren't you going to read more ? I think we would all like that."

Josh followed with;

"Please Tom, we would like to learn more of Bert."

Fred also joined with;

"I believe we are truly realizing that there is more to Bert than we were aware of."

This pleased Tom to hear these words but chose not to comment.

"Well, if you are sure you don't mind I would love to read more of Bert's memoirs."

For the next passage Tom chose the time he was arrested for helping another town's person with the desired results. He could tell they were visibly upset by what they just heard.

"No wonder old Bert was bitter." uttered Bill.

This simple statement was just the opening Tom wanted. In a calm, soft voice he replied.

"Ah ! But that's where you are wrong my friend. Bert was not bitter and least of all a crank."

Stunned by Tom's comment the teens stared open mouthed in surprise. Not waiting for any further comments Tom continued.

"This was his home. He grew up here. He dearly loved both his mother and father and was happy with them here. Yes, things took a dramatic turn for the worse, most of which was beyond his control. Because of a few self righteous individuals, a false reputation was built around supposed and made up circumstances. Again beyond Bert's control. But he was still not bitter. He wanted to stay here in the town of his childhood. As I said he considered this his home and here he wanted to stay."

"But he seemed like such a grouch." Mark chimed in.

"Did he really ?" Tom asked calmly. "Did you ever try to talk to him ?"

"Welll-ll no." Mark answered. We were sort of told to stay away from him."

"I realize that." Tom replied. "You boys are also a product of that mind set of two or three generations ago. No one ever attempted to know Bert, so a made up, false reputation persisted. Not one person ever attempted to get to know him, they all just assumed things because of the false reputation that was being spread.

Tom paused smiling.

"Before I get you too upset allow me to further read from these journals."

Tom read another anecdote. He picked out the one where he spent a few days and nights with Bert and burning up their dinner. Again the wanted results were shown. It put the teens in a joking mood with Tom being the brunt of the verbal barbs.

"Tell you what guys. I'm pleased you want to learn more of my friend Bert. I am more than willing to share these personal anecdotes with you if you allow me to. And after these stories I have other more personal information to share. I believe you will eventually see Bert for the great man he really was."

Though deep in thought the crew enthusiastically agreed with Tom's suggestion.

"Don't forget guys, pick a representative or two for the meeting with the ladies of the library. Let me know who in the morning and be prepared to work. Now if you will excuse me I have a dinner date with a very pretty lady."

Smiles and joking ensued ending the day as each went their separate ways.

~ ~ ~ ~ ~ ~

Tom arrived at Eileen's house at precisely six PM after a shower and change of clothes. Arlene flew into his arms as she answered the door.

"I missed you so much today but I'm learning that is something I'll have to get used to. And yes, we are both ready."

On the way to Aunt Martha's Eileen dominated the conversation during the short ride.

"I just loved your teenagers, Tommy love. They were so polite. I never realized how intelligent they were. They certainly were not the same boys I knew six months ago."

Tom smiled at her remarks while Arlene was beaming with pride.

Aunt Martha welcomed all with open arms with special attention to Arlene. Now it was Tom's turn to radiate with pride.

Dinner, as expected was a pure delight with every one enjoying seconds. Tom mentioned his planned representatives to meet with the library ladies and cautioned about being prejudgmental.

"Give the boys free rein and I'm sure you will be surprised."

Both aunts agreed telling Tom not to worry. They would make sure everything went well.

After dessert and coffee in the living room Tom drove Arlene and her aunt home. Eileen said her good nights and politely disappeared. Tom and Arlene cuddled on the couch for a short time speaking vaguely about future plans each not wanting to push the other. It was about eleven when the couple kissed good night.

Tom entered his log home still filled with the scent of Arlene about him. Once the lights were on his attention was instantly drawn to Bert's portrait.

"Well, my friend, some progress was made today on restoring your good name in this town."

Tom continued talking to Bert as if he was physically there.

"I know you kept your life accomplishments secret but I think it's time the world, or at least this town, knew who you really are. For keeping this town alive economically they should have built a monument to honor you properly."

Tom paused staring at the life like painting. He remained motionless, not knowing for how long.

"That's it !" he yelled aloud. "Why not ? Planning can be done slowly and quietly until the time is right."

Satisfied with this new idea his head filled with never ending thoughts. Happy thoughts.

"Good night, old friend." Tom addressed the painting and took himself to bed.

~ ~ ~ ~

Not wanting to be the last one at the yellow barn this time Tom set his alarm for an early rise. He awoke well rested and looking forward to a day with the teens. Arriving at the barn at nine AM gave him the time he wanted to review the five different reports the crew turned in. Combining the suggestions of the trouble spots he was able to come up with a comprehensive work plan that he figured would be approved by all.

The rearing to go crew arrived at nine forty having chosen Fred and Josh as the groups spokespersons. Tom nodded his approval and directed the two to the meeting room at the library proper. Then outlining his plans to the remaining three youths he praised all five crew members for being so thorough. He pointed out the things they picked up on that he himself missed. This, of course, just added to the confidence level of the crew. They then divided up the work stations according to desire and work expertise.

No sooner had they finished the assignment portion ,when Fred and Josh returned. The crew and Tom were anxious to hear the results of the meeting. The two returning representatives were all smiles. Although Tom was happy for them he tried not to show too much emotion.

"What suggestions did the library committee have for us ?" he asked.

"None really." replied Fred. "Nothing that we have not discussed ourselves."

"That's a credit to you guys for being so thorough. Personally I'm quite proud of you for being so alert as to what had to be done."

Both boys acted a touch embarrassed though you could tell they wanted to say something. Josh eventually overcame their shyness and spoke softly.

"To be honest, we did not know what to expect from the ladies. In the past it appeared they always wanted to avoid us. But today they treated us like adults or equals."

"Why do you suppose that was." inquired Tom casually.

Stuttering slightly Fred answered.

"Because we behaved and tried acting like gentlemen. We showed them respect for their opinion and answered by outlining our plan. They all agreed and gave us their approval."

"They even offered us tea." added Josh excitedly.

"See what a little politeness can do for you." commented Tom again casually. He knew a good lesson had been learned.

Purposely not dwelling on his comment Tom spoke a little more officially.

"Okay, guys, I really think it's time we got to work."

All smiles and filled with renewed enthusiasm, the work crew each went their own way after choosing the necessary tools for their particular job.

Tom remained by his truck looking at the planned tasks wondering how he was going to accomplish every thing after Thursday when the teens community service was over. His confused doubts were suddenly interrupted by a familiar voice. Sam McCort smiled as he said,

"I thought I would find you here. How's your project coming along."

"Actually it's going better than I expected. Much better." Tom replied.

"As it would have if Bert were running it, if they had only given him a chance." Sam added.

"What brings you to this part of town." inquired Tom.

"I have a message from Judge McCallister. I was in court earlier and he asked if I knew where you were so he could locate you. He asked if you could see your way clear to drop in to his office around three this afternoon."

Tom looked puzzled as Sam finished with,

"I have no idea what about. I'm just being the messenger boy." he added quickly. "I'd like to stay and chat but I'm already late for an appointment. Let's make it a point to get together. I'll call you this weekend."

With that Sam rushed away.

Tom began his rounds to see how the work was progressing. He mentioned a lunch break but each one in turn made the decision to keep on working. Tom did not want to discourage their work ethic. The question did come up however, of the readings of Bert's journals. Sadly Tom had to disappoint them. He mentioned his appointment with Judge McCallister that was a must. He promised at the end of tomorrow he would take all the time they wanted to read from the journals. As they were leaving for the day Tom told them he would have nothing but good to report to the Judge about their completion of the community service. Proud smiles were exhibited by the teens.

Chapter 18

Tom, seated comfortably and confidently across from Judge McCallister, listened carefully as he outlined the beginning of the Restorative Justice program for Tylerville and surrounding area.

"It's thanks to you Tom for urging me forward on something I should have looked into a long time ago. You have my sincerest gratitude for showing me the merits of such a program. Which brings me to the reason I asked you here. I have heard nothing but positive remarks about your handling of this trial program. Now comes the big question."

Tom nodded he was ready for whatever comments the judge had.

"Are you still inclined to continue the program ?"

With a soft smile Tom answered firmly.

"I will follow through on my commitment as originally stated until such time as a complete and serious program is established with regular full time personnel. Even then I will continue in whatever capacity you may deem constructive."

McCallister relaxed back in his chair now wearing a smile of his own.

"I hoped that would be your answer, actually I was counting on it. The wheels are in motion as we speak establishing such a program but I imagine it will be a few months before we hear of official results. In the meantime we will forge on by ourselves if you don't mind me including myself in your already successful venture."

"I look forward to whatever way I can assist you, with my main focus on helping these youngsters see what life can really offer them." returned Tom.

With a broad smile Judge McCallister stood from his chair extending his hand to Tom which was received warmly.

"It is I who look forward to being a part of your work and dream."

"Thank you Sir for your confidence and support. I honestly believe we can make this work."

"From where I stand you already made this work and very well I might add."

Reseating himself the Judge continued.

"Getting back to serious business, I have two more candidates for your library project. I'm afraid these two are a bit more rebellious than your present group, but I still think it's worth the effort."

"I will do my best Judge." replied Tom

"I have no doubt about that Tom, just to reenforce the courts backing I will personally drop in now and then to let them know the seriousness of this program versus a court trial and sentencing."

"I think that would be an appropriate approach in defining the validity of this program. It will show them the benefits are for them and their place in society and not just a bunch of words from a judge in a courtroom. No offense Judge."

"None taken Tom. That attitude of yours is what makes you perfect for the job you so willingly undertook. Now that we know we're both on the same page I have already taken the liberty of directing the two new teens to you at the yellow barn at ten in the morning. Beyond that I will leave the scheduling of hours completely to you as you see fit."

Tom again nodded his acceptance of the responsibility.

"Oh, by the way the new boys are to serve forty hours each."

Tom's mind was already at work feeling relieved the library work could continue uninterrupted.

Another warm, firm hand shake ended the short meeting as Tom took his leave. Back in his truck he reviewed what had been discussed and was pleased. He kicked over the engine and excitedly headed for Eileen's house.

~ ~ ~ ~

Tom's cozy evening with Arlene ended with his explanation to her of the journal readings he promised the boys after work the next day. He was planning on spending the rest of the day with his crew as sort of a going away celebration. Arlene as usual, totally understood. She even proposed baking some cookies and bringing them by when the work day was over. Tom agreed this gesture on her part would please the teens and show them there were others who cared. After a lingering goodbye Tom finally made for home.

Chapter 19

By nine thirty Tom was at the yellow barn, assessing the progress made to date. This whole project was going better, and faster than he expected. He figured by the end of the original crews last day the major percentage of the work would be completed. The next major rehab to attack would be painting the exterior of the barn. "I had better check with Aunt Martha and Eileen about the color first." he said aloud to himself.

Hearing voices he left the barn and greeted his crew by his truck. The days assignments were doled out and just as the boys were about to move away a new voice was heard.

"**H**ey! Are you this Tom guy we're supposed to see about some stupid community work ?"

Tom turned to the sound of the voice with attitude and quietly, but firmly answered.

"**Y**es, I'm Thomas Thatcher if that's what you mean."

The five original crew stepped aside, each with a slight smile.

Tom glanced at his watch. It was about ten minutes after ten. Still holding a firm tone he commented while staring directly at the two youths.

"**I** believe you were supposed to be here at ten."

"**Y**eah, whatever." was their snide answer.

"**W**ell you'll just have to make up the time at the end of the work day."

Now Tom's original group was smiling to the point of almost laughing though they were trying to conceal their enjoyment. Tom noticed and before it went any further announced,

"**Y**ou guys have your assignments, I'll check on you later."

The crew knew they were being dismissed and walked away still chuckling under their breath.

His attention refocused on the two new lads, Tom trying to stay firm but friendly addressed them again.

"Okay, I have your names and addresses, so which is which."

The dark haired teen wearing a cut off black T- shirt, arms covered with tattoos, replied snidely,

"They call me Ace."

"That's all well and good but I do not have an Ace written on my paper. What is your real name ?"

In a mumbled voice, eyes to the ground he answered, "Jonathon."

"A good strong name. I had an uncle named Jonathon. He was quite a man."

"Big whoopee." was Ace's reply.

Focusing on the other boy, Tom asked,

"So Dirk, do you know why you're here ?"

"Yeah, so I don't go to jail." was the sarcastic answer.

"Actually, it goes further than that." Tom responded calmly. "This program is to help you to a better future. Hopefully to give you something constructive to base a future on. A future where you fit into today's society rather than always fighting against it."

"Do we have to listen to your preaching all day or are we here to work ?" interrupted Jonathon.

"I didn't realize I was preaching, and yes you're here to work. It's called community service. To pay back to the community what you took away by your misdeeds."

Tom outlined the various projects at the barn inquiring if the teens had any preference or experience at anything in particular. Jonathon surprisingly answered.

"I used to build things with my Dad before he died so I know what a hammer is."

"Good!" Tom responded.

"I know just the spot for you. What about you Dirk, any hidden talents ?"

"My Dad's an electrician although I don't see him very often. He's a lineman with a big power company."

"Good, I think we can use your talents. Both of you follow me."

The first person Tom went to in the barn was Fred. He introduced the two new boys explaining that Jonathon was to work with him for a while. Looking at Jonathon Tom said,

"He'll show you the ropes."

To which came a quick sarcastic answer.

"I know what a rope is."

This surprised and shocked Fred, building an instant dislike. To cover his feelings he called after Tom.

" Are we still set for the journals this afternoon ?"

"You bet." Tom answered without looking but waved his hand in the air.

Tom and Dirk continued on, at last finding Josh.

"Josh, this is a new crew member who may be familiar with what you're doing. He will work with you for a while."

"Okay Mr. T." was Josh's friendly reply as Tom returned to his truck.

Josh returned to putting the light fixture back on the wall with Dirk following.

"Here let me do that. You're doing it wrong."

Dirk took over as Josh stepped aside.

"This piece goes first so you don't cause fires." Dirk added. "Do you always treat that guy like a friend ?"

"If you mean Tom, he is a friend."

"But he's the law." protested Dirk. "They are not out to help us. They just want to keep us in line with their stupid rules."

Josh stared at Dirk not believing what he just said.

"What are you looking at me like that for ? Those cops are all alike." Dirk stated with his wise guy attitude.

Josh, half laughing calmly returned.

"First of all Tom Thatcher is not a cop. He's not even connected with the law."

"Then what's he doing here ? Making us work on stuff we don't care about. Like this broken down building. They should just let it fall down. Maybe we can even help it fall down, if you know what I mean." Dirk ended with an evil snicker.

Presently, but not wanting to, Josh could feel himself getting angry. With difficulty controlling himself he slowly, but face to face, confronted Dirk. He spent the next six or seven minutes explaining the facts of life, his life, and that of Tom Thatcher and of old Bert, at least of what he knew, to Dirk. He refused to let Dirk say one word until he had completed his tirade. At this point he was literally in Dirk's face with only about seven inches separating the pair.

Dirk was speechless from the verbal assault not knowing what to say. Josh stepped back allowing a three foot distance between the two. Somewhat shaken from the affront just received Dirk, a bit subdued, however found his voice.

"I'm sorry. I didn't mean to offend you. I had no idea of the circumstances you just spoke of."

"That's how this whole thing started many years ago." Josh explained. No one cared enough to inquire about another persons situation. Rumors became truth which led to prejudice and persecution of others."

Josh paused thinking to himself, *"Now I'm sounding like Tom. I guess that's not a bad thing though."* He was inwardly pleased with his growth and maturity since meeting Tom.

"You guys really destroyed his garden ?" Dirk asked curiously.

"Yes, and we were thinking of starting on the house also."

"And now he's being nice to you ?"

"You got it pal. It's only been a month or so but he has really gone to bat for us, and he will probably do the same for you too if you let him. I have to admit he has really made some changes in us all. I for one am very thankful for having met him."

"So, all them stories you just shouted at me was all true ?"

"Yup, they were as real as you can get. Today is the last day of our community service and I for one am sorry to see it end." admitted Josh.

"You're kidding." exclaimed Dirk. "You mean you want to go on doing forced labor ?"

Smiling Josh answered. "It's not like forced labor when you're working with Tom. It's learning and fun. It's not the work I'm going to miss, it's being with and learning from him that I think we will all miss.

Fred, in the meantime, was also having difficulties with Jonathon who kept insisting he be called "Ace". He did not at all seem interested in doing any work.

"I'm here cause they are making me be here, that doesn't mean I have to like it or do their dirty work for them." claimed Ace.

Fred very casually asked, "Who is the they you are referring to ?"

"You know, the cops and the court idiots."

"Seems to me you're the only one being an idiot." Fred replied.

This caught Jonathon's instant attention as he swung around to face Fred.

"Who you callin an idiot, suck up ? Just because you want to play their silly games doesn't mean we all have to."

"Fine with me." responded Fred calmly. Then go ahead and serve some jail time and get a black mark on your record that will follow you for the rest of your life."

This statement got Jonathon to pause for a moment.

"You mean this here community service doesn't go on your record."

"That's exactly what I mean sport." smiled Fred.

Fred realized he now had control and was not intimidated by Ace.

"I guess being friendly with this guy Tom, you know the policeman in charge out there, helps keep things off the record too." Ace inquired.

Fred laughed yet again.

"You have got to stop being suspicious about everything in the world and start seeing things as they really are."

Jonathon was looking confused now which led Fred to try an explanation.

"You're not from around here are you ?" he inquired of Ace.

"No, the court in Heberd County sent us here to Judge McCallister, then he sent us to this guy Tom Thatcher."

"That my friend was your first good break."

Confusion reigned again on Jonathon's face. Fred made himself comfortable on an old wooden barrel.

"Tom Thatcher, for your information, is not a policeman, nor is he connected with the court. He started this program to help guys like us. Yes, I was in serious trouble also. Me and my friends destroyed his garden property and were planning to wreck his house, but we got caught.."

Ace interrupted with, "But you seem to be friends with him now."

"That's right, and I hope to continue being friends. This man fought for us in court so we didn't have to go to jail. He spoke with the judge about starting this program to help us, not to have us start out life with black marks against us. So if I were you I would keep my mouth shut and perhaps you too can learn something."

Wanting to end it there for now Fred firmly suggested,

"Let's get back to work now, follow me."

Jonathon, without argument trailed after him.

Tom signaled lunch time but as before the crew decided to continue working munching on the sandwiches provided.

"Jonathon, mumbling under his breath said, "You guys are really suckers."

Fred just smiled inwardly.

The last two hours passed quickly and all tools and work stations were secured for the night. The young men anxiously gathered around the large picnic table near Tom's truck. The group also included the two new recruits. Tom appeared wearing a genuine smile.

"A little business before the journals." he stated.

Good humored grumbling filled the air.

"First, for Jonathon and Dirk, you two will report here to me next Tuesday at ten AM. Please try not to be late."

Right away Jonathon rudely interrupted,

"Why can't we come again tomorrow so we can get this community thing over with ?"

Tom keeping an even demeanor replied looking directly at Ace.

"Because I have other plans for tomorrow and I have to assess progress to date."

There was no reply from either boy.

"I promised some journal readings to the crew, you two are welcome to join us."

'"We don't need any bible preaching." voiced Ace in his cocky attitude.

Mark was quick on the uptake.

"These are not bible stories. These are short anecdotes about a man we all wish to know about."

"What's an anecdote ?" asked Ace.

His pal Dirk answered him softly.

"It's like a short story of someone's life."

Jonathon snapped his head around, nastiness showing in his eyes. Mark saw this and instantly took over the conversation.

"This particular gentleman had a somewhat difficult life and these stories show how one can overcome hardships and turn out to be a warm loving person. No one is saying you have to stay. I believe Tom was just being polite."

Mark said this in a very adult tone not showing malice. Tom thought to himself that he could not have put it any better. Dirk, obviously the more subdued of the two prodded his friend,

"Why not stick around Ace, we ain't got nothin else to do."

"Yeah, I guess it's okay for a while. There better not be any preaching though." mumbled Ace.

Tom was proud of Mark's words and glad he stayed out of it. Under the circumstances he decided to change readings, for now anyway. He reached for the journal of the Korean War stories.

"I thought as a change of pace I would read of a few of Bert's Korean war experiences."

"Wow, you mean ole Bert served in the Korean war ? I don't think anyone knew that." Steve yelled out.

"There are a lot of things about Bert that no one knows or even bothered to find out." Tom offered, then realizing he said too much at this point in time anyway, referred right back to the journal. He chose this particular story because it was not a battle per se but their ongoing struggle with the frigid cold winter without the proper clothing. How they suffered frostbite and frozen weapons.

A short way into the story Arlene showed up with the as promised fresh baked cookies.

Jonathon was the first to notice her approach.

"Hey now, who's the hot chick ?"

By the time Tom stopped reading and turned around to look in Arlene's direction the five boys of his original work crew were on their feet completely surrounding the "ACE".

"We would suggest that you show respect to women, not just this one because she is our friend but to all women no matter the age. You may find you will get along better."

Fred followed with,

"If you need courtesy lessons we will be glad to oblige and at no charge."

As he finished his little speech he turned to Tom with a big smile. It was then Tom understood the boys had used the same words he used on them. Unaware of the words just spoken, Arlene, being polite, walked straight to Dirk and Ace her hand outstretched.

"Tom said there were two new men on the crew. Hi, my name is Arlene."

Dirk was first to respond. "H—H–Hi, I'm Dirk and this is my friend Jonathon."

Taking Jonathon's hand gently Arlene commented.

"I just love that name. That was my fathers name. Welcome to the crew."

Turning to the original crew she added,

"Since this is your last day I thought we could celebrate your success with some fresh baked cookies. Please guys help yourselves to all you want. You two may as well join in also." She smiled at the newcomers.

Fred took that as a cue and indicated with a smile and an arm movement to join in. Befuddled by the apparent acceptance and not really knowing how to react Jonathon and Dirk just stood there. The other boys did not wait for a second invitation and all at once attacked the cookie tray. Arlene, with her winning grin turned her attention to Tom saying for all to hear,

"And yes, you may have one also." Which brought laughter from the group.

She stood by Tom for only a few minutes watching the crew enjoy her baking efforts. She kissed him on the cheek preparing to leave.

"I'll leave you to your stories. Aunt Eileen and Martha are waiting. So long guys and congratulations. Hope to see you again."

She walked away all eyes following, including Tom. Grabbing another broken snack Tom refocused his attention,

"Okay guys back to the war."

All settled down including Ace and Dirk. Tom pretended not to notice.

For the next half hour he read of the hardships of a Korean winter where survival was the toughest battle. Tom paused for a while fielding questions from the guys. Steve spoke up rather shyly.

"Tom could you read some more from the other journal, you know, about Bert's personal experiences ?"

Trying not to show pleasure about the request Tom replied.

"Are you guys sure about wanting to hear more of Bert's experiences ?"

All quietly answered in the affirmative. Tom switched journals, thumbing through looking for something not too graphic at this point. He settled on the incident when he was with the last foster home where he came to the rescue of his foster sister. This turned out to be the right choice because of the dialogue it created between the boys in reference to the injustice of the situation. Even the Ace had comments in favor of Bert.

It was well after four thirty when Tom called a halt to the gathering. Thanks seemed to be the unanimous sentiment.

"There's one last cookie left Mr. T and we decided you can have it." joked Fred.

"Are you sure now ? I wouldn't want to deprive you boys of your proper nourishment." quipped Tom in return as he stuffed the cookie in his mouth.

Turning serious for a moment Tom addressed the crew who would be leaving, their community service at an end.

"I'm very proud of what you have accomplished and I truly hope I never see you again under these circumstances. I also hope we can remain friends and I look forward to seeing you all again, like at the noisy luncheonette."

This remark brought laughter from the five. Tom shook the hand of each, warmly with all the sincerity he could muster. Turning to the other two and with a still friendly tone, stated.

I'll see you both here Tuesday at ten in the morning and by the way wear some older clothes since we may get into some painting of this old place.

One by one they all drifted away leaving Tom feeling satisfied sitting on the tailgate of his truck. It was another ten minutes or so before he started for home.

~ ~ ~ ~

Comfortable at home he spoke to Bert's portrait again.

"**W**ell, old friend, you would have been proud of the youngsters today. I don't want to jump to conclusions yet but this may be the beginning of getting through to this town."

Tom gently touched the painting, his eyes damp. Moving to the kitchen to make coffee, his thoughts again drifted to a monument for Bert, but how do you go about such a thing. *"I can't force the town. I must convince them. Perhaps a small stone here on the property. The town folk can't stop that, or a headstone at the cemetery, tastefully done of course."*

Tom felt his mind was not working correctly at the moment. He let himself get too emotional. He poured a large mug of coffee returning to the living room. He just sat down when the phone rang. Arlene's sweet voice lifted his mood instantly. He mentioned his quandary which she picked up on right away.

"**I**nstead of fretting about it all night let's discuss it openly tomorrow at lunch with both our aunts." she posed.

"**I** guess that's why I need you around, you always know just what to say to get me out of a funk. I'll pick up Aunt Martha and lunch and we'll come to your place."

"**T**hat sounds wonderful Tom, I look forward to seeing you as always."

"**D**id you call for something special ?" Tom inquired.

"**J**ust to hear your voice." Arlene answered softly. "I just wanted to say good night."

"**I** feel better now because of you. I'll see you tomorrow." Tom returned the phone to its cradle gazing at the portrait.

"**Y**ou were right Bert, she is more valuable than gold."

Out went the lights as Tom drifted to bed.

Chapter 20

The warming suns rays streaked under the bedroom curtains nudging Tom into a new day. He was well rested and content. He quickly dressed and with a mug of coffee ventured out to greet the day. He circled the house and garden finally settling in one of the porch rockers. Sensing the serenity of the area the birds increased their morning songfest joined by the noisy squirrels. With further stimulation from the dark black liquid Tom's thoughts set in motion.

"The idea I had about a monument intrigues me, but where do I go from here. Not only how but where do I go. If nothing else a nice head stone at Bert's grave site is a start."

A sudden feeling of guilt encompassed Tom. In all his efforts and involvement with clearing Bert's name he realized he himself had not yet visited the burial site.

"That I will correct as soon as possible." he firmly said aloud.

Tom cleaned up, dressed and called Aunt Martha about the lunch plans which she readily agreed to.

"Pick me up early, in the meantime I'll call ahead to the Country Kitchen for a nice takeout lunch." Martha suggested.

Tom had not felt this good in a long time and smiled to himself on the drive to his aunt's. After escorting his aunt to the truck, the Country Kitchen was the next stop.

Brenda was genuinely happy to see Tom and then urged her best wishes be passed on to Arlene. She mentioned again the tremendous change in the teens behavior particularly here in the luncheonette.

"I threw in some special cookies with your lunch as thank you for what you did for us all."

A blushing Tom accepted her thoughtfulness.

Arlene was waiting on the porch as Tom turned into the driveway. She rushed to Tom nearly knocking him over as he exited the truck.. After her bear hug attack on Tom she gave the same welcoming hug to Aunt Martha. The hugging routine was repeated by Eileen once inside. During lunch the monument idea dominated the conversation with all in favor. The stone for the cemetery would be the first thing.

"Perhaps a small memorial garden at the cabin." posed Eileen. "He loved his "Farm" so dearly."

"By then we can work out something bigger for the town green or the park." Aunt Martha added.

The happy lunch was over a little after one with Martha needing to return home for a sewing club appointment. Tom with Arlene's enthusiastic approval continued on to the cemetery following Eileen's directions. The right location was easily found. Old Bert was resting peacefully next to his beloved Mother. Still being sensitive to Tom's moods Arlene let him have his alone time and space for a while. Seeing his composure perk up she went to his side enfolding his hand in hers. He, in turn clasped her hand tightly, looked at her smiling, whispering the words;

"Thank you. I'm okay now and always will be with you at my side."

He turned her face up to his and kissed her ever so gently.

"Bert approves. He just told me so."

Arlene was all aglow now. She knew they were right for each other. Another few minutes of silence was finally broken by Arlene.

"You're right Tom, a nice tasteful marker should be put here with a few small shrubs, perhaps small boxwood plants."

"Then that's what we will do." Tom confirmed.

Before leaving the cemetery Tom stopped at the administration office to inquire about the best place to acquire a proper stone. Satisfied with the information he received Tom returned to the truck explaining to Arlene they would have to go to the next town, home to a granite quarry. They planned to do that the next day.

Home to the cabin was the next stop.

"Did you ever finish the second journal ?" asked Arlene.

"No, not yet. I got busy with the boys and haven't returned to it yet."

"Then let's just enjoy the porch and some lemonade and we can read some more stories." was Arlene's bubbly suggestion.

"Sounds good to me." responded Tom as he turned into the driveway.

The homemade rockers on the porch were extremely conducive to relaxation. Along with the tall glass of lemonade and Arlene at his side Tom was content beyond his expectations. Arlene settled herself in the chair next to Tom gingerly clutching the journal to her.

"Please may I read today, I would like you to just relax."

Flashing the catching smile Tom knew he couldn't resist.

"It looks like I don't have a choice the way you're guarding that book."

"Good, now just sip your drink and listen."

Arlene turned to the page marker and read.

Tom ! If you are still reading these journals and haven't burned them yet, you might enjoy this next tale. It sort of shows my life wasn't all sour grapes. Where ever you were involved was pure pleasure to me. I'm sure you would rather not be reminded of your learning to drive experiences.

Tom quickly interrupted,

"Just skip that entry and go on to the next."

"Oh no you don't Mr. Quiet man. If Bert wrote about it then I want to read it." Arlene smiled while holding the book protectively away from Tom.

"Okay, okay, you win." Tom said sitting back in his chair.

Arlene laughed as she reopened the book.

"Now be a good boy and listen."

You were fifteen and kept bugging me to let you drive my old broken down jeep. I finally figured it couldn't do no harm, what with all this private property. You wouldn't be out in any real traffic. Actually you did quite well and learned fast, particularly since it was a stick shift. You were doing well enough that I was able to continue some farm work while you made circles in the grass at the top of the driveway. One day I guess you were feeling brave, while I was in a giving mood, my mistake, you asked if you could go up and down the driveway. Stupidly I said okay, just do not go out onto the main road. So up and down the drive you went. Then I didn't see you for a while. I started walking down the drive only to meet you walking up the road. You heard right "Walking". I very calmly asked about the jeep. You answered without looking at me that it some how got stuck down in the drainage ditch on the side of the road. It's funny you didn't seem to know how it got there.

By now Arlene was almost laughing while Tom was wearing a crimson glow.

Do you even remember the difficulty I had getting a tow truck or even someone with a tractor. Especially with my popularity. We did, however, accomplish its retrieval and then you suddenly had to return to Aunt Martha. What you didn't know at the time though, was that I was not even angry, just thankful you weren't hurt. You never did explain how you managed that. Have to go now, the coffee pot is calling.

Bert.

There was a soft pause with Tom now totally red faced and Arlene dressed in a broad grin.

"**S**o, you weren't always the good boy you appear to be now. Why don't you explain how you managed the ditch, and perhaps Bert is listening ?"

Tom joined in the laughter.

"**I**'m going to hear about this for the rest of my life now, won't I ?"

"**W**ho knows, I may remind you every now and then." was Arlene's happy answer.

"**S**hall we read some more ?"

"**S**ure, why not." replied Tom. "Anything to change the subject."

Opening the journal Arlene proceeded to read.

I just returned from Korea and purchased this land. Not too many of the locals knew I was back, or if they did, obviously didn't care. One mid- afternoon on my way back from Laurelville shopping for supplies I decided to stop for a beer. There was this out of the way pub on Rte 6 that caught my eye so I stopped. There were two mem playing pool and two at the bar and of course the owner/bartender. I started to take a seat at the bar as the bartender mumbled "What can I get you ?" He than looked up at me, surprise showing on his face. With a wicked sneer he nervously stated, "We don't serve your kind here, you might as well leave right now." The four patrons at once turned to see what was taking place. I politely said, "I beg your pardon, I just want a cold beer." The owner looked me directly in the eye saying, "You're that Bert fellow aren't you." I was a little shocked by this response because I had not been around here for four years let alone ever in this particular bar. Calmly I answered. "Yes, my name is Bert, Bert Morrow." You could tell by now the man was really getting nervous. "I told you mac, we don't serve your kind here." Still playing it cool I inquired. "And just what is my kind?" "You're a trouble maker and always have been. Now get out of here before - - - " I cut him short by asking. "Before What." The man was truly scared and shaking now. "I'll- - I'll- - call the police." "For what reason, I haven't done anything." I said smiling. One of the men at the bar also asked. "Yeah, what did he do, he just asked for a beer?" "Not in my place." shouted the bartender, red faced. "Get out you bum, go cause trouble some place else." I replied with a calm smile. I enjoyed messing with his head. "I guess you can forget the beer, this doesn't look like a friendly place to drink anyway. Have a nice day." I yelled over my shoulder as I left the pub. I sat in my truck for a few minutes to compose myself and to stop shaking before I drove off.

This experience really threw me for a loop. I never saw that man before, was never in that bar before and had been away for more than four years.

This is just to show you Tom, how evil and damaging false rumors can be. Not just to the one who is the brunt of the falsehoods, but how the hate has warped judgement of those not even involved with the beginning of the untruths. I'm just one particular person. Imagine, if you will, how many other parts of the country and the world that this is taking place.

With moist eyes but smiles Tom and Arlene gazed at each other not knowing whether to laugh or cry.

"**I**'m sorry I never got to meet Bert. Now I know why you loved him so much." Arlene then added firmly. "Yes! we will get this injustice corrected."

She moved to Tom's lap, hugged him and kissed him.

"**O**kay, now big guy, how about some supper ?"

Chapter 21

The sun and blue sky of Saturday morning faced Tom on his way to pick up Arlene for their trip to the granite quarry in hopes of acquiring a headstone for Bert's resting place. Carefully wrapped in a blanket in the back seat of the truck was Tom's beloved portrait of Bert. He had no idea if it was possible but thought a likeness carved in stone of Bert would make a pleasing tribute.

With Arlene's ever smiling face lighting up the trucks interior Tom set his course for the Quarry. On the way the young couple discussed the size and color that would be appropriate, although they were also aware of possible restrictions they may face once they spoke to the stone mason. Reaching their destination they were graciously welcomed by a most pleasant middle aged man. Tom briefly explained his desire for the head stone which were met with total acceptance. Looking at Arlene then back to the stone artist he hesitantly asked about the possibility of a semi dimensional image of a head and shoulders, something that would show depth. The stone mason was not at all put off by the idea of such a thing.

"We have often accomplished that very thing you desire, but would require some sort of image to go by."

Tom's spirits soured upon hearing this and hurriedly said,

"I'll be right back."

With that he rushed out to the truck, returning with the portrait of Bert.

"What a beautiful piece of art." was the instant comment.

Arlene self consciously felt a flush come over her upon hearing this yet remained silent.

" I would love to work from this original but dare not have it here in the shop, though I would take every precaution to guarantee it's safety it is not really the proper venue for such a work of art. Would you allow me to photograph it and then work from that."

Tom gave his willing approval to the photographing.

"By the way, my name is Norman Conrad." he said extending his hand and continuing to speak. "Of course the more desirable way would be to have the outline drawn directly on the chosen stone at proper scale, but obviously that's not possible."

Both Tom and Arlene were sporting smiles now. Without hesitation or asking Arlene, Tom stated confidently.

"I would like to introduce the artist.", the sweep of his hand indicating Arlene.

Looking a little surprised Norman replied,

"My compliments young lady, this is an exquisite piece of work."

Blushing slightly but enjoying the praise Arlene answered.

"Why thank you kind sir." modestly adding, "I try my best."

"This is the perfect answer. Let's pick out the right stone for quality and size and have this wonderful young artist start us on our way." Norman said excitedly.

"But, I have never carved in stone." protested Arlene. "Isn't there any other way ?" Couldn't you do it ?"

"I have the proper tool for this and in just ten minutes I'll have you working like an expert. Trust me, your knowledge of the arts you will find to your advantage, plus I can promise you it will be a far better likeness than I could come up with."

A nervous Arlene, not wanting to disappoint Tom looked at him hesitantly. Tom was all smiles and proudly stated.

"I know you can do it. Do it for Bert."

She could not refuse now and turned to Norm who already had the etching tool in his hand, handle side pointing at Arlene. She smiled, accepting the unfamiliar tool as Norman took her by the hand moving to a sample stone. As promised ten minutes of teaching and Arlene was etching like a pro. Tom made himself scarce yet continued looking at Arlene knowing he found the right woman to spend his life with.

In a very short time and with the confidence of a professional Arlene was busy transforming the chosen piece of granite with the basic outline of Bert's portrait.

In the meantime, Tom was already making future plans for the memorial project with Norman. They discussed various suggestions put forth by Norm. Without making a final decision they were in agreement on the details to be included. A warm hand shake solidified the verbal contract.

Some forty five minutes later Arlene's smiling face reappeared.

"That was actually fun." Handing the tool to Norman she voiced, "I just need your approval."

The three drifted to the work station staring in awe at what they were viewing. It was the perfect replica of the original portrait.

"I must admit, I have never seen anything so beautifully done, and in such a short time. I never could have accomplished that myself. Would you like a job young lady ?"

Flushed in total embarrassment Arlene was stuttering for words.

"I think not kind sir, I'm only here visiting for a time."

Too bad." Norman mumbled. Speaking more distinctly Norman directed his eyes to Tom. "This is more than a great start and along with the photos I should be able to produce what you want in a week or so. Leave me a number to call and a small deposit and I'll get started right away."

Carefully re-wrapping the portrait in the blanket Tom carried it to the truck. On his way to the truck Tom recalled Arlene's comment about only visiting here for a time. This upset him somewhat and he knew he would have to ask her about this yet he did not want to show her that he was alarmed by this. Putting on his best smile he returned to the shop. The pair said their good byes with Norm still making a pitch for Arlene to work for him. Perhaps on a single job basis every now and then. She still politely but graciously refused. No offence was meant and none taken.

As soon as they started for home, Tom proudly commented.

"I was so very proud of you back there. You are truly an artist. I couldn't believe that etching you did, especially knowing you never did that before. You obviously impressed a fellow artist also."

"I did that for you and Bert. I thank you for your faith in me but I didn't think it was anything that special. You're just being prejudiced." she replied with a loving smile.

"I don't care what you say, I'm still very proud of you. In fact that deserves a proper dinner and I know just the right steak house."

"No, not tonight Tom, I'm not properly dressed for such a thing. How about tomorrow when I can properly dress for the occasion with my special man."

Knowing she would feel more comfortable Tom agreed.

"Then back to Aunt Martha's it is, where I can throw something together for both of you. I don't have to be at the library until Tuesday morning, so that gives us lots of time together till then."

"I like the idea of having you all to myself for a couple of days." she replied as she moved closer to him in the seat.

Aunt Martha was more than happy to have the young couple join her for the late afternoon and evening. She had just finished making a beef stew and was thrilled to share it. Tom and Arlene filled Martha in on all the details of the afternoons trip to the quarry. Pleased with their efforts she volunteered what ever help should be needed in fulfilling their wishes. She went on to say how pleased she and the library committee were with progress being made at the yellow barn. They truly looked forward to its completion.

The next two days found Tom and Arlene inseparable, totally enjoying each others company. Now back at Aunt Eileen's, Monday evening was a difficult parting even though both knew it was for a very short period of time. Eileen chose to take advantage of the situation with her usual teasing.

"Now Tommy love, you had better get on home now before you grow too tired of this pretty lass. That will come soon enough down the road."

"Auntie ! What a mean thing to say. Don't go giving him any ideas."

Tom was smiling now,

"Aunt Eileen is right you know. I better go before you throw me out. You know what they say, absence makes the heart grow fonder."

Arlene was pouting now as Tom gave Eileen a good night hug.

"Look at the sad little lass, you had better give her a hug also."

With that Eileen quickly disappeared.

Still maintaining her pout Arlene quietly asked.

"Are you growing tired of me ?"

"Absolutely ! I'll have to put up without seeing you until tomorrow.", replied Tom as he enfolded her in his arms and kissed her.

The kiss lingered till Arlene finally broke apart.

"I hope that will keep you wanting more, I don't want you to tire of me."

They hugged tightly once more and Tom departed. His ride home to the cabin was filled with nothing but Arlene.

Chapter   22

Tom's drive to the yellow barn was a bit uneasy. He had nagging thoughts that Jonathan the "ACE" and Dirk were to be no shows. Arriving at nine thirty five he made himself comfortable with his mug of black coffee. He conducted a mental review of things completed and those to do. Progress was better than originally expected. Just as thoughts of Arlene were creeping into his work sheets an old beat up sixty five Mustang drove into the yard parking next to the truck. Ace and Dirk waved and sort of smiled. All three exited their respective vehicles at the same time with Tom extending his hand to welcome the younger boys.

"Glad to see you guys."

"I hope so." replied Jonathon. "We want to get this thing over with as soon as possible. It's interrupting our personal schedules."

Tom did notice they truly wore beat up old clothes but chose not to make it a point. The three just started to review what was left to do when Fred's old truck pulled up with the five original crew members. Tom was happy to see them but was curious as to why.

"What are you guys doing here ? Your service commitment has been completed and I already submitted a most favorable report on your behalf to Judge McCallister. The five youths looked to each other wearing smiles of thanks. Fred, as usual took the lead, though almost shyly.

"Well Tom, we know how much work there is left to do and with only two crew people, three counting yourself, we figured it would take quite a while. We all would like to see this job finished." He hesitated here looking at his friends. All gave affirmative nods. "So we all took a vote and want to be in on the completion. So if you don't mind we are here to work."

Tom overcome with pride, warmly said.

"Welcome back." And with a huge grin added, "Well what are you all standing around for, we have work to do."

Ace in his cynical attitude mumbled, "You guys are crazy."

Work assignments were given and soon the place was buzzing with activity.

At eleven o'clock Aunt Martha and two other library ladies showed up, just out of curiosity. They were treated most respectfully by all the teens. Tom pulled his aunt aside asking her to get in touch with Eileen referencing the changes in lunch plans with seven teens to feed rather than two. Martha confirmed it would be taken care of as the impromptu visitors left. Tom could not believe how well all the guys were working together. There was still the odd comments being made by Dirk and Ace, but even those appeared to be tempered with a smile or laugh.

Twelve thirty on the button Arlene showed up carrying a large cooler filled with lunch for the boys. She was followed by Eileen hauling a giant carafe of lemonade. Some of the boys seeing this rushed to relieve the ladies of their heavy burdens. One of the boys being Dirk. In no time at all the seven were gathered at the picnic table and Arlene began handing out sandwiches. As she approached Jonathon the original five stared intently at the Ace.

"Thank you Miss Arlene." Was the only comment which drew smiles and relaxed posture of the five.

Lunch went quickly and the boys returned to work without being pushed.

"What's with the five originals ?" asked Arlene. "I thought their time was completed ?"

"I'll explain tonight, right now even I have to get to work."

With a quick kiss to her cheek he vanished.

The rest of the day went well and just after two PM all were gathered at Tom's truck.

"Could we hear some more journal stories, Tom ?" asked Josh.

"I'm afraid not today fellas. I didn't expect you and do not have the journals with me."

To the surprise of everyone Jonathon inquired without hesitation.

"Could you bring them tomorrow ? Dirk and I would like to hear more of this Bert guy."

"That's a promise guys. I'm glad you are still interested. To change the subject just a bit, with what you accomplished today we can start on the painting tomorrow. I have already arranged for ladders and scaffolding. The paint will also be here first thing tomorrow. Remember! Old clothes. Okay guys, that's about it, I'll see you in the AM."

The boys headed for their respective cars leaving Tom alone. As an afterthought he called to Fred as he was just entering his truck.

"Can I see you for a minute ? I won't keep you long."

Fred walked to Tom's truck asking,

"What's up, Mr. Thatcher ?"

"Just curious I guess as to what's motivating you guys. Why return here ? You all are free men again."

With a confident smile Fred replied;

"Because we are free again we are free to do what we choose and we choose to be here."

"But." Tom started and was politely interrupted.

"Look Mr. T, what you did for us was a wonderful and generous thing. Let's just say it's our way of saying thanks." He paused momentarily and quietly added, "Besides we have another more selfish motive."

"Oh !" Tom's curiosity was now working.

"It's a little early to say yet. Please give us a couple of days and all will be revealed, I promise."

"Okay Fred, I respect your feelings and will not push. See you tomorrow."

Halfway to his truck Fred called over his shoulder.

"Don't forget the journals."

Tom laughed and was feeling good about everything. He jumped in his own truck and steered it to Eileen's house.

~ ~ ~ ~ ~ ~

A quiet restful evening with Arlene allowed Tom an early rise filled with renewed energy. He looked forward to his time with the teens. Making sure he himself had on old clothes Tom set off for the yellow barn, soon to be a warm cream color with contrasting brown trim. Not exactly his colors but that's what the library committee chose.

Arriving at what he thought would be early there was a big surprise waiting for him. The teens were already at work, including Ace and Dirk. The scaffolding was almost completed with paint buckets and brushes being divided up. Tom exited his truck to the words from Josh;

"Your coffee is over on the picnic table."

It wasn't just a single mug but a whole pot was brewing away thanks to an extension cord from the main library building.

More than pleased with what he was seeing and with a genuine happy smile Tom yelled at the young crew.

"I hope you guys realize I don't pay overtime."

"Reading from the journals will do." answered Fred.

"**O**H ! The journals. Aaa – I —A – Oh yeah, the journals. Well it seems" Tom guiltily stuttered.

Suddenly the area was quiet. It was almost as if the traffic noise became silent also. Serious looks of disappointment could be read on every face. Steve, after glancing at the others, replied sharply.

"**N**o journals, no work."

With that all seven boys sat where they were, dropping whatever tools they had. Total silence reigned. The quiet remained for a half a minute or so with Tom giving in. Smiling again he softly stated,

"**O**kay you guys, you win. The journals are in the truck."

"**W**e know that." replied Mark. "I saw them on the seat as you drove in."

Laughter started along with continued work.

"**I** give up, I guess you guys are one up on me. Do I get a job in your work force ?"

"**S**ure." Ace answered. "You can make sure we don't paint each other."

"**T**hat might be an improvement." Tom laughed back.

The boys turned to and by lunch more than half the barn was looking bright and new. The area turned even brighter with all the smiles from the boys as Arlene showed with lunch. Eileen also was bearing food and drink. The boys quickly helped themselves while Arlene brought a special sandwich to Tom mentioning she would like to stay for the afternoon. Knowing she would be disappointed he turned down her request.

"**I** don't need your pretty distraction disturbing my crew, besides after the workday we're going to be involved with journal reading."

Disappointed Arlene was, but understood Tom's reasoning. She left with her aunt, her mood down a wee bit. Eileen, her usual wisdom free of charge, soothed with,

"**D**on't go gettin yourself so down lass. Ye cannot control the man too much. It's not good for either of you. He truly loves you and you should know that by now. Give the man his space and you'll love each other all the more for it."

Arlene smiled at her aunt and leaned over to kiss her cheek.

"**Y**ou know me better than I know myself. Thank you."

She accepted her aunt's words and was content again.

The work day ended with only a little more than half the trim to do. By two fifteen all was cleaned and put away for the night.

"**B**efore you start on the journals Tom, could we talk for a moment

?" inquired Fred.

"**S**ure thing, what's on your mind ?"

"**W**ell Sir, there's only some trim left and not enough work for all seven of us. So we thought if you could bring some of your garden tools tomorrow, some of us could do some much needed work to what little landscaping there is. That is of course, if it's alright with you."

Ace added in his own tough guy way.

"**L**et's face it, this place could use all the help it can get. The building looks okay now but it can look better with some bush trimming and stuff."

Tom could tell, Ace's rough ways aside, he really did seem to care.

"**O**kay ! It seems you guys are calling the shots so who am I to stand in the way of true beautification. I will bring the garden tools."

"**T**hanks Mr. T, now how about some Bert stories ?" asked Josh.

Grabbing journal number one Tom decided to really let these teens hear about the cruelties pushed on Bert having no basis in fact. He read the short anecdote of Bert's mother's reburial. The youths were in shock that such a thing could happen. Why did the burial of a good woman cause any problems at all. This was a normal courtesy that should not have been interfered with. The delays were caused by just plain ignorance. Tom cut the discussion short by reading another excerpt. This one was the rape and murder of Bert's fiance that he had absolutely nothing to do with. Tom continued on immediately to another story. This was the one concerning himself and the boy scouts. As simple as this situation was it really stirred up the teens discussions. They, again, could not understand why this isolation even took place. Tom was a total innocent thrown into the middle of an impossible situation he had no control over.

Tom paused here seeing the effect it was having on the boys. He realized he had to calm them down so they did not start any trouble because of what he had read to them.

"**O**kay guys, let me have your undivided attention, please. I don't want you going off half cocked because of a few stories."

"**A**re these really true ?" asked Ace.

"**I**'m afraid they are Jonathon. It took years but they can all be verified as to their accuracy.

"**A**re you doing anything to correct these wrongs against Bert ?" inquired Bill in a very concerned voice.

Tom hesitated a moment then decided to go all out.

"**Y**es I am Bill. But it is easier said than done. I don't want to cause any town wide problems because I carry a personal hurt. It took too long to get accepted myself. That's probably how this whole thing started way back when. I would like, though, to show this town that Bert wasn't really the bad guy as the rumors have it. He was anything but, to this town. There are things about Bert I choose not to reveal yet. But once they are known I believe they will help me clear his name. That's the goal I am working towards."

The boys were silent. Shocked as it were that things like this actually took place and by people they probably even know or know of.

Tom, for the present moment, thought that he possibly went too far and would himself be causing the same problems for others. Mentally changing tactics he addressed his young friends with a different tone.

"Look fellas, I feel I got you too stirred up. The last thing I want to do is to cause another situation like Bert's, and since Bert helped raise me , that connection is already there. I am not looking for vengeance, I just want people to see Bert in a more realistic light. I want to dispel the false rumors about him that never should have started. I feel that, at least for now, I have been accepted by Tylerville. I do not want to undo that acceptance. By using the wrong approach to achieve my goals I could totally undo what I have accomplished to date.

Tom's work crew were slowly looking at each other along with some whispering.

"I think we all understand Mr. T." Fred commented. "I believe we know exactly where you are coming from. We may appear young but we are not uncaring about what you are going through. Right now, because of what you have read to us about Bert, if we started talking to people the wrong way it could really undermine the very basis of what you are trying to accomplish regaining Bert's reputation."

Jonathon then raised his hand shyly.

"Believe it or not even I can relate to this. I have had my own experiences of what Bert was going through. Nothing as bad as he had, but I know what bad rumors can do to a person. I don't know about the others, but if I can help in any way to clear Bert's name without destroying yours I'm all for it. Please let Dirk and me help, if you think we can."

Tom was impressed with Ace's feelings and genuine humility. He grew in Tom's eyes with this sudden insight to himself.

"That goes for me too Mr. T." added Steve.

"And me." said Mark.

One by one they were all aboard. This was more than Tom expected. He could feel his emotions welling up in his chest but he did not want to show it too much. The boys picked up on this and willingly changed the mood that was building.

"So you tell us how to go about this Tom." Josh voiced for all. "We'll take our direction from you. You tell more about Bert and we'll help you clear his name."

Tom recovered himself answering.

"I appreciate your feelings guys, but this is my problem. I don't want to get you involved in something that could cause trouble for you."

Steve spoke quickly cutting Tom short.

This is our problem too because this is our town. The town that almost destroyed someone's life. That is also a reflection on us because we live here. I for one want to help you fix this so that it doesn't happen again. I may not be an adult yet, but I don't want such a reputation before I become one."

Josh followed suit with.

"You got us with you whether you want us or not."

Tom sat silent for a moment with seven smiling faces staring at him. Finally speaking softly he said.

"Okay guys, but give me time to figure out where I go from here. So from here on out mums the word about Bert. I don't want to cause you any trouble. I promise I will welcome your help. I know it's getting late but one last story you may enjoy."

Tom quickly read Bert's entry about his driving experience. It ended with laughing and ribbing.

"How did you get the jeep in the ditch Mr. T?" asked Dirk.

"That's one secret I'm going to keep to myself." Tom laughed in answer. "Okay men. I'll see you tomorrow, garden tools and all."

Eventually the parking lot was cleared except for Tom sitting behind the steering wheel of his truck wiping his eyes his thoughts running rampant.

"This is more than I could have wished for. But do I want to get these kids involved ? They seem to be all newly reformed now, why feed them a possible set back. Even Ace and Dirk have changed in a very short time. I do hope they listen to my cautions and not say anything yet. Actually, I really do believe they will take my lead. Tomorrow I will talk with them again."

Feeling better Tom drove almost automatically to Arlene. Eileen almost crushed him in her bear hug the moment he stepped through the door.

"Tommy love, I thought you would never get here. The supper's already on the table so you can't refuse. Rejuvenate that tired body a bit and I'll leave you two kids alone. Quilting club tonight you know."

"Do you ever allow yourself free time ?" Tom questioned with a smile.

"Don't you worry about me love. I'll always be here for you both."

Arlene had her arms around Tom this whole time.

"Let the man eat first lass, then you can smother him."

Slightly embarrassed Arlene released Tom and led him to the table and sat next to him.

"So, how did your day go without my distractions ?" she quipped.

"Very well, thanks and ended up even more interesting."

Tom then went on to outline what had taken place because of the journal readings.

"Looks like your support group is growing." volunteered Eileen. You did a marvelous job with those boys and I for one believe they will stand by you. Just take it slow love and you will clear the old geezers name."

Again Tom knew she meant nothing disparaging by her reference of the old geezer.

Dinner over, Arlene volunteered to take care of the dishes.

"You run along to your meeting and have fun."

"Can't wait to get rid of me, can you lass, so you can smother this poor man again."

"Auntie ! You're impossible." cried Arlene though a bit crimson.

Tom was quietly laughing through this whole thing.

They had a nice evening together including a walk under the stars. Conversation was light which was more than satisfactory with Tom. He needed the non stressful time. Tom was back in the cabin by ten PM. feeling totally relaxed. He knew tomorrow was a busy day.

~ ~ ~ ~

At the yellow barn, garden tools in tow, Tom was greeted with much enthusiasm. The teens had already decided who was going to paint and who was going to work on the landscape. Fred and Jonathon approached Tom with a few thoughts.

"Mr. T. Do you think it's possible to get the library ladies to part with a few dollars to get some new shrubs ? Ace here has some great ideas for dressing this place up. I think his ideas are pretty good."

"A man of hidden talents I see." Tom replied looking at Jonathon. "I know they don't have much of a budget, but I'll tell you what. I'll give you my credit card and you guys get whatever you think is appropriate."

"You would trust us with your card ?" asked Ace with a strange look on his face.

"Why not, is there any reason I shouldn't ?" Tom inquired staring directly into Jonathon's eyes.

"No sir, none whatsoever." was the reply.

"Then go and do whatever. By the time you get back we will all be able to give you a hand."

Tom was really feeling good now. He decided then to make sure the library committee would do something special in the way of a thank you. He would definitely talk to Aunt Martha regarding this.

It appeared that Jonathon, in spite of his tough exterior, had a special affinity to landscape design. The other teens, recognizing this followed his direction without ridicule.

"This is the way it should always work with people." Tom thought. It reminded him of his days in the Corps. Total cooperation was the key to any success.

By day's end all was accomplished. The added touch of the landscaping made the old barn look like a new structure. The curb appeal increased by a thousand percent. Even Tom could not believe the transformation.

Lunch time came and went without a single sandwich being touched. The young crew could taste the finish line and wanted to see its completion without interruption.

At one twenty P.M. the paint brushes and garden tools were returned to Tom's truck and the sandwich cooler was attacked by a mob of happy teens. It was obvious they were proud of what they did. Tom was doubly proud. Proud of what they accomplished and proud of them for their thoroughness and follow through. He definitely wanted Judge McCallister to see these results.

Tom joined in the late lunch celebrations and once the crew settled down wanted to put forth a few ideas.

"The playground by the town green had obviously lacked attention for some time." He stated. "You original five have already been dismissed so I guess Just Ace, Dirk and I will handle what repairs we think are necessary."

"Why should just you three have all the fun." returned Fred. Ace and Dirk are part of us now and what they do, we do also."

"Do you know what you're saying ?"

"We know exactly what we're saying." Fred answered firmly. "Which brings us to a proposal we would like to make."

"Okay, let's have it."

Fred took a deep breath and looked around at the whole crew to various nods and smiles. Making himself more comfortable on the bench and more directly to Tom he spoke slowly.

"Well, we all have been talking, and what we have been doing lately, well is sort of fun. Yes, we know some of it was hard work, but it has given us a sense of accomplishment. A sense of who we are. We feel like we count now. People look at us differently. People talk to us now, not at us. We have you to thank for that."

Tom started to say something but was instantly cut off as Josh held up his hand to stop him. He did this with a grin, not out of rudeness. Fred continued in all seriousness.

"As I said we have you to thank for that for showing that you cared, for making us feel important, for making us care about ourselves. We know now what we can do, which is just about anything. We also realize we still have a lot to learn, especially regarding people. I sound like I'm getting long winded now, so to cut it short we want to go into business for ourselves."

Toms expression changed but remained silent.

"Not to make a lot of money, but to give ourselves a purpose."

Fred paused, then looking eye to eye with Tom asked.

"Would you help us, or join with us, or at least help us to get started."

Here he stopped, a nervousness showing on his face.

Tom gazed around at the anxious teens before speaking. Without emotion one way or another he asked.

"What kind of business do you propose ?"

A slight smile now showing, Fred replied confidently.

"Just exactly what we have been doing. General handy man stuff, light rehab of buildings, landscaping and the like."

"What about the professionals who already do that sort of thing. You could make a lot of enemies right here in your own town. That could lead to another Bert bashing scenario with a lot of bad repercussions. And this time it will be you who will be receiving the verbal bashing."

"That's why we are asking you for help to get started. To get started without causing problems. We have been discussing this for a few days now and think we have a good plan."

Tom relaxed his position showing serious interest. Josh took over the presentation.

"We don't want to compete with anybody. We would like to do just what we have done here." He waved his arm indicating the barn. "To help the non business's who can't afford the real professionals. Like the library here, seniors who still own their own homes but can't physically do the work anymore and can't afford to pay a professional. We would only charge the cost of the supplies necessary and perhaps a small percentage on top of that. It would not have to be much, just a little pocket money for us. You know, movie money, gas money, burger money."

"Take a girl out money." Steve threw in to some laughter from the others.

Ace joined in back to a serious mood.

"We could eventually build up a reserve for equipment of our own instead of borrowing from our parents. We could start here in Tylerville and spread out to other communities. I'm sure there is a lot of work around that we could do that a lot of people could not afford to have done otherwise."

The enthusiasm was wild now with all the guys throwing up ideas. Tom finally threw up his hands to calm the runaway chatter. Once all was quiet he addressed the group softly.

"Okay I'm in."

Excitement rose again as Tom stood, "But" he said a little louder. This killed the chatter again with curiosity showing.

"Give me a few days to fine tune some of your ideas. I will consult with both Sam McCort and Judge McCallister for the legalities of such a venture."

The expressions changed on the teens.

"You mean we may not be able to do it." Steve posed.

"No, that's not what I'm saying. But to keep everything on the up and up we must know certain ramifications, such as what licence may be necessary, if any. I don't really see a problem but it is better to be on the safe side."

Tom's friendly explanation satisfied the group and all became calm again congratulating each other for a good start.

"How about a journal story before it gets too late ?"

This they were all in favor of. Based on what had recently happened Tom chose to read the story about Bert's garden being trampled by unknowns along with Tom burning dinner, to be followed by the flat tire tale.

"This first story may have a familiar ring to it. It just shows how long a hateful rumor can carry it's destructive power."

As Tom read he could sense how uncomfortable the boys were getting. The latter part of the story about the burnt dinner helped relieve the tension. Tom further lightened the air with his words.

"Not to worry guys, I don't hold grudges. That's all water under the bridge as they say. This next story is a short one, then we can all go home."

Tom read the short epic of the flat tires which had no serious damages, just a slight inconvenience.

"So that's where Mr. McCort comes into the picture." commented Bill.

"Right you are, and he has stayed an important part of the picture ever since. You will learn more of that important relationship further down the road. Okay men, have a great weekend. Dirk and Jonathon, I have your contact information and will be in touch at the end of the weekend. Until then I will be working on your proposal."

The teens left reluctantly taking one last look at their masterpiece, the new cream colored barn which took its place among the better sites in Tylerville.

Before leaving to see Arlene, Tom managed to secure an appointment with Judge McCallister at nine A.M. the next morning which was Thursday.

Chapter 23

"Thank you for seeing me on such notice sir." Tom said as he was ushered into the Judge's office.

"I guessed it was important since It wasn't that long since we last talked." replied the judge. "Have a seat, what's on your mind ?"

"The simple things first. The library's yellow barn project is finished as is my garden, both beyond my expectations.. It would be appreciated, when you get a chance of course, if you could take a look at the now cream colored barn." Ton commented smiling.

He went on to explain how the five original youths chose to work beyond their thirty hours even though they had been released. The judge was struck with surprise at hearing this asking;

"You said five boys, there were only four in court as I recall."

Tom explained that the fifth had managed to get away before the police showed up. But after hearing the court results chose to join his pals in doing their community service. By the way, they are all good boys and I believe totally changed."

"What about the two toughies from the other town ? How are you making out with them."

"That's another surprising story."

"I thought so." interrupted McCallister. I felt bad giving them to you."

"Dirk and Jonathon ?" Tom stated.

"Jonathon" asked the judge.

"Yes Ace, as he preferred to be called. Well Jonathon and I and the rest of the group are getting along just fine sir. As a matter of fact he is a very good worker, they both are."

"Who are you anyway ? The Pied Piper or Willy Wonka ?"

Tom laughed at this though a bit embarrassed. He relayed the whole story of the work being done and shared by all the teens.

"Now for the one of the two reasons for my being here."

"Two." questioned Judge McCallister.

"Yes sir. Regarding Jonathon and Dirk, they have both served close to thirty hours for me and willingly I might add. Your original judgement was for forty hours."

Hesitantly Tom continued.

"I know it's not my place but I'm asking if you could consider their time finished."

The judge stared in silence.

"My request sir ties into the second reason I'm here.

"Go on." the judge said almost sternly.

Tom took the next almost ten minutes to talk about the teens wanting to start a business. He went into full detail including his own involvement in the plan and the type of work they wanted to do.

"You could consider it a voluntary extension of Restorative Justice. I'm also sure the guys would be willing to accept any future Restorative Justice candidates into the group."

Tom finished his plea and sat back in his chair. The judge was silent, deep in thought. Time dragged on even though it was less than thirty seconds. A sly smile appeared on his face as he slowly commented.

"Not only are you a good litigator but I believe you should be on the bench."

Tom also smiled at this but could feel a flush come over him.

"No need to be embarrassed Tom, I was sincere in what I just said. Your requests are sound and logical. I also know by now they have your solid backing."

He shuffled some papers and finding a folder, opened it.

"On your word I am commuting the balance of hours of both Jonathon and Dirk to completed as served."

Tom felt good about his decision and was pleased for the teens. He sincerely believed the two were changed youths.

"Now let's talk more about this business of theirs." The judge smiled. "You stated that you already warned them of competition by professionals and how it could possibly affect them and the town as a whole."

"Yes sir." Tom answered "And there will be more discussion about that very thing as we go. I believe their idea of a customer base came from my community service talks. You know about the elderly and poorer folk who can't afford to make necessary repairs. Not only that, it could be like a permanent Restorative Justice venue. An ongoing community service outlet so to speak. It would also put any new candidates in touch with this corps of boys, which, in my opinion would be a definite benefit.

The judge put his hands up as if surrendering.

"Enough councilor, you have me convinced and sold on your idea."

"Their idea sir." Tom corrected.

McCallister smiled and nodded.

"If you need anything else from me, please do not hesitate, or maybe it should be the other way around."

They both laughed as they shook hands. Tom took his leave as if he were walking on air.

~ ~ ~ ~

Tom was at Eileen's house by eleven o'clock still excited from his meeting with the judge. His explanation of the mornings events was non-stop to Arlene and her aunt.

"I'm all out of breath just listening to you Tommy love. I'm going to have to rest a while before I go out." She further chided, "Why don't you take this pretty lass here and go someplace so I can get something done."

"That's a request I have no problem following." Tom replied.

Once in the truck Tom asked;

"Where to my lady ?"

"How about a trip to the quarry to see the progress ?" suggested Arlene.

"Great idea. I have some additional wording for him to add to the stone."

"May I see it ?"

"Not right now, I want it to be a surprise to all."

"I understand Tom and I won't pry, I will abide by your wishes."

Down deep inside she respected Tom's feelings and knew the time would come when she would share in everything.

The stone carving was moving along nicely and was absolutely beautiful. Tom dropped off the additional instructions to Norm for the text inscription, then the couple left. At Arlene's request they went straight to the cabin.

"I just love this place. There is nothing pretentious about it. It is just plain homey. Is that even a word ? I could live here forever."

"Are you saying that you would be happy living here ?" Tom inquired matter of fact.

Thrilled beyond her dreams Arlene answered instantly.

"Is that a proposal Mr. Thatcher ?"

Taken a little by surprise Tom hesitated thinking about what he just said. Turning to look at her Tom lovingly replied,

"I guess it is my love, I guess it is."

Arlene ran to his arms.

"Yes my darling, I'm saying I want to live here and with you and you alone."

Arlene on tip toes kissed him and as they parted she added;

"And that makes it official."

"I guess it does." Tom answered with a big hug. "Thank you." he whispered into her hair.

"Do we tell Aunt Eileen ?"

"No" Tom replied instantly. Let me make it official with a ring."

"I don't care about a ring Tom, I just want to be with you."

"You have been since the first time we met. I knew then you would be my wife, and I know Bert would approve."

Arlene was literally glowing now. She was like a child running loose in a toy store. She sat down then immediately got up running and jumping into Tom's arms. She poured kisses all over his face while laughing.

"You don't know how happy I am." she spouted somehow.

"I think I have a pretty good idea." he smiled in answer.

"I guess I am being rather silly, but I don't care. I love you and that's all that matters. I want to celebrate, but with just you."

"How about that dinner you shunned the other night."

" That would be perfect.. A perfect dinner for a perfect occasion with the perfect man to end a perfect day." stated Arlene in a sing song voice.

"Do you think you're getting carried away a little, Miss Perfect." Tom ribbed.

"Perhaps, but don't you understand I am the happiest woman in the world right now and I don't care who knows it."

~ ~ ~ ~ ~ ~ ~

This particular steak house was the ideal setting to end the day for Arlene. The soft, quiet atmosphere with candle lit tables, each separated from the other for maximum privacy yet still part of the whole coziness of the double fire place room. Arlene was stunned into silence as she took in the total picture. Tom smiled at her with the words;

"To end the perfect day."

Arlene clasped his hand and squeezed hard.

While being escorted to their table Tom heard a familiar voice.

"Are you too successful now to say hello to friends."

Tom snapped his head around only to see Sam McCort and his wife with their glowing smiles. The four passed on the usual pleasantries before Tom and Arlene moved on to their own corner.

Dinner with the right bottle of wine was ordered as Arlene actually outshined the table candle.

"May our life always be like this." she whispered softly.

"You mean eating in restaurants all the time ?"

"Don't ruin my day now you clown." as she politely slapped his hand.

They dawdled over dinner letting the world go by. They were not quite finished when Sam appeared at their table.

"I don't want to spoil your dinner but I did want to mention McCallister and I spoke this afternoon. That's a great idea your kids have. See me early Monday morning. There is a town council meeting this Wednesday and I think you should be there. Think it over and I'll see you Monday. Have a great night folks."

Tom and Arlene were alone again toasting to their special day. Tom's thoughts went to the town meeting but quickly discarded them so as not to ruin their day.

After saying good night to Arlene, Tom set out for his cabin in the woods. His thoughts again drifted to the council meeting on Wednesday.

"I don't know why Sam thinks I should be there but perhaps it's not a totally bad idea. I'll have to wait until Monday to see Sam but this may be my opportunity for me to tell about the headstone memorial for the cemetery. It might be just the opening I need for my change the opinion of Bert campaign."

Relaxed and satisfied because of the day, once home he grabbed Bert's first novel and took himself to bed. He awakened Saturday morning with a stiff neck, book still in hand. A few exercises and a hot shower had him back to normal. After breakfast he drove to Aunt Martha's who could not stop talking about the barn, its appearance and the many more uses they could get from it now.

"Last night the library committee voted to host a nice lunch for your youth corps as a thank you. Do you think they would like that or even come to such a thing ?"

"I think that's a wonderful thing and yes I do believe they would come." replied Tom happily.

They spoke of general plans for the luncheon but that was to be decided upon by the ladies.

"Before you see Arlene today I have something for you."

Martha disappeared for a few minutes while Tom slowly sipped at his coffee. She returned with a loving smile and handed him a dark blue velvet covered ring box.

"I've been keeping this for you at your mother's request. I'm sure you can put this to good use now."

Tom, a bit red faced, looked at his aunt questioningly. Still maintaining her warm smile she put her hands on his clamping the box and kissed him on the temple. Tom just stared at his aunt confused.

"Everyone knows about you two, except you two." Martha said. "This ring was your mother's. It was the only thing she truly treasured from your father that, the bum didn't steal. She wanted you to have it when the right girl came along." Smiling her biggest smile she added, "She is the right one, isn't she ?"

Tom was speechless.

"Come now Tom, It's quite obvious. Did you ask her yet ?"

Laughing to himself he finally answered his aunt.

"As a matter of fact, yesterday was the day."

"I just knew it, Eileen had the same hunch. She's going to be so happy."

"I guess you were right, you two knew before us."

"I'm so happy for you." Martha said as she hugged her nephew. Now you run along and give Arlene that ring to make it official and you two will have dinner with Eileen and I tonight."

Tom started to say something but was shushed.

"Ah-Ah, it has already been decided. Now scoot, I'm sure Arlene will be waiting for you."

Eight minutes later Tom was being hugged by Eileen.

"Tommy love, it took you two long enough."

Arlene looked on as stymied as Tom.

"Apparently we are open books." Tom held the open box before Arlene. "I guess we can now make it official."

With tear filled eyes Arlene was frozen in place.

"Well, take it lass, before he changes his mind and offers it to me." ribbed Eileen.

As luck would have it the ring fit as if it were custom made.

"**T**his means even more to me now that I know it was your mothers." sobbed Arlene between large intakes of air.

"**I** do love you Tom, so very much." she cried into his chest.

"**O**h, stop it lass, you've got me all teary eyed now." teased Eileen. Looking at Tom she continued teasing with, "See what you have caused now Tommy love."

All eventually calmed down with Arlene extremely proud of the ring and naturally the engagement.

The four had a cozy celebratory dinner, of course with a lot of teasing of the young couple.

Sunday was a quiet day for Arlene and Tom at the cabin. They enjoyed being together, not necessarily conversing but knowing the other was there. Tom fussed with nothing in particular and read more of Bert's novel while Arlene sketched and painted the dreams before her. They luxuriated in each others company knowing the upcoming week was going to be busy.

Chapter 24

Tom and Sam arrived at the same time at Sam's office, Tom naturally being nervous about what Sam had to say.

"So, give me the whole spiel about the kids business like you gave the judge."

"I hope you did not take offense Sam, by me talking to McCallister first ?"

Sam smiled; "Put your mind at ease my friend. The thought never crossed my mind, besides that would have been my first step also. Now fill me in on what you told the judge."

Tom went into the same detail he gave to McCallister. Sam listened, not out of politeness but was genuinely interested.

"I'm glad to see you already brought up the competition problem. Even the judge was impressed by that. I see no real problems with the plan except for the money end."

Tom was instantly alert.

"Bookkeeping, taxes, workman's comp., liability insurance, etc."

I guess my thinking did not really go far enough." Tom mumbled sadly.

"No need to get down on yourself my friend. There are always answers."

Tom's spirits perked up a bit.

"Organize your teens into a charitable group. They can do what you just outlined on a volunteer basis. What money they get for their services can be by donation. This way everything is kept legal and above board. If you wish I can provide you with a good accountant who I'm sure will work gratis."

By now , Tom's head was spinning. He had not yet been involved in the real world of finance and legalities. He now treasured Sam for his knowledge and help.

*"**O**ld Bert was no fool."* he thought. Then thinking out loud for Sam to hear, Tom voiced his thoughts.

"**I**f we formed a group, say the Tylerville Youth Corps., we, the boys I mean, could do the work they have just been doing for donations. Enough to cover the expenses they incur and then some. The accountant could then keep tabs so that no abuses occur."

"**Y**ou got it pal. That's it in a nutshell. Naturally the accountant will fine tune that thinking and then it's up to you to pass it on to the teens. Knowing your rapport with the group I don't think you will have any problems. If something should arise you have me and the judge and the accountant to fall back on. The teens deserve to be compensated for their labors. As long as they realize it will not be a salary based wage. The accountant can work that out for you."

Tom replied in a more than happy tone.

"**Y**ou don't know how good you have made me feel. I'm sure the guys will love it. This can actually solve a lot of problems. The main one being to keep the young folk busy and learning. While listening to you another possible idea came forth. We could work on getting the professionals in this town to actually help. Not necessarily financially but in teaching some skills. That could possibly lead to some of these youths getting an actual paying job."

"**Y**ou were born for this job Tom. You're a natural for working with the young. Who knows, we may be able to get some young women involved also. That way your Youth Corps could reach out to many more."

"**W**hoa, slow down, Sam. We are not even started up yet and you have me employing the entire state.."

Laughing Sam answered; "You're right of course, but what an idea this is. Allowing young people to work, helping them feel important, helping them help themselves. Once the town takes hold of this idea all kinds of opportunities could open up. Opportunities for the young. In time perhaps we will no longer need Restorative Justice."

"**A**gain slow down Sam, you're sort of overwhelming me."

Smiling and laughing Sam responded,

"**Y**ou're right, I'm talking as if it was my program."

"**I**t could be !"

"**N**o thanks, I have all I can handle now, what with advising youth groups and all." he grinned.

"**Y**ou mentioned the town council meeting on Wednesday ? What's that all about ?"

"**Y**es, I almost forgot. Judge McCallister is going to address the council regarding the Restorative Justice program. He is requesting the teens two lawyers be there also. I think this is something you should really consider."

"**Y**ou bet I will, be there I mean. It will be a great opportunity for me to also address a memorial service for Bert."

"**D**o you think that's wise ? Do you really think this is the right time for that ?"

"**W**hy not, I'm going to do it sooner or later. I think this will tie in nicely."

Tom could read the concern in Sam's face.

"**N**ot to worry Sam. I will not cause any trouble. I will approach the subject calmly and matter of fact. I have gained some recognition in town because of this Restorative Justice project so I will try and capitalize on that."

Sam sat back and smiled again.

"**I** know when your mind is made up so I will just wish you good luck."

"**T**hank you Sam, I knew you would understand." Tom replied calmly. "By the way Arlene and I are now officially engaged." he added proudly.

"**W**elcome to a whole new world." Sam teased. "I assume that's what Saturday nights dinner was all about. My wife called it right."

Tom laughed again, mostly at himself.

"**I**t appears the whole world knew of this before Arlene and I did."

"**I**t's a woman's intuition thing." commented Sam. "Don't try to figure it out. I guess that's about it, see you on Wednesday night. Starting time is usually six forty five."

Sam extended his hand, "Congrats on the engagement and your great success with the yellow barn, sorry I mean the cream colored barn."

Tom left feeling quite good about his future projects. He couldn't wait to tell Arlene.

~ ~ ~ ~ ~ ~

On the drive from town to Arlene's Tom, as usual, was all thought. *"I forgot to mention the unpublished book. Along with everything else I think the timing is right for the book at least to get the wheels rolling.*

I know Arlene is going to want to go with me on Wednesday evening. I guess there is no harm in it. I just don't want to expose her to any unwanted ridicule I may get. Particularly when I bring up the Bert memorial."

Changing thoughts again he muttered aloud.

"**N**ote to self; call Jonathon and Fred when you get to Eileens."

Arlene, being her bubbly self welcomed Tom as if she had not seen him in weeks. Eileen teased as usual. Tom used Eileens phone to call the guys referencing meeting on Tuesday at the playground. He put off their questions about the business saying he would explain to all Tuesday morning. He reviewed the meeting with Sam while Arlene and her aunt listened quietly. As expected, Arlene asked immediately if she could go with him on Wednesday evening. Eileen chimed in that she and Martha would like to attend also. At this point Tom didn't dare say no.

The rest of the day was filled with trivial keep busy projects at the cabin. Arlene lost in painting and Tom planning for Wednesday evening.

Arlene agreed to be taken home right after supper so Tom could work quietly on his presentation.

~ ~ ~ ~ ~ ~

Tom's thoughts were not coming easily. *"How do I talk to the towns people about a topic they don't want to hear ?"*

This really bothered him but he also didn't want to let it go.

*"**P**erhaps Sam is correct. Maybe this is not the right time yet. This meeting is for a few other topics. If I was to bring the Bert thing up now I may be killing a later opportunity for a true explanation."*

Tom sat back letting his thoughts drift to Arlene and then to her artwork. This made a natural connection to the head stone being carved now.

"**T**hat's it !" He said in surprised tone. "I'll ask if I can make a short announcement and then very carefully mention the memorial service for Bert. I won't push or try to sell the idea. I'll do it as just a piece of information and let it go at that. I'll just wait then and see what food for thought will turn up. I'll write something down to read, this way I can make sure it's non confrontational."

Tom was satisfied with this for the moment.

~ ~ ~ ~

Tuesday morning and Tom was completely focused on the playground and the guys. He no sooner parked the truck when he noticed all seven teens walking the perimeter of the playground. They were so involved in making a list of things that needed attention they failed to see that he had arrived. Josh was the first to notice.

"Hey there, Mr. T." he yelled. "We decided to do our own inspection. There's a lot more dangerous things here than meets the eye at first glance. It's a good thing you picked this project."

Astounded, yet again, at the guys willingness and self motivation to tackle things on their own, Tom replied.

"I thought you would like this. It's totally different than the barn. At least this way you can play as you work."

His remark drew a few laughs.

"Gather round and make yourself comfortable, we have a few things to discuss first."

"Did you check into us starting a business ?" Fred inquired.

"I have information on that very subject that needs to be discussed."

Doubt showed in the teens eyes but none dared vocalize that fear.

"Not to worry, everything looks good, there may have to be a few minor changes in the original plan. We will get to that but first I have some other news."

They all grouped by the swings, a few of the boys actually sitting on them. Tom laughed inwardly at this, thinking, lucky them.

"I managed to secure a meeting with Judge McCallister last Thursday morning. I was there for two reasons. The first regarding Ace and Dirk."

The pair suddenly looked serious as Tom directed his eyes to them.

"Based on what you have just worked, the hours I'm referring to, along with your cooperative attitude, he agreed to my recommendation to consider your time served as a completion of your community service. You have fulfilled the courts requirements and are released from any further obligations."

Of course this went over big with the two teens along with congratulations and pats on the back by the other five. Ace looking grateful but serious politely inquired.

"You did that for us ? Even after the hard time we gave you in the beginning ?"

"Why not." Tom commented. "Personally I think you earned it. You did that for yourselves. You both committed yourselves to the group and pulled more than your share of the work. I believe in fairness that goes both ways."

The group mood was now one of extreme comradery. Tom, as an after thought, continued.

"Oh, I almost forgot. The library committee was so pleased with what you accomplished on their sacred old barn that they want to thank you by preparing a celebratory luncheon. Very soon I imagine. Although it is not a requirement that you attend, I think it would be a nice gesture if you did."

"What ? And not go to an offer of free food, are you kidding." spouted Bill.

This sentiment was carried by the seven unanimously.

"I figured you would all agree, besides it will be good for P R especially for your new business. Which brings me to what you are all waiting for I'm sure."

You could sense the eagerness of the young men.

"Well, I spoke at length to both the judge and Sam McCort. They are both in favor of your new venture."

This news, of course went through the group like fire. Tom let them have that moment of excitement before finishing.

"However, there will have to be a few changes in your thinking and structure."

Eyes filled with curiosity as the group waited for Tom to finish. Tom laid out all of Sam's suggestions, answering that they were more than just suggestions. Keeping it positive Tom went on with a more detailed outline. Eventually, after much back and forth discussion the teens understood the reasoning behind the suggested changes. The guys did , however, raise the question that this would actually hinder them in making any money and wasn't this the reason they wanted to start a business in the first place. Thinking to himself Tom agreed with them. He was also pleased they were using intelligent reasoning. He hesitated a moment searching for the right words wanting to stay positive.

"Both Judge McCallister and Attorney McCort agree you should receive financial compensation for your labor and at this very moment are working on that very question. You must not concern yourselves with that. I believe all will work to your satisfaction. In fact I know it will."

Tom instantly thought to himself of Bert's foundation to anonymously help out the people of Tylerville and put on a big smile of confidence for the guys to see. His smile was contagious and the group was happy accepting his words

"Please give us a few more days to work out a few more kinks to this plan. In the meantime you've got a volunteer business established.

The teens were also satisfied with the title of "Tylerville Youth Corps." The light chatter that started was interrupted by Tom.

"Okay men, now that the business part of the meeting is over what say we take care of the reason we are here in the first place. But before we actually start anything let me remind you about the fact that at present none of you is under obligation to community service anymore, which means we do not have to do any work on the playground. You can all go home if you so choose."

Looks were exchanged among the teens until Fred spoke up.

"You mentioned earlier, Mr. T. About good P R. This little project would be a perfect example of what we could do and to show the community that we are serious."

"I couldn't agree more." answered Tom. "So lets get to work. By the way the town council meeting is tomorrow night and the judge is making a presentation on the success you guys have made with the Restorative Justice and the yellow barn. He may not outwardly show it but he is quite pleased with what you have accomplished. Not just for the physical work but for your own character building and self esteem."

All the guys acted a bit shy about the praise given but inside you could see they were happy for the recognition.

"Okay, let me see this list you have been working on and see what we can accomplish today." Tom willingly inquired.

The day went well after that and the guys worked happily non stop up to four P M. when they called it quits. It was again agreed by all they could finish by late Wednesday. Tom was pleased and felt secure in the knowledge that the playground would be a lot safer. He cared not about the money he threw into it, because of the self worth it was giving the boys. It again reminded him of his earlier days in the Marine Corps and what pride can do to a person's growth in character and self.

Everyone left for the day looking forward to tomorrow and finishing the playground. Just as Tom was climbing into his truck Josh called his attention.

"Hey Mr. T. We know you are busy tomorrow night but after that you still owe us some more Bert stories."

Tom smiled, happy at receiving the request.

"I promise guys, perhaps Thursday for a few hours, at my place."

"You're on." was the combined reply from all seven.

~ ~ ~ ~

Tom pulled into a parking slot near the playground at ten minutes to ten only to find the new Youth Corps already at work. A new border had been built around the perimeter of the swing area and the guys were filling it with fine beach sand and raking it evenly. This they thought would decrease the risk of serious injury if some child fell off. This was not the only detail they were implementing. The group had come up with many safety features Tom had not thought of.

They cheered his arrival with jokes about how the boss is allowed to come in late.

The day went well and even the boys themselves were amazed at how much had been accomplished in just two days. By three o'clock they were all resting by the trucks deciding who was going to the town about their completion. Tom suggested they report the completion to Judge McCallister since the town had never been notified that such a project was even being thought of by the group. Ace and Fred volunteered so that the judge could see they were serious about their work corps. Tom chose not to interfere with the guys wanting recognition.

The boys departed and Tom returned to his log home to shower and dress for the town council meeting.

~ ~

After picking up his aunt Martha he went on to collect Arlene and her aunt. They were all surprised at how many cars were already there. The town Hall was not that large and it appeared they would have a full house. Tom could feel a certain nervousness come over him. He was not accustomed to addressing this many people who were not marines. They found four chairs toward the back of the room and seated themselves. Tom thought he recognized Josh from the back of his head but dismissed the idea.

"Why would they waste their time at a dumb old town meeting when they could be hanging out some where more interesting."

By the start time there was pretty much a full house. With the preliminary usual business stuff out of the way Judge McCallister was given the floor. Well respected, though he was, the immediate reception was not exactly a warm one. The judge introduced the Restorative Justice Program going through its boring details with little interest to be had. That is until he brought the program closer to home.

"I am not telling tales out of school since the courts proceedings are open record. As some of you know we initiated just such a program here in Tylerville under the watchful eye of a young man not exactly new to the community. It's just that the last six years of his adult life were spent serving our country with the Marine Corps both here in the states and in the Middle East. It was at his behest, after he himself suffered some malicious destruction of his property, that this program was started. Rather than start off some of our young teens with a black mark against them he urged the start of this program. I am here tonight to prompt you into acceptance and support of this venture. Once we get full acceptance of the community and the State Department of Corrections it will be fully funded by the state. In the meantime this man who pushed for the start of this has generously funded this out of his own pocket."

At last there was a stir in the audience. Apparently this was not known by many in the town. Breaking the general quiet of the room, a not too loud voice could be heard.

"Way to go Mr. T."

The judge instantly showed his disdain for the outburst but on closer observation there was almost a hint of a smile that lasted for only a few seconds. Tom did not turn around as others did but could tell the voice belonged to Ace. He gave a quiet snicker to himself to the obvious smile of Arlene. Judge McCallister, ignoring the short outcry, continued.

"This venture, I might add, has met with much success. I don't want you to take just my word for it so I brought with me tonight a few people who have first hand experience and knowledge of the outcome of this first try. I will not bore you with long winded testimony but I do want each to say a few words regarding this. Sgt. Donald Adams is here representing the State Police. He was the initial arresting officer."

Sgt. Adams very convincingly spoke for just under two minutes. It was obvious the interest of the room stirred. The judge next introduced Janet Whitmore of the Library. Her praise for the program and the work the boys did on the library unfortunately went on and on to the point the judge had to interrupt and thank her for her input, to the smiles of relief of the audience.

At this point Martha leaned over to Eileen and whispered, "That woman never did learn to shut up." Eileen concurred with her own smile.

The judge promised not to go on too much longer urging the peoples backing for the program. He did , however, mention the playground that was just refurbished voluntarily by the boys. With this he introduced Fred much to the surprise of Tom. Fred spoke briefly but eloquently for a sixteen year old, outlining what the program had done for him and his friends. He nicely swayed into a brief outline of the business the teens wanted to start. With this he seriously solicited help from the professional businesses of the area to show they were not in competition or out to hurt anyone, only to help the less fortunate. There was an outburst of applause in which even the judge took part in. When the applause died down Fred humbly added a thank you to the people for their acceptance and support.

"We sincerely appreciate your support but the real thanks should go to Mr. Tom Thatcher."

At this the six other teens provided a short applause of their own. Fred smiled at this.

"Mr. T. Treated us like people not wayward teens. He accepted us for who we were and allowed us to take part in discussions about the work we were doing. He made us feel like adults and equals. We were not slighted or talked down to. He made us feel like an important part of the project. For that we seven are very thankful."

Fred quietly took his seat while Tom tried very hard not to go red and to hold back the tears of pride. After a slight pause the chair of the Town Council asked Tom to speak about the program and why he took such an interest.

Tom, feeling confident, reiterated what the judge and Fred already said with a slight variation. Then feeling this was his opportunity he decided to touch on the subject of Bert Morrow.

"This whole thing came about under odd circumstances. I'm sure you all know by now that I now occupy Bert Morrows log home and property. What some of you may not know is the fact that Bert was like a second father to me. He actually help my aunt raise me so that I didn't end up in a restorative program myself. The damage to my property was a spillover from what Bert had to put up with all the time. But that's all done and forgotten."

Tom spoke the last sentence with a sincerely positive tone.

"I came home from Afghanistan too late for my good friends funeral which was attended by only three people. This great man deserves more than that. I would like to make sure he is honored properly. That's the least he deserves. In a few weeks time I will hold a proper memorial service for Bert Morrow. No one is obligated to come but personally I think you, the folks of Tylerville, owe it to him. That is your decision, not mine. I will post the exact date on the Town bulletin board."

Tom said this, not as a challenge, but with the voice of determination. He would not be deterred from this goal. This was Bert's home town and now his. He was not about to throw away all of Bert's service even though the folks of Tylerville were unaware of what he did. The room was quiet and Tom chose not to challenge that with his eyes. He thanked the Town Council for their time and almost over politely thanked the towns folk for allowing him to speak. He retired from the podium returning to his seat looking at Arlene who instantly grabbed his hand and squeezed. By the time he was seated the town agenda continued as all appeared normal again.

When the meeting was over and they were exiting the building Tom, surprisingly was approached by a few folks. A few congratulated him on his success with the teens, while a few said they would definitely be at the graveside memorial service. Arlene showed extreme pleasure hearing these commitments. She did not want Tom's efforts to go for naught.

Back at Eileen's house they indulged in cake and coffee while talking over the meeting reaction. The consensus was that it all went well and was readily accepted. Tom arrived home in good spirits and settled in bed reading Bert's first book.

-165-

Chapter 24

The dust cloud moving up the driveway readily alerted Tom of a visitor. In this case, visitors. A truck followed by two cars circled at the top of the drive and stopped. His memoir audience had arrived. The seven founding members of the Tylerville Youth Corps jumped from their respective vehicles sporting broad smiles. Loud but respectful greetings were given as Tom returned the smile.

"What beautiful landscaping you have here Mr. T. This must have been professionally done." stated Bill grinning ear to ear.

"Naaa, just a couple of bums passing by who wanted coffee money." responded Tom with an equal grin.

The group gathered round the picnic table finding their favorite comfortable spot. Tom playing dumb asked.

"Did you guys want something special or are you just bored with life ?"

"We're here to collect what you owe us." Ace answered.

"Oh really, and what might that be ?" rebutted Tom.

"Stories, you owe us stories. You know, Bert's journal." Josh joined in.

"Gee, I don't know if I have time for that. I was planning on sitting in the rocker and talking to the trees."

"Not a bad idea. First read to us , then we'll all talk to the trees." Steve threw out.

Just then there was a light breeze winding its way through the trees echoing their arboreal whisperings.

"See ?" pointed Josh. They are all in agreement."

"Okay, you win." Tom answered sounding disgusted. "I guess I can't argue with nature."

Tom retrieved the journals from the cabin settling himself in a rocker by the table.

"Before you start reading." interrupted Fred, "We do have some good news. Harry Tanner, you know the guy who owns the hardware store in town, well, he was at the meeting last night and spoke to me this morning asking about our Youth Corps. He said he is willing to talk to people on our behalf and dig up some work for us. He mentioned talking to some of the local contractors about throwing some small jobs our way. He also said he would seek some teaching help for us."

"That's great news guys." Tom exclaimed with sincerity.

"Looks like you're on your way. This can really turn into good things for you and the whole town for that matter. You can always recruit more help and eventually give the total community a face lift. I'm sure the less fortunate folks will be more than pleased to get some help. I'm quite proud of you men. This can't hurt your future either. Remember also that I'm more than willing to help you guys any way I can." Tom added as an afterthought.

"I have to admit, I was rather surprised at seeing you at the meeting. I figured that kind of stuff would be rather boring for you." Tom further commented.

Fred replied instantly, "That was Judge McCallister's idea. A few of us went to see him Wednesday afternoon. Believe it or not we found him very easy to talk to."

"That's exactly what I have been trying to tell you guys all along. Talk to and treat people like you want to be treated and most often it will be reciprocated. Of course, there always the one percent who won't, but don't let that change you're approach. The judge may appear to be a hard man but he is fair. Respect him and his position and he will respect you. That, by the way, goes for anybody. Enough business talk. I'm glad it's working out for you guys. Now for the journals. I almost forgot. Arlene made another batch of cookies and some lemonade for you. We can enjoy the snack while we read.

Tom was not picky this day about which anecdotes to read. He read them in the order they were written. Letting them see what Bert went through on a continuous basis, would he hoped, drive home the message of the damage of falsehoods. He read each entry in a calm non judgmental way allowing the tale to speak for itself. It did prompt comments from the teens but Tom managed to keep them toned down. He did not want a lynch mob mentality to take over. The group understood this and was more than cooperative. They enjoyed the epics along with Arlene's tray of goodies.

To keep things on the light side, Tom finished the days readings with some of the narratives of Bert's Korean war experiences.

Close to three hours had passed when Tom called a halt to the gathering.

"Sorry guys but I have a very pretty Irish lass waiting for me to take her to dinner. We'll have to continue this another day, that is when you're not working." he said with an encouraging smile.

"I think we would like that, as long as you don't mind Mr. T."

"I don't mind at all guys. I'm proud of Bert and like being able to share him with others."

Fred then quietly inquired.

"This memorial service for Bert, is that something we could attend also ?"

"I would consider that a compliment, fella's. I would like nothing better. I would be proud to have you there."

Smiles of acceptance were displayed on all the young faces. The boys thanked Tom for the day and sent their thanks to Arlene for the treats. Keeping it light Josh added.

"She could bake cookies for them as often as she wanted and they would try not to hurt her feelings when they forced themselves to eat them."

Smiling Tom agreed to pass the message on to Arlene. The yard emptied out leaving Tom alone with his thoughts.

~ ~ ~ ~

Though dinner plans were changed, Tom was not upset. His aunt Martha and Eileen got together and planned dinner for the four of them to celebrate the young couples engagement. Tom's success with the Restorative program was an added reason. Martha even supplied a great bottle of wine.

It turned out to be a most pleasant, relaxing evening. A rather late one too, for both the aunts. Tom eventually felt the effects of the calm evening and the wine and said his good nights. Home safely in his cabin in the woods he retired with Bert's novel.

Sleep overcame him in short order. He awoke, book in hand and birds singing. Before even leaving the bed his thought went to the unpublished novel.

"Wouldn't it be nice to have on hand if and when he could get the town together to review Bert's life and show, in spite of the harassment, what he did for this town and the people in it." Tom followed this thought by voicing out loud

"Note to self. Try and get to see Sam today to discuss the book publishing. After a quick breakfast he called Arlene. He arranged to meet her for lunch at the Country Kitchen after he met with Sam McCort.

Sam was delighted to see Tom. He had not had a chance to speak with him after Wednesday nights meeting.

"I'm glad we could meet. I wanted to pass on some feedback about the town meeting. Most comments were positive. There was only one or two negative remarks about the meeting. Not about the Restorative Justice but your remarks about the memorial service. Not to worry though, those comments came from what I would call old codgers who happen to be negative regarding anything and everything."

The two men laughed softly, both familiar with that type personality.

"What were your thoughts on Wednesdays gathering ?" asked Tom anxiously.

"The whole program appeared to have been accepted. Your work with these youngsters impressed just about everyone. Not to take anything away from you but McCallister is well respected in this county. His backing of this idea carried a lot of weight. Don't take me wrong, but since the trial, or hearing if you will, the fact that you started this whole idea is well recognized. You seem to be building your own reputation. I think many more folks will be coming around to your thinking in the very near future."

"Thanks for the input Sam, I really needed that positive feedback. Do you think I was too forward with my memorial service plug ?"

"Well, to tell you the truth I was a little shocked when you brought it up. I wasn't expecting that. But, all in all, I think it went as well as could be expected for this town. I have heard a few positive comments and some definite yes's on attendance. You sure like to grab the bull by the horns." added Sam with a grin. "No wonder you and old Bert got along so well. You're very much alike."

"I'll take that as a compliment." smiled Tom in return.

"Do you have anything special planned for the memorial service ? Stupid question I guess. Knowing you I'm sure you do."

"As a matter of fact I do. I'm having a headstone carved for the gravesite."

"Not a simple one, I'm sure."

Tom smiled. "Depends on your point of view. It will have his image carved into it and a small dedication I wrote."

"How did you arrange for the personal likeness."

"I'm sorry, I thought you knew about Arlene."

"What does Arlene have to do with Bert." Sam inquired.

With a very proud grin Tom answered.

"She happens to be a very gifted artist and with a few old pictures supplied by her aunt she did a wonderful life like portrait. She then transferred it to the stone. It was so good Norman even offered her a job. The next time you're in the area stop by the cabin and have a look."

"I will make it a point to do that. Probably next week, I have to go that way for an appointment. Looks like you have quite a woman there. You better hang on to her."

"I plan on it." Tom answered smiling again.

"Is that all you came to see me about ?" Sam asked.

"Oh, no, I almost forgot. The unpublished novel ?"

"I was wondering when you would get around to that."

Speaking firmly and positively, Tom replied.

"Let's do it. The sooner the better."

"Fine leave it up to me. I'll get on it today."

"How long does something like that take ?" questioned Tom not having any experience with such matters.

"Frankly, I don't think it would be very long. I'm sure the publisher will expedite it ASAP knowing it's from Bert. Let's face it, every thing else he wrote has been a very good money maker. They will push this through as quickly as possible. Trust me."

That's just what Tom wanted to hear. He already felt his day was complete on hearing this."

"I'll leave it in your capable hands then. Fill me in about the time of release. That I'm really anxious to know."

Sam felt his statement rather odd but did not question the request.

Their chat concluded, Tom walked to the luncheonette. He passed a few people on the way and was cheerfully greeted with smiles and normal salutations.

Inside the eatery he also was met with a variety of head nods and smiles. Tom received his biggest smiles from Arlene and Brenda. In fact Brenda's welcome could be taken as more welcoming than Arlene's. The two women were talking at a booth toward the rear of the eatery.

"Congratulations on your talk last night and of coarse your engagement. Most of all my personal thanks for working your miracles on the boys. I have never seen such a transformation. Those course teens are the perfect gentlemen. More so, I think then some of the adults."

Tom, almost feeling awkward again, gave his thanks. Arlene was all aglow with pride for her man, even more so when Tom kissed her hello in front of Brenda.

The owner/waitress took their order and as she turned away warmly exclaimed.

"You sure are a breath of fresh air for this town."

Alone now the newly engaged couple discussed the night before and this mornings visit with the attorney. Tom then directed the conversation to the preparations for the memorial service. Arlene suggested a two or three week date. This would give them a proper time to arrange everything. Arlene also added, much to Tom's surprise.

"It would also give the two aunts time to talk it up around town some more. And let's face it, you know the boys' are going to help spread the word."

Tom was immediately chagrined but knew Arlene was right.

Brenda reappeared with the chosen lunch and could not stop talking about the totally changed teens.

" I have never before been treated with such respect even by the grown men of this town." Smiling and looking directly at Arlene she quipped, "You better hold on to this man, because if you don't I'm going to steal him."

"Wait a minute." objected Tom. "Don't I have anything to say about this ?"

In unison, both women turned to him and said "NO".

With a hurt look on his face Tom turned to his lunch mumbling.

"I guess I know where I stand."

Brenda left laughing while Arlene also turned to her lunch plate quietly saying.

"I'm glad to see you know your place."

She peeked up at Tom to see him staring back both enjoying the fun.

Lunch over, tab paid, Tom and Arlene were on their was back to Tom's cozy cottage.

"I have something to show you when we get home. No one else has seen this yet. Something I want your advice on. You're artistic advice."

Still in a playful mood Arlene inquired professionally,

"And what do I get in return for this artistic advice ?"

Playing along Tom answered seriously.

"A ride home tonight. Remember it's a long walk."

"Well, in that case, since you're going to be nasty about it, I'll be kind to you this time and advise you for free."

"I'm honored your Ladyship."

"I thought you would be."

By the time they pulled into the driveway both were laughing like silly children. Once in the house Tom fixed a pot of coffee while Arlene prepared tea for herself.

"**O**kay now, where is this art you need my advice on ?" Arlene further probed curiously.

"**I**t's upstairs, I'll get it."

"**I** didn't know you had an upstairs."

"**I**t's just a storage loft." Tom answered as he reached for the fire place poker. He lowered the stairs and proceeded up. Arlene, without asking followed.

"**H**ow cute. Just another thing to love about this place."

"**P**ull up a trunk and sit down." Tom indicated smiling.

He reached for and proceeded to open the last metal box Bert spoke of. He handled everything lovingly finally reaching the medals. Proudly, yet softly speaking Tom explained that these were Bert's medals and ribbons he was awarded, most for heroism in the Korean War. Arlene stared open mouthed, not saying a word. Tom proceeded to display each one explaining its significance. His words choked him, and Arlene could see tears in his eyes as he unveiled the very last one. Before he named it Arlene whispered.

"**I** know what that one is. I have seen it displayed on the Telly. Was he a marine also ?""

A voice shaking whisper answered a quiet "Yes"

"**M**ay I." she asked softly as she took the box from his hand. He reached for the picture of the award ceremony with the president.

The pair sat quietly for a time, Arlene allowing Tom the necessary moment for composure. At last breaking the silence and with a very upbeat voice she stated.

"**A**nd you want a display of honor for the memorial service ?"

"**V**ery much so, but I want, no, need your help. Will you ?"

"**O**f course my darling. You needn't ask. I am always here for you."

She turned and with her hand caressing his cheek, softly kissed him. A few tears showed in his eyes.

"**C**an we bring these downstairs ? Then we can have the table to display them and discuss a design format."

Soon the ladder was again secured making the ceiling whole again. Tom spread the award medals on the table in correct order explaining the priority sequence and significance of each. Arlene marveled at the finished sight.

"**B**ert was a genuine hero." she whispered

"**A**n unsung hero." Tom furthered in the same whisper. "No one knows of his heroic exploits except me. Now the two of us. I don't believe Sam even knows."

"**A**nd you want to show the town at the memorial service." said Arlene in a questioning curiosity.

"**T**hat's the general idea. Do you think it's wrong of me ?"

"**I** don't think anything could be more right." she replied as she moved to him and kissed his cheek.

They embraced for a moment with Tom finally moving back to reality.

"**S**o young lady what do you think you can do for me."

"**W**ell, you can work with wood, my aunt and I can work with fabric , so I'm sure we can come up with something. Can you supply me with some paper and a pencil and leave me for a while, I need to think."

"**F**or you anything my love." Tom said as he stood.

Arlene loved hearing these words and her glow showed as much. Her request fulfilled Arlene drifted into another world. Tom smiled to himself and returned to the loft. He remembered Bert mentioning his military sword hidden somewhere. Tom methodically started his search. It wasn't too long before its discovery. It hung from two nails on the flat side of a roof joist partially hidden by the roof insulation.

It was exactly like his own. *"Of course stupid, it's called Marine Corps tradition.."* he thought as he recovered it from its hideout.

Tom had not handled his own for some time and holding Bert's sword filled him with pride. Shaking himself out of his reverie he went back to Arlene.

"**I**'m sorry to disturb you but do you think there is a way to include this in your display ?"

She smiled softly as Tom lay the sword across the table before her.

"**T**hat will do just perfectly." she responded and went right back to her paper.

Tom found the book he was reading and relaxed on the couch.

The soft kiss on his forehead gently awakened Tom. Arlene was sitting on the arm of the sofa affectionately admiring him.

"**N**ice nap ?" she said quietly not to disturb the mood. Tom breathed deeply with a sigh.

"**N**ot long enough." he teased.

"**W**ell, while you were in lala land I was slaving away trying to earn my ride home."

"**A**nd did you ?" Tom asked seriously

"**Y**ou tell me, come take a look." replying she grabbed his hand pulling him back to the table.

There before him was another example of Arlene's perfect artistry. Her sketch showed a wind blown U.S. Flag with a shield shaped design superimposed topped with the Marine Corps emblem under which were displayed the medals in their proper order. Hanging from the bottom of the shield was the sword.

"**T**hat is absolutely perfect my love. How big will it be ?"

"**A**s big as you want it, but remember you don't want to overpower the medals. They should be the main focus."

Arlene then went on to explain the details involving the colors and fabric, with identifying names. Large embroidered letters across the bottom spelled out ; "Bert Morrow – S.Sgt.. And the years served. The words were in gold on the scarlet background."

"**C**an you do all that ?" Tom inquired dumbfounded.

"**N**ot by myself silly, but the four of us can."

"**T**he four of us ?" questioned Tom again.

"**Y**es. You and I and our two aunts." she answered as she hooked her arm in his and snuggled into his shoulder.

"**I** love it, I absolutely love it." Tom gushed.

"**N**ow do I get a ride home ?" Arlene pleaded.

"**I'**ll carry you home in my arms if I have to." He answered pulling her closer.

"**I'**ll go get the lumber first thing tomorrow." He thought out loud.

"**T**hen you can take us to a fabric shop." Arlene threw in. "Let me use the phone to call the ladies and start the ball rolling."

Hanging up the phone , Arlene addressed Tom. "Okay, we're all going to meet at Martha's tonight. I said we would bring home Chinese. Is that okay ?"

"**S**ounds great to me." answered Tom not taking his eyes off the drawing.

The remainder of the afternoon the pair spent in the porch rockers reading the last of Bert's journals not including the war journals.

~ ~ ~ ~

Tom opened the last book indicating to Arlene there were only two entries left.

"**O**kay, if you're willing to share, we can each read one." suggested Arlene.

"Sounds good to me." Tom replied. "I'll kick it off." he said as he put his coffee mug aside.

Here's a good one for you Tom, if you are still reading these journals. I received a special delivery letter one day threatening foreclosure on my house and property for many years of unpaid taxes. Rather than put shame on myself it was strongly suggested I just quietly move out and not return and no court action would follow. Did you ever hear of such silliness. I guess who ever it was that sent the unsigned letter was desperate or plain dumb. The truth of the matter was that I always paid the taxes in full on the first day they were due and had been doing just that for years. I even filed the cancelled checks documenting that. Again, the wonder man, Sam McCort came to my rescue. He not only researched the town records but the county records as well. As it turned out I was one of only a few who actually paid their taxes that quickly and in full. With further scrutiny on Sam's part it turned out that neither the town clerk or town treasurer had any idea of such a letter. Someone out there must really hate me. No matter, I guess I'm more stubborn than they were. I'm still here and intend to stay so that you, Tom, have some place to come to.

Waiting for you,   Bert.

"**C**an you believe people ?" Tom sighed. "The nerve."

"**H**ow could anyone hate that much ?" rhetorically questioned Arlene. "What that poor man went through yet stayed steadfast to his principles. He was obviously a man among men."

Tom, a touch upset by the story, was now beaming from Arlene's statement.

*"**B**ert was correct when he said find a good woman."* he thought gazing at her with a love filled heart.

"**O**kay my turn." she said holding out her hand for the transfer of the journal.

Tom, most reluctantly, handed it over. Before reading aloud Arlene glanced at the writing, instantly realizing this was going to be emotionally rough on Tom.

"**W**ell." he urged. "Don't keep it a secret."

"**S**orry love." she replied and settled herself to read.

Tom,

As much as I hate to say it, I believe time is catching up with me. My eyes seem to be growing dimmer with each passing day. Things just don't appear to be as bright as they used to be. I'm sure when you get home all things will be bright again.

Arlene quickly raised her eyes to Tom observing his faraway glance. Hesitantly she continued.

She said this

The mind still wants to take on any and all challenges the world or Tylerville wants to throw at me but the physical body is somewhat hesitant of late. If you were here at my side I think we could literally take on the world together. And win too!

A hurried second glance by Arlene caught a quick smile by Tom.

I am aware, because of your last letter that you will be mustering out soon. I may appear selfish, but it can't be soon enough.

If it wasn't for dear Eileen keeping me on my toes with her nagging, who knows where I would be by now. She is such a love, without you she is the only thing that keeps me going sometimes. Don't you dare tell her I said this.

A low chuckle was heard from both.

The farm needs you, our friends of the forest need you. Most of all I need you. Forgive the rumblings of a foolish old man. Truth be known, you're the only thing I have lived for all these many long years. Your six years in the Corps filled me with a pride no one can take away. That is probably something only we Marines can understand. There are so many things I am eager to talk about. Come home soon, Son. We are anxiously waiting. Except for my time in the Corps, I have lived my life just for you. To show you what pride, honor and dedication really mean. Remember Son, never betray your principles.

I love you, and always have loved you.

— Bert —

Very much concerned for Tom, Arlene quietly closed the book, but hesitated to say anything, waiting for Tom's overall reaction. Tom, inwardly sobbing turned away from Arlene to hide his sure to be uncontrolled emotions. She went to him gathering him in her arms, guiding his head to her bosom.

"Let it go love, let it go. I totally understand. I share your pain and your love for Bert."

Tom, putting his arms around her pulled himself closer and let the tears fall. He felt a touch of embarrassment yet could not overcome the feeling deep within him. Arlene, attempting to stay strong could feel her own tears streaking down her cheeks as she slowly rocked him back and forth. Not a word was spoken. They remained this way for countless minutes. Time did not matter now.

Tom eventually severed their bond, pulling away. He wiped his cheeks and started to shamefully apologize. Arlene immediately hushed him putting two fingers to his lips. "We'll have none of that." she whispered.

With a strong and cheerful smile she voiced.

"Okay, now what size did you say you wanted the medal display ?"

She said this as if nothing had occurred

"When you purchase the necessary wood don't forget the paint for the flag. OH, and some gold paint for the emblem."

She kept talking as she walked into the house. Once inside she could feel herself well up with tears. She headed for the bathroom, secured the door and let it all out. Emotions that were held in so to appear strong for Tom. She hurt for Tom but wanted to remain as untouched as possible, at least for the part he could see. Tears gone, cheeks dried she exited the room only to find Tom still outside. She let him be and returned to her drawing.

Late afternoon arrived to find all was normal and the couple prepared to leave for the Chinese take out.

Neither Tom nor Arlene mentioned the afternoon episode. For now, at least, it never happened. On the ride to pick up dinner and to Martha's the enthusiastic couple seriously conferred about the design for displaying Bert's heroic awards. A size for the flag outline was finally chosen. All the rest was determined based on that. They were both pleased with the flag size of approximately three foot by four foot. Of course they realized they were yet to have the input of their respective aunts.

Arlene's design, as expected, was received with praise. What was addressed was the fabric work. This part of the discussion Tom purposely stayed out of. Here he felt his only job was to put the final stamp of approval on the outcome, then sit back and watch it happen.

Arlene tried to keep a close watch on Tom all evening staying close to him. This did not go unnoticed by Tom. It did give him an added sense of security knowing he could openly share his deepest emotions.

"I guess she really does love me." he thought and smiled inwardly.

By ten PM. All ideas were beat to shreds, and they agreed it was time to call it a night. Tom took notice of Arlene's concerned look and spoke before she did.

"I'm alright. I'm okay now, thanks to you. I'm glad you were there when we read the last entry. With you at my side I believe I have become stronger. I will go home and get some sleep. I'll be back first thing in the morning. You can go with me to get the wood necessary. And, oh yes the paint also.

Good nights were said all around and as Arlene hugged Tom she whispered "I love you." with an extra hard squeeze.

"I know." Tom smiled. "I love you too." He hugged back.

"Enough, you two, there will be plenty of time for that after you're married." teased Eileen

"That is if you still want to do it then." joined Martha with a laugh.

Tom handled the drive home well. He kept his thoughts on the new task of building the medal display. When he arrived at the cabin he ignored the journal totally as well as Bert's portrait. He prepared for bed and continued with Bert's novel which he found most interesting.

Chapter 25

After the morning shower and good breakfast, Tom was feeling refreshed and happy. He closed his mind to yesterday and was strongly looking forward to the challenge of the memorial service. Putting time and thought to this medal display was just what the doctor ordered, and he welcomed it willingly. He put together a list of materials needed for the display, reviewing it twice making sure he covered everything. He even remembered to include small lumber to build an easel strong enough to carry the main display.

The drive to Eileen's seemed shorter because of his up mood helped along with some classical jazz on the truck radio. Arlene was more than happy upon seeing Tom's improved attitude. She, herself let yesterdays experience fade away. Today was a renewed start. She alone went with Tom to the lumberyard for some private time with him before picking up both aunts for fabric shopping.

Headed back to Eileens with the truck carrying the necessities Tom asked in a pleading voice.

"Do I really have to go fabric shopping with you gals ? You don't really need me there."

"But you said you would go the other night." answered Arlene.

"I know nothing about the material you girls are going to buy, so why drag me along ? I could be home working on the flag and shield cutouts."

Arlene knew he was correct, they really did not need him purchase the needed materials. They had already agreed on the color choices.

"Well. Okay, if you're going to whine about it. I guess we could do without you."

"Thank you love, I'll make it up to you tonight by taking you to dinner."

"You've got yourself a deal, fraidy cat."

"Thank you, I feel better already.

Anxious to get started on his part of the project, Tom sang with the radio all the way home. He turned into his overgrown dirt drive only to find it blocked by a small bull dozer with a drag rake attached to the rear. He became confused and slightly upset until he saw a few of his favorite teens working with various rakes and shovels.

"Hey, Mr. T.." smiled Ace. "I guess you're wondering what we're doing here."

"The thought did enter my mind." Tom smiled in reply.

By then Fred was at Ace's side.

"We were getting tired of this disaster of a driveway you have.. It was making our cars rattle, even more than normal. So rather then just complain we decided to fix it."

"That's what our Youth Corps does, in case you didn't know it.." added Steve.

The others commented on the wood and paint in the truck bed. Tom explained the story behind the wood without divulging too much. It was decided he leave the truck on the side of the drive as the crew helped carry the lumber and paint up to the barn.

"By the way Mr. T. This job is on us, for all that you have done for each of us. Just our way of saying thanks." volunteered Josh.

"Besides, it will save us on the repairs on our cars." Ace added with a laugh.

Deeply touched by the boys generosity, Tom was actually at a loss for words.

"I don't know what to say guys." he muttered.

"Then don't say anything." Fred replied. "Let me get back to work and obviously you have work to do also by the looks of the wood you were carrying."

The young ones left Tom standing there with a big smile. Would he ever cease to be astounded by this particular group of teens. At first, he thought he would go and supervise what they were doing but instantly concluded it would be a bad idea. He would show them he had trust and faith in them. He happily went about his own project. In fact he became so absorbed he lost track of the time and what the young ones were doing. Had it not been for sudden noise of the small dozer he would have completely forgotten. Leaving the barn he could see they were just about finished the top circle of the drive. His truck was already parked by the side of the barn. What he was now observing was another whole driveway. One by one the boys appeared all sporting sweaty brows and large grins. Tom walked part of the new drive with them. Gone were the pot holes and bumps. Left was a well manicured roadbed. The side shrubs had been trimmed back or removed completely allowing for a don't scratch the truck drive all the way. Tom was also now all smiles.

"I don't know how to thank you guys. If I hadn't seen this with my own eyes I would swear this work was done by professionals."

This sent a look of pride rushing through the group, including Tom himself.

"You're probably all starved by now. I don't have much to offer, but come sit down and rest and let me see what I can dig up."

"No need Mr. T. We came prepared and already had our lunch break." Fred advised.

"But you know what you can do for us while we rest a bit, is read us a Bert story." interrupted Bill.

Dirk followed with,

"Yeah, one of them Korean things. They're better than going to the movies."

Tom had wanted to continue with his project yet realized he owed them that much.

"I would be more than happy to do that. I'll be right back."

In less than a minute he returned with a journal. He read two entries to the guys satisfaction.

"We have to run now, the truck to pick up the dozer should be here soon." said Ace.

Rested and happy they started the walk back to the road. This time Tom accompanied them marveling at the work that was accomplished.

"Don't forget Mr. T. You promised to let us know about Bert's memorial service." reminded Bill.

"And I will keep that promise guys. It looks like about three weeks from now. Most likely on a Saturday."

Then with a genuine smile of gratitude he also promised to spread the word about the fabulous job they performed on his now real driveway. He shook the hand of each individual young man, thinking to himself. *"They really are young men now."*

Alone once again Tom casually walked back up the drive in utter amazement and a happy heart.

"You would like these kids also Bert." he said aloud looking at the trees.

Checking his watch he realized he himself would have to quit work for the day in order to clean up for his dinner date with Arlene.

~ ~ ~ ~ ~ ~

Just after six PM, Tom was knocking at Eileen's door. He could hear Eileen calling through the door.

"Come in Tommy love." Once he was inside she continued. "She's almost ready, she'll be down in a minute. Come see the fabric we got today."

She led the way to the den where it was laid out.

"You were right to beg off today, you would have been bored stiff."

Tom liked what he saw and just knew this was going to be a dynamite exhibit thanks to Arleen's artistic talent. He was already looking forward to tomorrow and working on the wooden model. Arlene descended the stairs and lit up the room as always. Tom gave a low whistle to which Eileen responded.

"Now Tommy love, you will have to stop that when Arlene's around. You might make her jealous."

"Are you trying to cause trouble again Auntie ?" Arlene scolded with a laugh.

"You two go on and have fun tonight. I'll just have some leftovers alone."

"Now stop that, Auntie. You know darn well Martha is coming over tonight." scolded Arlene once again.

~ ~

In the truck and on their way Tom excitedly told his story of his day at home.

"Guess what the guys were up to today ?"

"You saw them today." questioned Arlene accusingly. "You said you were going to work on the display."

"I was home and did work on the display. They came to the cabin in sort of an official capacity. In fact they were there when I arrived there."

Arlene showed confusion.

"As a thank you to me for helping them they redid the whole driveway. You know, graded it and got rid of all the potholes and ruts. They were showing off what the Youth Corps was capable of. They did a great job on their own, I took no part in it. I can't wait for you to see it."

"Perhaps tomorrow I can get a look. We can't do too much in the way of sewing until we get the model to work with."

"I would love to spend the day with you. In fact you can probably even help me."

Arlene smiled at this idea, she adored being with Tom.

They arrived at the steak house looking forward to a quiet evening.

During dinner Arlene proposed an idea to make things easier for Tom.

"Why don't I stay at the cabin tonight with you ? That way you won't have to be constantly driving back and forth ?"

Tom was both pleased and shocked at this idea. Being a bit old fashioned under the influence of Bert and Aunt Martha, he immediately answered.

"That wouldn't be right, as much as the idea intrigues me. Your Aunt Eileen would never go for it and neither would Martha, and you know it. We would be upsetting a few people no matter how innocent it was."

"I know you're right, I was just thinking of you going back and forth all the time with no breaks in between."

"Silly girl, I love you and will do whatever it takes to be with you. And if that takes driving back and forth every day, than so be it."

"You're such a sweet man." Arlene gushed and reached out across the table to touch his hand. They were both quiet as they sipped their wine. A few minutes later Arlene bubbled out.

"Then tonight you will stay at Eileen's. She has another bedroom or there's always the couch. I'm sure she wouldn't mind. This way you save some time and get your proper rest."

She finished with a big smile and wide pleading eyes.

"You have all the answers, don't you." Tom commented smiling.

"Please !" Arlene said sweetly as only she can.

"Okay, we'll see what Eileen has to say about it." Tom gave in.

"Oh goody, I get you for the whole night."

"And so does your aunt."

"Party pooper." she laughed.

~ ~ ~

Eileen instantly thought it was a great idea.

"You'll be giving the poor man a chance to get some rest, the way you have him running all over for you. Now not another word Tommy love. There's the bed room at the top of the stairs. It has it's own bath too. So that's settled."

Shyly Tom answered, "Yes Mam." to the glow of Arlene's face.

"And this time I'll cook breakfast for you." Arlene added.

"**D**o you know how ?" Tom teased as Arlene slapped him on the arm.

The three relaxed listening to some light jazz music. Tom was surprised and asked Eileen about the music.

"**I** may be from Ireland Tommy love but that doesn't mean I'm ignorant about the world. My father, God rest his soul, was the one who taught me to like traditional jazz. In the old days he worked for a while in New York City. He used to spend his limited free time in a place called the "Metropole". That's where he learned to love your jazz. He didn't stay there too long. He missed the simplicity of the quiet life of the old country. But I'm boring you with useless chit chat. I think I'll turn in now. Don't you young ones stay up too late."

Eileen sweetly kissed each one on the temple and took herself upstairs. Tom and Arlene continued to listen to the music while cuddling. Tom, trying not to be rude was hiding his yawns, not too successfully though.

"**D**o I bore you that much that I make you yawn ?" she taunted lightly.

"**I**'m sorry my love, but its been a long day. To be honest with you I'm beat, and I will admit this was a great idea of yours. You know, staying over."

"**S**ee that proves I love you. I'm only thinking of what's good for you. Come, it's time we both turned in."

She hugged and kissed him good night at the bedroom door pledging her love. Tom went to bed falling into a contented sleep.

~ ~ ~

A light tap on the door slowly brought Tom back to consciousness.

"**A**re you going to sleep your life away ? Breakfast is almost ready." Arlene whispered through the door.

Tom answered Arlene's soft lilting voice with a sleepy, "I'll be right there."

Ten minutes later, dressed and refreshed, he was sipping black coffee and enjoying bacon and eggs topped off with Eileen's homemade sweet rolls. He was teased by both women for sleeping the day away.

"**N**ow see, didn't I tell you, Tommy love, you needed some decent rest. Next time listen to me and don't be as stubborn as Old Bert.

It was after nine thirty by the time he and Arlene were headed back to the cabin.

~ ~

"This isn't the right driveway." chided Arlene. "Did you move yesterday when I wasn't with you ? This drive looks too good."

"Didn't they do a fantastic job ?"

Arlene was in awe of the marvelous transition. "This is absolutely beautiful."

After Tom changed clothes Arlene followed him to the barn to continue the work on her design. Oblivious to time and each other the pair worked uninterrupted. Tom was deeply involved in working the shield in layers giving it a slight curved feature. Sort of a three dimensional effect. He periodically consulted with Arlene that her chosen fabric would stretch over the design. By early afternoon both agreed lunch was overdue. They complimented each other's efforts and headed for the cabin. Arlene again praised the work on the driveway and circle drive by the house.

They joined together in making lunch even snaking a bit during the preparations. They chose to rest a while in the rockers on the porch, each with their chosen beverage. Their enjoyment of the silent serenity was suddenly broken by Tom.

"That's it !" He voiced aloud yet softly.

Arlene turned to him waiting for further clarification.

"How would you like to take a ride to the capital city early this week ?"

She agreed but still had questioning eyes. Tom smiled and understood her confusion.

There are certain proceedings usually followed for military funerals. I just decided that would be the appropriate thing for Bert considering he was a medal of honor recipient. It is a time honored and sacred and touching ceremony. It involves uniformed personnel. I know there is a Marine Corps recruiting office in the city. They can help us with the right connections to get that underway."

Arlene could tell from the way Tom spoke that his heart was set on this ceremony for his friend Bert. Tom described in some detail what took place which peaked her interest and joined his enthusiasm. Not having viewed this before she was truly looking forward to it. Tom felt confident this could be arranged. He grabbed her hand saying.

"It's because of you that these ideas are possible." and kissed her cheek.

She hardly understood what he meant by that but accepted his show of affection.

"Back to work young lady, we're burning daylight."

He laughed pulling her up from the rocker.

"Aye, aye, Sgt." She saluted with a broad grin.

~ ~ ~

Building the shield was more involved than Tom anticipated, nevertheless it turned out better than expected. Once covered with the scarlet cloth it would make an extremely eye catching array that would show off Bert's medals beautifully. By the end of the day Arlene had also finished the painting of the wind blown flag construct. It was then Tom determined he would need tomorrow to finish up alone. Of course Arlene was disappointed in not being able to see Tom, and doubly disappointed in having to go home early tonight. She totally understood his reasoning but that did not satisfy her discontentment. She pouted openly trying to change his mind with no success. She then changed back to her normal happy self admitting she was being selfish.

On the ride back to Eileen's they openly tossed about ideas for the final touches on the shield. There was the longest kiss good night until Tom found the courage to back away. Arlene let him go but her eyes said otherwise.

~ ~ ~

Next morning in the barn Tom missed Arlene yet knew this was the right thing. He needed unbroken concentration in order to finish this project correctly. And finish he did by mid afternoon. Cut, shaped, sanded and painted. Tom was proud of what he had accomplished, what they accomplished, he corrected himself. Deep inside he aspired that this would go a long way towards rebuilding Bert's ill gotten reputation and hopefully to heal old wounds of Bert and himself. Putting away his tools he closed the barn doors and decided a stroll through the forest would be a good mind cleansing reward.

The wonderful scent of the dampened earth and decaying leaves and other vegetation along with tree growth filled his lungs. It was really a long time since he breathed the real earth. *"A far cry from desert sands and heat."* he thought. These pathways, all too familiar to him, having walked them countless times, both alone and with Bert, somehow it was all new sights, sounds and smells. He rested on a fallen tree spanning a small rippling creek, letting his mind be taken over by natures wonders. The sun dappled its rays through the trees catching the slow trickling water and making little diamond sparkles dance over the well worn stones. He found it amazing that, like snowflakes, no two created ripples were alike. His concentration was suddenly yet quietly disrupted by a pair of small red squirrels chattering away at him. He, unknowingly was blocking their pathway across the creek. Tom laughed softly.

"I'm sorry little guys, am I in your way ?"

They chattered their very upset answer as if they understood him.

"They most likely did." he thought. Another short minute went by and the forest critters chattered their annoyance once again, a little louder.

"Okay guys, I get your message." Tom answered as he stood up allowing the pair of red imps passage over the log. Once achieving their goal they turned as if to say "Thanks" and were on their way through the underbrush. Smiling, Tom continued his walk, crossing the log himself. The silence of the forest had its own sound, that most take for granted. It was anything but still. There were so many different noises intermixing, one could almost not distinguish them without extreme concentration. That was also the beauty of the silent noise. It was a music of its own. Each movement, whether animal, water or tree contributes to the cacophonic symphony of the forest. Its incongruous rhythm was its own musical rhythm. The natural orchestrated music had a calming effect on all who chose to listen. Unfortunately some only hear noises. "I feel sorry for those people." Tom thought aloud. They are missing something that could change their lives.

He stopped again at a small pond created by a natural spring. It's own rhythm added to the forest mix. Tom watched as the water started on its journey fulfilling its contribution to the forest life. Contentment reigned in Tom as he nodded off to the music and scent of nature. A curious doe and her fawns awakened him while satisfying their thirst at the pond's edge. Neither deer nor man was disturbed by the other. An understanding of nature, you might say. The animals went their way while Tom stood and stretched and ambled on in the opposite direction.

Returning to his own world Tom was almost sorry to leave the woods. He made a promise to himself to try and spend more time there. For right now he was totally at peace with the world.

~ ~ ~

Before leaving to pick up Arlene, Tom checked his handy work in the barn. The paint was dry and all appeared ready. Wrapping the three pieces in old car blankets he gingerly placed them in the truck bed, securing them from sliding. He was now set to leave. "Oops, I almost forgot." he said laughing out loud. Returning to the house and retrieving the box of medals he sat them on the seat beside him knowing there would be no bouncing on his brand new, rut free drive. "Thanks guys." he smiled as he turned onto the main road. He sang along with the radio again the whole time to Arlene.

As expected she was ready and waiting for the trip to the big city of the state capital. The contents of the truck were carefully carried to Eileen's den. Arlene proudly transported the medals to the den also. Content that all was secure the couple left for the city, a ride of just under an hour.

The recruiting office had not changed much in six years. A few new pictures had been added and that was about it. Tom was surprised that there were four Marines in attendance, A Gunnery Sgt. being the ranking man. While introducing himself to the Gunny a familiar voice rang out behind him.

"Tom, you old bastard, how the hell are you."

The owner of the voice then saw the smiling Arlene.

"Excuse me Mam, I didn't see you. I meant no offense."

All four recruiters were now staring at the Irish beauty. The Sergeant friend of Tom's noticed Arlene's engagement ring. Looking back to Tom said.

"You sure are a lucky one."

Arlene did not blush but smiled proudly.

"Be nice to him gunny, Staff Sergeant Thatcher here saved my ass. Oops, sorry again Mam."

Arlene, not offended remained cheerfully smiling. After all proper introductions were made Tom explained the reason for the visit. When Bert's name was mentioned in regards to the Medal of Honor, the corporal in attendance moved to a wall chart behind his desk.

"Here it is Gunny, Bert Morrow, 1953.

Further explanation revealed Tom's motive for his visit. Instantly all four recruiters were in favor of a memorial service done in the proper military fashion.

"Leave it to me Tom, the mouthy Sgt. volunteered. I'll take care of everything. How about a piper ?"

"That would be fantastic, the icing on the cake." replied Tom.

The Gunny followed with; "We'll be in touch shortly with all the details.

Tom shook hands and "Semper Fi'd" the four recruiters. The Gunny's parting words were.

"Now take that beautiful vision out of here so I can get my troops back to work."

This time Arlene did blush, yet managed to thank everyone.

Outside, Tom breathed easier.

"It's nice to know people in the right places when you need them."

Walking back to the truck Arlene softly inquired with a smile knowing what she was saying.

"Did you really save that Sergeant's ass ?"

Trying to make light of her inquiry Tom answered.

"If that's what you want to call it. Just doing what had to be done."

Arlene pushed no further, but moved closer to Tom her arm around his waste, cuddling into him.

"Now I know why Marines are considered a unique group. You all seem to think with one mind. I have to admit, I admire that. It gives me more insight into you. It explains a lot for your character and I'm the lucky one who benefits. No wonder I love you."

Tom felt a shyness overcome him and chose not to comment on her last remarks.

Back at Eileen's they found both Martha and Eileen busy with the exhibit. Fabric had already been stretched and adhered to the shield mock up. It looked perfect to both Arlene and Tom. Martha admitted to being a bit confused about the Marine Corps emblem. She felt the intricate detail required was beyond her skill. Eileen agreed with that statement. Even though Arlene maintained the artistic skills to draw the necessary details, transforming her sketch into fabric was questionable.

The emblem was to be about six inches in diameter and would highlight the center top of the shield. The medals were to be hung in proper order in rows below the emblem. Enough space would be allowed for the Medal of Honor with it's blue and white ribbon to be hung immediately below the gold emblem to finish the design. Bert's military sword would be attached across the bottom of the shield at a slight diagonal. The finished shield would then take its place of honor on the large model of the wind blown American flag.

While the three women threw out ideas and then discussed them in detail without reaching any conclusions, Tom drifted away to think with out the inane chatter mixing with his thought process. He stood by the front sun room windows gazing out at nothing in particular. An image of the emblem entered his mind. Behind it a wall took shape. A wall with pictures and certificates on it. This was the wall of the recruiting office.

"Double Bingo." he said out loud while snapping his fingers followed by, "That's just what we need."

Returning to the women he stated with finality.

"Problem solved ladies. An actual metal emblem does exist about the same size we need. All we have to do is pick it up.”

All three of his favorite women regarded him with questionable gazes.

Eileen, with her usual fast wit whispered.

“My Lord, he’s gone and lost his mind altogether. Oh Tommy love, what are we going to do with you now ?”

Exactly as the others Tom broke into a laugh..

“No, I’m serious.” and as he pleaded he was interrupted by Arlene.

“The recruiting office.”she blurted out. “Your friends at the recruiting place.”

Tom smiled at her, “You got it my love. That will solve the whole issue.”

Arlene went on to explain to the aunts the wall emblem they saw and how it would be the perfect solution.

“It’s just a matter of getting it.” Tom countered.

Arlene with a glitter in her eyes and a wry smile quietly spoke.

“If you can’t, I bet I can.” She winked at Tom.

“I bet you could too lass, with them eyes to conquer any man.” laughed Eileen.

Tom had to agree, then added. “I think I’ll go alone to get the emblem. That office is no place for an innocent young woman.”

“I do believe you’re jealous.” Arlene teased.

“You bet I am.” Tom confirmed.

Martha, trying to break up the fun proposed.

“Now that the problem is solved let’s see what we have to plan next.”

“I’ll call tomorrow to the recruiting office and see what I can arrange.” Tom finalized the discussion.

“I have a good way to end the day.” offered Martha. “I’ve got a roast beef cooking in the slow cooker at home. What say you all help me eat it.”

A dinner party it would be, they happily decided.

Chapter 26

The next few weeks appeared normal for Tom and Arlene. Anticipation was slowly building for the memorial service. Every day news and reports were garnered pertaining to attendance at the service. The numbers were growing slowly, thanks to Eileen, Martha and the teens. The teens in particular were very active in talking up the affair.

Tom, urged on by Arlene, gave the boys a sneak preview one afternoon of the finished medal display. Because of their insistent questions about the medals, Tom took the time that afternoon to expound in a rather detailed way, what each medal stood for. All but the Medal of Honor. Of course the guys knew basically what it stood for but Tom convinced them to wait for the full account which would be read at the ceremony. Again another step in the regaining or rebuilding of Bert's reputation.

Tom was delighted with the way things were shaping up. Arlene had been with him every step of the way with both her encouragement and participation. The two aunts were not to be excluded either. They knew Bert for many years and knew who he really was as a person. They willingly ignored the rumors and gossip about him which they truly knew to be false.

Tom was feeling convinced he was doing the right thing, for himself and for Bert. Even if no one showed for the memorial he knew he would see it through. This is what you do to honor a fellow Marine. Any armed forces participant for that matter. This particular case was special for a number of reasons. First of all it was Bert, a more than special friend; second he was a recipient of the nations highest award for valor. Then and most important, Tylerville was long overdue on learning who Bert Morrow had been and in Tom's mind this was only the beginning.

On the advice of attorney McCort, Tom would keep this as a-political as possible. He knew Sam was correct in this thinking. He could feel it in Arlene's reaction to Sam's advice. He, in turn, promised both that this would be so. Tom vowed to himself that this ceremony was to honor a valiant Marine who served his country well. His personal feelings would be best served at another venue.

Tom's alone time was well spent writing his presentation and reviewing it to ascertain that all remained neutral.

Arlene was growing as excited as Tom waiting for the big day. She had never witnessed a true military funeral before.

The everyday life of the newly engaged pair remained quite normal in spite of the building excitement. Time with each other, time with their aunts, and time with the newly formed Tylerville Youth Corps. Whether alone or with each other they remained very much attached. When the final date was fixed a last check was made on the head stone progress. All was in order. The stone was to be in place two days before the actual service. The last definitive arrangements were made in person with Gunny at the recruiting office. It was actually just an excuse for Tom and Arlene to spend some quality time together and enjoy the ride to and from the capital city.

Tom was overjoyed when the full scope of the ceremony planned was outlined which was to include the flag presentation, even though there was no casket for draping. It was then he was also informed that a Captain Hodgson would be attending. The gentleman was unfamiliar to Tom but would complete the military protocol perfectly.

Arlene still unfamiliar with such things was amazed at the attention to detail being observed by those men in uniform. She too was pleased that Bert was being recognized, though it was some sixty years later.

~ ~ ~

Tom returned to home via a different route and stopped at a diner for lunch. He did not discuss any more of the ritual service but Arlene could see that Tom was extremely happy. After a quick lunch they continued back to the cabin by a round about way. Sort of sight seeing you might say.

~ ~ ~ ~

The day Tom was anxiously awaiting was here. He was attired in full dress uniform complete with medals. Arlene was again glowing with pride for her man. Tom, Arlene and the two aunts arrived at the cemetery early yet were not the first ones there. Arrangements had been made with the Youth Corps to assist the grounds keeper in setting up chairs and a small podium. Amazed at seeing the teens dressed in jacket and tie he thanked them with a tear in his eye.

At ten past ten people began to arrive. Some, Tom was familiar with, others he had not seen before. Sam McCort and his wife made their presence known and Tom did spot Judge McCallister in the background. Brenda, from the luncheonette was actually in conversation with the guys . They were obviously on a whole new footing based on mutual respect.

Some sixty plus chairs had been set up by the teens with four in front by the graveside for Tom and his three lady friends.

A sudden hush overcame the attendees with the appearance of many uniformed men, all in Dress Blues of course. The Gunny and Capt. Hodgson introduced themselves to Tom immediately. The balance took their places necessary for the ceremony. Seven riflemen stood at attention at the grave, the recruiters were to handle the flags. The bugler and bagpiper were off in the background. At ten thirty six Tom moved to the podium. A stillness came over the crowd who had been marveling at the display of marines in full dress. The teens most of all, were awestruck.
Tom noted to himself to introduce the boys to some of the Marines when this was all over.

"Thank you all for coming, this means a lot to me. Now if you will all please stand we will address the colors." Tom said formally.

On a silent command the color guard quietly marched up to and stood at the head of the grave. With the American flag held high and the Marine Corps flag dipped in respect Tom started the pledge of allegiance. Following that the piper played the National Anthem. The Marines, of course stood at attention while saluting. When the anthem ended it appeared as if a silent commands were given and all uniformed men stood at rest. Tom again addressed the gathering.

"Once again I thank you for coming. We are here today to honor Bert Morrow who passed from our midst not too many months ago without proper recognition. No one knew of his accomplishments in the service of his country.   Today we are here to honor the man and those accomplishments."
Tom nodded to Fred and Josh who reverently removed the drapery from the new headstone. Tom read the inscription.

In honor and memory of a man who selflessly dedicated his life to serving his family, community, Corps and country. May his example inspire generations to come.

After reading, he paused allowing this to settle in. It also gave time for the people to reflect on this. Additional time was given so they could stretch necks to see the 3 D carving of a lifelike Bert Morrow.

Tom continued sounding completely professional while nodding to Ace and Dirk. The two teens, with as much reverence as their work mates, slowly unveiled the wooden display to everyone's admiration.

"I will now turn over the proceedings to Capt. Hodgson."

Showing nothing but military professionalism the Capt. quietly said "Thank you Staff Sergeant." Looking out over the crowd he continued speaking. "What you now see before you are one man's heroic accomplishments. These medals show in a very small way the unselfish valor of that one man."

The Capt. proceeded to describe each medal and reviewed the circumstances of its award, pausing here and there to let Bert's accomplishments be absorbed.

"And now ladies and gentlemen, as if that weren't enough for one man, he went on further to top that himself."

Capt. Hodgson then carefully read the certificate of award of the medal of Honor that Tom had read to himself weeks before.

It has been attested to that S/Sgt. Bert Morrow did on the day and evening of 12 February 1953 almost single handedly hold off a company of Red Chinese regulars. During the course of the day he received his second Purple Heart, all the while helping his fellow wounded Marines to safety. He alone saved countless lives while inflicting a heavy toll on the enemy. He was still fiercely fighting hand to hand as friendly reenforcements arrived. He continued in command until the enemy was totally subdued. Even then he had to be forcibly and physically carried from the field of conflict under protest."

Here the Capt. paused again. A few moments passed when he was heard to say, "Proceed."

Again under silent command all uniformed men snapped to attention. A folding wooden table held the draped flag in place of the casket. Two Marines began the folding ceremony of thirteen folds, representing the original thirteen states. During this procedure the seven riflemen fired three rounds each before returning to a silent attention. The folded flag was passed to the Capt. Who formally presented it , on behalf of a grateful nation, to Eileen and Martha, much to their surprise. They were speechless with tears streaming down their cheeks. During the presentation the bugler sounded taps off in the distance. Upon completion of taps the piper, not quite as distant, played Amazing Grace, slow and strong. At the end of this piece the uniformed men marched as united and majestic away from the grave site. Tom, once again stood at the podium.

"Thanks again for helping me to honor my friend Bert Morrow. To show my grateful appreciation there are refreshments being served by the administration office. Please partake. This will give me a chance to personally thank each and every one of you."

Before Tom wandered over to the food he turned his attention to his three special ladies. There was not a dry eye among them. Aunt Eileen and Martha were speechless at being the recipient of the ceremonial flag. They were finding great difficulty in trying to speak. Tom did not push, he just kissed each on the cheek.

Arlene, on the other hand, although with tear filled eyes, threw her arms around Tom's neck kissing him.

"That was so beautiful. I have never seen such a thing."

"Just tradition." Tom smiled.

The teens approached Tom with smiles of respect. Turning to Arlene he asked.

"Could you stay with them" indicating the aunts, "I want to introduce the guys to some of the Marines."

"Recruiting, are we ?" joked Arlene.

Tom smiled in answer. "You never know."

The guys were truly fascinated at meeting the uniformed Marines, who in turn were more than happy to answer the boy's inquiry's.

Before actually returning to Arlene, Tom was sought out by Judge McCallister.

"Tom, I can't tell you how impressed I am by this whole affair. I'm even more impressed by these teen aged gentlemen walking around here. I know now that in the future I will consider you one of my advisors when it comes to problem teens."

Tom was a little embarrassed by this sudden praise.

"Keep up the good work and remember you always have my backing."

The judge shook Tom's hand firmly and with sincerity.

~ ~ ~

By late afternoon all was quiet. Martha and Eileen were recovered enough to speak again and could not express their thanks enough for the honor they received today.

"If anyone deserved it you two did." Tom commented.

When they were ready to go home Martha asked about the medal display.

"The weather is supposed to be good for the next few days so I decided to leave it for further viewing."

Martha followed with, "Aren't you afraid of vandalism ?"

"Not really." Tom replied. "I discussed it with the guys and was told they would take care of everything.

Arlene, on hearing this was reassured and remarked.

"And I'm sure they will . It couldn't be in safer hands."

Eileen joined with.

" Martha and I were thinking that it may be a good idea to put it on display at the library for a while. You know, hometown boy is hero, that sort of thing. Perhaps you could write a little information sheet, you know a quick explanation of the medals such as that nice Captain did today. After a while it could go back to it's permanent home, "The Log Cabin."

Neither Tom or Arlene had any objections.

Chapter 27

$\mathbf{T}$om was riding a high after the successful reception of the honor ceremony. He felt that part of his promise to Bert had been fulfilled. There were now those who knew who Bert was, at least partially knew.

Autumn was beginning to show herself. Even on a clear day the forever blue was taking on a different hue. The warmth of the sun's rays though still warming, were giving way to northern chills. This definitive seasonal change, with its briskness was a welcome change for Tom. His days in the heat of Afghanistan drifted further from his mind. School began another year and the teens availability was now limited. Their new business was doing well. Tom made himself available to help with school problems no matter what they were, scholastic or personal. He persisted in stressing the importance of their education. Not that they had to be straight "A" students but to gain a well rounded knowledge that would keep them in good stead into adulthood. Tom did, however, put some emphasis on math and physics, reminding the boys how useful it was in their work on the yellow barn this summer and how it would always come into play for the rest of their lives.

Eileen was aware that her small old barn needed some minor repair. A paint job to freshen her up was not out of the question either. She willingly engaged the Youth Corps, which, of course made Tom happy.

"Since the old goat gave me all this extra money I decided I may as well put it to good use." she playfully told Tom. "Now with school was back in session the boys would do some of the small repair jobs after school and work on the painting on week ends."

On the first Saturday when all seven were present Arlene was there to greet them also.

"I'm glad you're all together. I wish to express my thanks also for your wonderful work on Tom's roadway to the cabin."

Huge grins showed on all the faces. Arlene then approached each young man taking their hands in hers as she leaned over and kissed each on the cheek. They all gladly accepted her thankfulness. Believe it or not the only one who showed any shyness was Ace as he quietly whispered "thank you Miss Arlene."

"Now when you're finished for the day perhaps I can twist your arms into sharing some fresh baked cookies." she smiled.

Steve answered instantly. "Well if you insist Miss Arlene, we'll try and help you out. We wouldn't want them to go to waste."

The other guys gladly agreed.

"One more thing guys. I do appreciate your politeness but it is not necessary to say Miss Arlene all the time. Just plain Arlene will do just fine, after all we are friends, are we not ?"

When the teens drifted back to work Aunt Eileen commented.

"That was a wonderful you just did lass. Showing them respect is good for their character building."

Now it was Arlene's turn to blush.

The boys worked well by themselves. Decisions were made maturely. They did, however, from time to time, defer to either Fred or Jonathon for a final yes or no. There was no jealousy in the group. These teens operated that way out of natural feelings. They considered themselves equal knowing each others strengths and weaknesses and who to follow depending on the given situation. Tom would critique now and then or volunteer advice but the real decision making came from the collective. Eileen, as usual would have her say, but generally left the group to do their thing knowing Tom kept an oversight.

Every so often Tom and the youths would gather, sans Arlene, for a men only gathering. Bert's war journals were usually the key topic with a periodic visit to an unjust incident of Bert's younger days from the earlier journals.

Tom's relationship grew both with the teens as well as Judge McCallister. The judge had two other youngsters sentenced to the Restorative Justice program. Tom had assigned them general cleanup of the park and playground as part of their community service before introducing them to the original group. The guys welcomed them explaining the Youth Corps function as an extension of community service only this time to earn a little money for the corps and for themselves.

As Tom planned and expected, the cockiness of the two new candidates soon disappeared, helped along by the newly converted teen group. At the end of their mandated twenty five hours, they too voluntarily joined the Youth Corps.

The judge was again delighted with Tom's success strongly

suggesting he apply for a position with the state Department of Corrections advising for the state wide program. Tom, naturally flattered with the offer, politely declined. He justified his reasons to McCallister of just wanting a quiet, private and simple life without great expectations from him. Disappointed but understanding, the judge accepted his refusal, for now. He did, however, warn Tom that he might try again.

Chapter 28

Life was going well for Tom. Of course he had Arlene to share everything with. Their respective aunts made a family complete. Since the funeral ceremony more people recognized him as a town member. Bert's whole name was even discussed once in a while.

Inwardly Tom had a good feeling about his dream of cleansing Bert of those harmful, vindictive false accusations and rumors. Down deep inside he actually believed things were turning the corner for Bert. Life was looking good again. He had Arlene, family ties, respect in the community and emancipation for Bert from the dark side of peoples minds.

That is until that one dark Thursday afternoon when he met Mr. Charles Thompson. Not only did Tom feel his dream going up in smoke, to him it was like a shadow dimming his bright rays of hope. Not knowing why, but he let it hang heavy on his heart which in turn dulled all his prospects for happiness. Tom had never before experienced such a fast transformation of spirit.

He was in town on his way to the hardware store when he was stopped on the street by Charles Thompson. Tom was addressed in a harsh, not too polite voice.

"You're that guy, aren't you ? That Tom fellow."

"Yes, that's my name." Tom replied politely.

"Well, I'm here to tell you right now, you stay away from my son."

Tom totally perplexed asked softly.

"I'm sorry sir, you seem to have me at a disadvantage. What is it you are referring to."

"Don't play coy with me Mr. Fancy Marine. I'm talking about my son Richard. He was in your Restorative Justice thing. Now your corrupting him with all this Bert Morrow crap. You got him in your work group doin all your jobs for you. Well, not with my son you ain't. We put up enough years of that nere do well Bert, we don't need another one to take his place. What's with you anyhow? You're trying to make this no good into the all American hero. We know what the bum was really like."

Tom could feel himself slowly burning inside. Better judgement told him to keep his temper under control as he answered.

"So far, Mr. Thompson, everything you have said is wrong. I don't suppose you would like to hear the truth of things."

Tom said this slowly in a quiet tone looking directly into Thompson's eyes as he tried to keep his fists from clenching.

Red faced and angry Charles replied even louder.

"Are you calling me a liar ? That figures. It just goes to show you, that you're no better than he was. It seems no matter what real people did we couldn't get rid of the old recluse. All he did his whole life was cause trouble for us decent folks."

Now Tom was not only angry but he was hurting, deeply hurting inside. Using all the courage he could muster to speak without a cracked voice or crying, he asked directly.

"Have you ever met Mr. Morrow ?"

Mr. Thompson stood there mute and red faced while Tom pursued this further.

"Perhaps, had you known Bert Morrow your opinion would be unlike it is now."

Thompson's silence was broken but only by guttural stutters from an extremely frustrated and hate filled face. Tom knew he had the upper hand now, at least for the moment. He physically held his ground, staring but not moving. Thirty some seconds ticked off slowly neither man moving. Charles Thompson turned suddenly and walked away without turning his head and yelled back.

"You just stay away from my son if you know what's good for you."

Tom remained frozen in place until his verbal attacker was out of sight. Snapping himself back to reality he looked around at the few people who were silently gawking. Composing himself as best he could Tom resumed his mission of going to the hardware store, his mind going every which way, mostly filled with confusion. Because of the few witnesses there he was glad he restrained himself from getting physical. While still in the Corps that man would have found himself on the ground and hurting.

He managed to purchase what he needed and left. Trying to bring order to his jumbled mind he walked aimlessly for a while, nodding to and accepting greetings from various townspeople. He suddenly found himself in the neighborhood of Sam McCort's law office.

"Fate making decisions for me I guess." he mumbled quietly.

He turned and walked straight to the office hoping Sam was there. Luck was with him this day.

Before Tom actually spoke, Sam could tell he was distressed and to keep things light warmly said.

"What's up ?"

"Sam how do I go about setting up or calling a town meeting? Either in the town hall or high school auditorium."

Sam McCort answered with a smile.

"You don't do anything in a small way do you ?"
Looking humble now Tom replied pointedly.

"I want to rebuild Bert's image with the town. The only way I know how to do that is to confront them directly.

Gazing at Sam's concerned expression he followed with.

"No Sam, this is not for revenge, nor will I do it antagonistically. Knowing all that has come to light I want to show Bert in that better light. I want to discuss the negative attitudes. The towns prejudice against Bert, which has carried from generation to generation and has now carried over to me, must be shown for the hateful act it is. I believe by bringing to light all that Bert did and was can help tear down this wrongful passed down attitude. The younger generation, such as my teens, are carrying on a rotten tradition that they had no part in nor understand why."

Sam let Tom have his time and voice. He knew the air would lighten then. When Tom finally paused, a bit embarrassed by his tirade, quiet though it was, Sam lightened the air.

"Are you sure you're not a lawyer ?" he said with a sly grin.

Tom smiled in return and without showing embarrassment answered.

"I just feel strongly about such things, and injustice is one of them."

Tom paused for a moment then went on to layout for Sam what had just occurred on the street.

"Who did you say this was ?" inquired Sam

"A Mr. Charles Thompson."

"Oh yes, his son just recently was sent to you for Restorative Justice."

"Yes, and he did not appear to be a bad kid."

"I know of Mr. Thompson. A stubborn, very ignorant man without much education. His biggest problem in life is himself. He has no tolerance for any ideas or opinions other than his own. His biggest fault lies in not pursuing the truth of matters."

"That I found out the hard way." interrupted Tom.

"**I'm** glad to hear that you handled him as you did. That always stops him, but I still would not trust that this is the end of him."

"**I** didn't think it would be and I promise you I will play it calm and cool."

"**T**hat is your best defense with someone like Thompson. I'm glad you came to me instead of letting it eat you up inside. Tell you what, give me a little time and I'll see what I can come up with. I admire your reasoning and will help all I can."

For some reason Tom felt better already. The idea of sharing this burden with someone who understands his reasoning and goals helped to lift his spirits even though only a little.

A few other unrelated subjects were briefly discussed and Tom left the office. There were no other incidents out of the ordinary on his walk back to his truck. Tom drove straight home, not stopping to see Arlene as promised. He would call her later. He did not want to burden her with this confrontation, at least not right now.

Once home he grabbed a beer and sat in the living room looking at Bert's portrait. He reaffirmed his vow, "We'll get through this and successfully, I promise."

It was early evening when he finally called a disappointed Arlene.

"**A**re you alright Tom. I was worried, I expected to see you this afternoon."

Tom hesitantly answered.

"**I'm** fine. I just got held up with some things in town and it was late before I knew it and rather than disturb your dinner I came home to eat."

He had a feeling that Arlene was not buying his excuse yet still did not want to upset her.

"**A**re you sure you're alright ? You sound as if something is upsetting you. Are you angry with me ?"

"**O**f course not my love, you are much too wonderful to be angry with. I guess I'm just tired. Can I see you tomorrow ?"

"**Y**ou had better or you will really be in trouble." she jokingly scolded.

"**H**ow about ten tomorrow morning my love."

"**T**en it is, my darling, I love you" she whispered.

"**A**nd I you. Have a good night."

Tom hung up the phone feeling a bit uncomfortable. It was not his intention to deceive her. Perhaps tomorrow he will be able to explain everything. He read himself to sleep.

~ ~ ~ ~

A restless sleep did not help Tom's conscience. Reflecting on the last two or three weeks Tom realized he committed a major blunder with Arlene. His rationalization that he did not want to upset Arlene was all hog wash. He knew that now. It really would be unfair of him to hold back from her. Had she not been at his side always. Her support was endless, physically, morally and spiritually. Her encouragement of his dream allowed him to continue under the darkest of circumstances. She had truly become a part of him that he did not want to lose. He tried to imagine how she would feel hearing of this incident from others and not directly from him. She would be devastated to think I did not love her enough to share all with her.

His mind now made up, he would explain the whole troublesome day to her as soon as they were together this morning. Inwardly he felt better as he headed for the shower and a light breakfast.

~ ~ ~ ~

At one minute to ten Tom was smothered in a hug by his Irish beauty. Eileen had departed earlier for one of her many club meetings and for this Tom was thankful. He would feel more at ease apologizing and explaining to Arlene. He could fill in both aunts later.

As expected, Arlene's first words were.

"**A**re you sure you're okay. Your tone last night did not set right with me. Please don't keep secrets from me." she smiled softly and kissed him with the love he knew was genuine.

"**Y**ou're right my love. Please forgive me. Let's sit and I will explain all."

Tom replayed the days frustration to her leaving out no detail. He finished looking deep into her eyes for her negative reaction. Instead she showed a loving smile and with eagerness in her lilting voice responded with;

"**I** think that's a wonderful idea of having a town wide meeting. I can help you with the planning. We'll show the world who Bert actually was and there will be no shame either. I am at your side darling as I know our aunts will also be."

As his mental rambling's of earlier that morning told him, Arlene was truly the catch of a lifetime. Almost silently he muttered to himself while smiling "You were right Bert."

"**H**uh, did you say something ?"

"**N**ot really my sweet, just a little thing between Bert and myself."

She laughed , and moving closer took both his hands in hers.

"**W**e will do this together as we will always do things together. I want to be part of your life, good or bad, so please don't exclude me because you think it may hurt my feelings. Now just forget about yesterday and we will concentrate on a successful town meeting."

Arlene lingered with her thoughts for a few seconds before adding with a smile.

"You know, I think I'm even looking forward to this. Now that's settled for now, so what shall we do today ?"

Tom joined her positive mood suggesting a quiet ride through the mountains with a few stops at different art gallery's and antique shops. She was beaming a broad grin replying.

"You certainly know how to make a girl happy. Let me leave a note for Auntie and grab my sketch pad and we can be on our way."

~ ~ ~

Tom used the day to settle his jumbled mind and nerves. The change of scenery and loving company was just what the doctor ordered. Arlene's ever bubbly disposition could heal anyone's psychological wounds. He let his spirit free enjoying nature's beauty and the Irish uplifting. They stopped periodically where she would make quick sketches of the landscapes that called to her. They slowly whittled the day away savoring the attractions of various antique shops and small art galleries, each making a few silly and actually useless purchases. The day was theirs to enjoy and enjoy they did finally ending with dinner at a quaint little restaurant in the middle of nowhere. It seems they were the only patrons at the hidden treasure of an eatery.

It was well after nine PM. When they returned to Eileens. Not accepting any arguments Arlene insisted that Tom stay over night, with Eileens backing of course. Tom put up no resistance and genuinely relished the idea. The perfect ending to another perfect day.

~ ~ ~ ~

Tom was up early and felt renewed. The head clearing day with Arlene as a distraction worked wonders. He now felt he could attack his latest challenge logically and without too much emotion to get in the way.

As quietly as possible Tom tiptoed down stairs only to find Eileen busy at the stove.

"Ah, good morning Tommy love. The coffee's waiting for you, black and strong as you like it. You'll not be leaving this house today with out some of my special buttermilk pancakes. And instead of just standing there gawking with your mouth open, you can fetch a new jug of maple syrup from the pantry."

Of course she said all this with her usual all loving smile.

Tom just walking from the pantry, jug in hand, was met by Eileen. She kissed him on the cheek saying,

"Thank you love."
A young jealous voice from across the room spoke out.

"Are you trying to steal my man ?"

"Not to worry, lass. But if'n I was you wouldn't stand a chance." smiled Eileen.

Tom met Arlene halfway in the room with a good morning kiss.

"I thought you were going to sleep the day away." he chided.

"I wanted to but I didn't trust you two alone." she joked back in reply.

"Now you sound like the old goat lass. Never trusting me to do things right, God rest his soul." commented her Aunt with loving eyes and smile.

"And what dear sir ?" inquired Arlene of Tom, "Are we going to do today ?"

"Well, you're on your own this morning, I promised the guys I would meet them at their new project, an old barn in need of repair."

Arlene put on her pouty face at which Tom smiled.

"Not to worry though I shouldn't be too long. I can be back here by eleven to pick you up."

"I guess I'll just have to do my laundry then." she said in a bored tone of voice.

"Oh my, the way you two go on one would think you were married for twenty years." chortled Eileen. "Sit down Tommy love, your pancakes are ready."

"Yes, Mama." he laughed in answer.

~ ~ ~ ~

Just outside of the town proper, the opposite of Tom's home, was the new location of the Youth Corps new project. True, it was an old barn but the repair work was minimal that the boys could handle. Tom was there only for initial guidance.

As was their habit, the boys had coffee waiting for him. After observing the greeting pleasantries, Tom inspected the barn and generally agreed with the guys on what should be done. He didn't see anything they couldn't handle. Tom also knew he would be doing a final inspection upon their completion.

He was getting ready to leave when Ace and Fred asked if they could discuss something with him. Though it was only the two that asked, all gathered around.

Fred hesitated a bit so Ace jumped right in.

"That new guy, Richard quit the group."
Fred quickly corrected him.

"He didn't quit on his own, his father made him quit. Apparently he had all kinds of bad things to say about you and old Bert."

"And none of it true." Tom was quick to comment.

He then mentally caught himself. He did not want to get emotional in front of the guys. Changing his tone he calmly followed with.

" Everyone is entitled to their own opinion."

"But Mr. T." Josh interrupted. "Rich said he was smearing your name all over. Rich doesn't know you like we do. He's all upset and confused."

"I am flattered with your concern but I don't want you guys getting involved in or getting stuck in the middle of something that's not really your affair. This is between me and Mr. Thompson." Tom said softly.

"Mr. T. ?" Steve questioned in a slightly subdued manner. "Isn't this just like the stuff old Bert was writing about in his journals ?"

Tom hesitated, considering how much further he should go. He really did not want the boys getting involved, afraid of the fallout on them also. That would not be fair at all. He had not anticipated this. He could feel eight sets of eyes burning into him with concern, yet questioning.

"Okay, look guys. Listen carefully and please heed all that I'm about to say."

Genuine interest was displayed on the eight faces.

"Steve, you are absolutely correct and it is something that should be stopped. There in lies the problem. I mentioned before that everyone is entitled to his or her opinion. It is changing that opinion that is the difficulty. The truth of things is not always the easier or most popular route to take. This particular case is extremely touchy. This is something that has been going on for decades with Bert. What we are seeing now is just a continuation of that narrow-mindedness. Why ? Your guess is as good as mine. An outright attack on someone's character can have severe repercussions and in turn defeat the actual truth."

Besides their obvious concern the boys were now becoming confused.

*"**Oh**, the innocence of youth."* thought Tom.

"**T**his recent addition to an already existing problem I had not foreseen. There is much more going on here then you men are aware of. And no, I'm not keeping secrets from you. In the short time we have known each other I have grown to love and trust you all which is why I don't want to involve you."

"**D**o you mean there is more involving Bert ?" questioned Josh.

Surprised at his insight, Tom answered with the truth.

"**Y**es, that's exactly what I mean, and no, it is nothing bad. Exactly the opposite, is what it is."

Tom knew he was probably going further than he should yet felt it was necessary. A more thorough explanation may help them to understand why he wanted to avoid their involvement.

"**A**s you all are aware from the journal readings, people get hurt. Not necessarily physically, although that can happen also, but get hurt mentally and emotionally. which can , at times, be even worse. Lifetime scars can be acquired. Luckily that is not the case here."

Tom could see the guys remained uneasy yet he still did not want to reveal all.

"**P**lease trust me on this. I am diligently working on a correction to this whole situation. You already helped me on step one."

"**Y**ou mean Bert's memorial, don't you ?" stated Fred.

"**Y**es, and all your work was greatly appreciated especially your participation."

"**T**hen why can't we help now ?" inquired Ace strongly, fitting his personality.

"**I** believe I will be asking for your assistance, but not just now. I have not solidified my plans as of yet. So I'll ask of you again, trust me on this. I could not bear to see you suffer any long term consequences, such as Bert did because of another's ignorance. When you do hear what I have planned I truly believe you will fully understand my motives not to involve you right now. And please promise me to keep today's conversation just between us. Early unfounded rumors could undermine all that I have worked for."

Slowly the youths, soon to be men, searched each others faces and readily agreed with Tom to keep silent if that was truly going to help him and Bert.

"**I** can't thank you guys enough for your trust and understanding. I believe we can eventually put an end to the matter. A proper ending for the good of all. Now, don't you guys have work to do ?"

Tom smiled with this last sentence.

"Oh and by the way Arlene sends her regards."

With this, the guys smiled.

"Thanks men, you have my number if you need me."

~ ~ ~

There was a touch of anxiety within Tom as he drove back to Arlene. Did he tell the boys too much ? Did he not tell them enough ? Should they be involved ? Is their innocence a protection or an enemy ? Could he trust their silence ? This last question was a definite yes to Tom. He truly believed in their loyalty. This self questioning session thoroughly convinced him a town meeting was the right course to pursue. The sooner the better.

Wishing it could be tomorrow only made Tom laugh at himself. There was a lot to prepare and plan for. When he did this, all contingencies must be thought out. He wanted to be well armed with irrefutable facts. The truth is always the hardest thing to believe. A backfire from a session such as this could be devastating to all those he loved and respected.

Out of nowhere an off the wall thought presented itself causing Tom to smile and comment aloud.

"This is not the Marine Corps and this is not Afghanistan and this is not a battle plan, although in a way I guess it is."

Silently he was thankful for such training. A sensation of confidence suddenly enveloped him and his mood lightened. The key to a successful mission is thorough planning. He remembered now one of Bert's axioms that he repeated often. "You can't go wrong with the truth boy. It will always serve you well."

So involved in his thoughts he passed Eileen's house then had to turn around. Embarrassed, he hoped no one caught on. He checked his watch exiting the truck. Five minutes to eleven. *"Perfect timing."* he thought. Arlene was waiting at the door.

Chapter 29

Eileen was still at home and in light of his talk with the teens Tom decided to fill her in. After all she was extremely active in many organizations in town and you know inevitably something would be said. Then of course the not so accurate rumors start.

Eileen listened quietly as Tom replayed the whole episode, this time including his recent chat with his teen group. She displayed no outward emotion but one could tell she was deeply disturbed. Putting on her best cheerful smile she addressed both her niece and Tom.

"Don't you fret, Tommy love, you're not in this alone. We'll get to the bottom of this. I know of this Mr. Thompson fellow, but never knew him to be this outgoing."

With an additional sparkle in her eyes she added.

"I like your town meeting idea. Martha and I will help of course. Have you told Martha yet ?"

"Not yet but I plan to."

"Don't you worry your head over it. Martha and I are getting together this afternoon, I'll fill her in on just what you told me. You two get on with your day."

Tom appreciated her willingness to help but politely cautioned her about doing anything else until further planning had been thought through.

"Mums the word Tommy love. We're here to help not hinder." she said accompanied by one of her bear hugs.

~ ~ ~

On the drive to his cabin in the woods Tom had thoughts soaring through his head almost to the point that his concentration on driving was not one hundred percent. Arlene, on a number of occasions, had to shake him back to reality. Tom eventually pulled over and stopped.

"I'm sorry my love. I guess I'm a bit overwrought and am letting this thing get to me."

"Do you want me to drive ?" she asked in a docile way.

Tom smiled shyly.

"I didn't know you could."

Returning his smile she replied.

"You never asked." then added, "Didn't you see the car in the driveway the first day we met."

"Yeah, I did, I just didn't put two and two together."

"I ask again, do you want me to drive ?"

"No, I think I'm alright now. Thank you for bringing me back from where ever , I don't even know. It's only a few more miles and we'll talk of something else."

Arlene felt more relaxed now and agreed to keep him occupied with more mundane chatter.

A sudden comfort overcame them both as they turned into the drive to their log home.

"Tell you what, let's grab some quick refreshment, then go for a walk in the woods. I could use some of natures music to calm my thoughts."

Arlene's answer was a huge smile as she cuddled closer to him on their walk to the cabin.

Their silent meander worked its magic on both. When they did speak it was close to a whisper as if in respect for the forest.

"This should be our church when we get married." Arlene murmured.

Tom squeezed her hand in answer.

"That would satisfy me just fine but I don't think our families would consider it very functional."

Both laughed, and both were thinking to them selves; "Who cares." The happy couple wandered around for close to two hours admiring natures beauty. Returning to the house Tom was refreshed and felt he could think again about his present dilemma. Having Arlene at his side he realized was a beneficial influence. Entering the living room Arlene spotted the flashing light on the answering machine.

"Looks like your public awaits." she joked.

Tom pushed the button to listen.

"Tom, Sam McCort here. I have some great news. Remember I said the publisher would jump at another book by Bert. Well they did that in spades. As we speak it's on its way to the markets world wide. I guess I didn't mention that part. His books were translated into many

languages. I should have a few copies in my hands by Tuesday. I'll call you as soon as that happens. Have a great weekend."

The message ended the usual uninteresting way, "End of message"

Tom was overjoyed and Arlene was the recipient of that joy as Tom crushed her in his arms and kissed her.

"I like it when you get good news." she murmured.

"Good news ? This is great news. The timing couldn't be better. Sam had mentioned earlier how well all his other books were received by the people of this community. I'm now counting on this one to have been read by the time I call the town meeting."

I'm glad you're feeling better now. Why don't you relax for a few minutes while I prepare us some lunch."

She kissed his cheek and pushed him out of the kitchen.

Tom found himself drawn to the other novels and the pseudonym under which Bert wrote. His mind became super active again on the planning for the big event. Deeply lost in his thoughts Tom was not aware of Arlene standing beside him. She softly touched his shoulder.

"Lunch is ready and I don't want to eat alone. Care to join me ?"

He gazed at her and she could see the love in his eyes. They held hands walking back to the kitchen.

"If nothing else I want to complete this mission for her rather than subject her to a life of my angst over my failure." ran through Tom's mind on the way to the table. Once seated he believed himself able to control his selfish feelings and asked Arlene for her thoughts on his town meeting idea.

Inwardly she was truly pleased that he would include her by asking her input and opinion.

"If you believe this will end these malicious falsehoods that have been going on for decades, then yes, I say go for it. I know you are aware of the difficulty ahead of you but I do believe this can be accomplished. I will do whatever you ask to assist you in every way, Except !"

The emphasis on the word except caught Tom's immediate attention. He looked at her with anticipation. Her face and eyes slowly showed her smile.

"Except for the speechifying. I'll leave that up to you since you seem to be so good at it, you know, you being a lawyer and all."

Arlene and Tom were almost laughing by the time she finished the sentence.

"Seriously speaking though, I think you can do this. There are a few people already behind you and I'm positive many more can be recruited. In particularly your loyal troop of teens."

"**I**'m trying to keep them out of it if I can. I don't want their innocence tarnished because of a few misguided adults of the past."

Arlene reached to touch his hand warmly.

"**W**e won't let that happen, my love, and that's a promise." her eyes highlighting her sincerity. As an after thought she added, "Don't under estimate your boys. Their minds and principals may be stronger than you think."

Not answering this comment Tom, did, however acknowledge her observation and did not disagree. To lighten the mood Arlene ordered Tom to assist her in cleanup.

"**O**kay, Staff Sergeant, you are now on KP duty. Then and only then we can get to some serious planning. While you think out loud I will take notes and then we can build a solid plan of attack."

"**N**ow you sound like my platoon leader back in the desert."

"**I** learned from the best." she smiled.

Keeping the serious thought on the light side is really what Tom needed so he did not wrap himself up in the wrong attitude and defeat his whole purpose.

"**D**on't forget now in your thought process you already have two good friends in Sam and the judge." she reminded.

"**I** have more than that." Tom smiled back, "And I intend to use them."

Arlene looked up at Tom, a question mark showing on her face. Chuckling softly Tom said.

"**T**he book publisher and the bankers from New York City."

"**Y**ou are planning big time." Arlene answered. "And we still have Aunt Martha and Aunt Eileen. Who knows, they might even know of others who knew and liked Bert.

The afternoon passed quickly as one by one , ideas were bounced back and forth. At five o'clock Arlene asserted herself.

"**T**hat's enough for today big guy. We don't want to wear your brain out totally. At least not yet. I suggest we quit for today and think about dinner."

"**I** know you're right so I bow to your wisdom O Pretty One." Tom replied along with an exaggerated bow.

"**I** think our two aunt's were planning an evening together. Why don't we join them, the distraction will do you good. I'll just call ahead."

~ ~ ~ ~

The evening with the aunts was a total success. Worries and concerns were cast aside for fun, food and joking, with Tom catching the brunt of them and being outnumbered three to one. Snacks and drinks were consumed freely which meant Tom, once again stayed overnight at Eileen's as did Martha.

Tom awoke earlier than expected and savoring the family life he had just experienced with Arlene and both aunts. This is what he wanted. What career he wanted to follow after the military was still a question unanswered. That would have to wait until this business about Bert was put to bed. Martha and Eileen were sipping tea at the kitchen table with Arlene no where to be found.

"I think the poor lass had a little too much of the spirits last night. Let her sleep. She'll be better for it." Eileen smiled.

"In the meantime we three will have breakfast, then you can run me home." joined Tom's aunt.

Martha, upon exiting the truck reaffirmed to Tom her support and help for the town meeting.

"It will work Tom, I know it will. There are a number of us who knew Bert the way you did and you will have their support also. Have a great day son, chin up."

He drove back to Eileen's in good spirits. Arlene was still sleeping and Tom did not want to disturb her. He chose to go back to his home alone. Eileen agreed to letting the young lass sleep. Arlene could call him later.

"Be of good humor Tommy love. All will work out I just know it will."

As much as he loved Arlene, he was thankful for this time alone. A man needed this now and then. He happily went about some routine household chores listening to some chosen classical music as he worked. Tom knew there was nothing more that could be done on this day regarding the town meeting. This helped set his mind at ease. He would see Arlene late this afternoon and evening. *"I'm sure she could use her time to catch up on her own needs."* he thought.

For reasons unknown Tom thought about starting his own journal following Bert's example. He put these thoughts aside, for now anyway, He had enough on his plate already. "A nice outing and picnic with Arlene would fill the bill for tomorrow." he spoke aloud. "I'll let her decide where she would like to go." Tom puttered around for another few hours before calling Arlene.

Her choice for Sunday's outing was to stay home at the cabin and just relax. Perhaps a short visit to the forest and then picnic right there in the yard. Surprised but not upset by her decision Tom planned accordingly. He even conspicuously placed a canvas on an easel along with her paints to the reception of one of her million dollar smiles.

The day proved to be perfect as they waited on each other with drinks and snacks and a tasty steak grilled for dinner. Their contented day ended with dancing on the grass to some romantic slow music. Late evening Tom returned Arlene back to Eileen's ending their dream date.

Ten the next morning found Tom at Sam McCort's office each with a cup of coffee. Sam, with an almost guilty grin stated.

"Do I have a surprise for you."

He reached into his desk drawer retrieving a hard bound book entitled, "The True Cost of Ignorance and False Judgement" by William McClain.

A sense of pride filled Tom as did a few tears in his eyes. Sam continued with.

"It's as if Bert knew you were going to call a town wide meeting. I knew you two thought alike some times but this is down right scary. Five copies arrived this morning by special delivery. I did not realize it but this was released in New York City last week and already sold over forty thousand copies."

"If this book reads anything like the title I'm going to love it." Tom finally said.

"I already peeked at a few chapters and it reads just what the title suggests. This will undoubtedly be unexpected ammunition for your meeting. In light of this I would suggest you hold off calling a meeting for a while. Let's see how the book sales turn out and then start your meeting plans."

"As long as we're on the subject of the meeting, do you have any suggestions on how to convince people to attend ?" inquired a serious Tom.

"There's an old adage that holds true most of the time, feed them and they will come." Sam smiled

Tom sported a very bewildered expression.

"You've got to be kidding. There could possibly be one, two or even four hundred people."

"Or more." added Sam. "Or you could only get thirty guests."

Tom was silent, remaining in his bewildered state. You could tell he was thinking.

"Where can you hold such a function." Tom asked slowly and not necessarily asking Sam. "Town hall is certainly not that big, and by the time we have a meeting it will be too cool to hold it outdoors."

Sam quietly interrupted his thought process.

"You said yourself earlier the High School auditorium, then you can also use the cafeteria."

"Then which comes first, the speeches or the food."

"Good question." returned Sam. "Either way, there are going to be people who will only attend one or the other.'

There was a silent pause before Sam resumed his own thinking process.

"Unless you want to wait about nine months and hold your meeting outdoors ."

Tom did not like that option as his expression showed. Before Tom put himself in too much of a down attitude Sam tried to lighten the air.

"Not to worry my friend, we'll come up with something."

The fact that he included himself when he said *"WE"*, did perk up Tom's spirits and gave a half smile.

"You're right, I'll just have to think about this some more. I guess I'll consult the eating and meeting experts."

Now it was Sam's turn to look confused. Tom picked up on this and smiling said.

"Martha and Eileen."

Sam joined with the smile.

"You're right, they probably are the experts. In the meantime let's both concentrate on Bert's book. Who knows what additional information he may throw at us."

Tom agreed realizing he had more pre-planning to do.

"Thanks Sam, I won't take up any more of your time." he said standing ready to leave.

"Don't get discouraged, we'll figure this out, especially now that you're going to consult the experts."

Tom knew he meant the aunts and laughed with Sam as they shook hands. He left with three copies of Bert's new book, knowing Arlene would want to read one also and most likely Martha and Eileen. He could not wait to get started on the book.

~ ~ ~

Arlene was home alone, Eileen away at one of her many club meetings. Tom automatically knew that Martha would not be home also. He would have to wait to talk about a location for the meeting.

Arlene, excited about the new novel instantly grabbed a copy from Tom. Hugging it close to her she asked.

"Do you have any plans for us today ?"

"Not really, I was going to leave that up to you."

"Good." she replied with her broad Irish smile. "Then let's read. Make yourself comfortable, I'll make some tea and coffee. We'll worry about lunch if we get hungry."

She kissed Tom and headed for the kitchen. Without argument Tom found himself a comfortable chair, put his feet up and turned to page one. Minutes later he was given his coffee without a word. Arlene then found her own comfy place, also put her feet up and proceeded to read. For well over an hour the only sound to be heard was a page being turned or a cup touching the table. As if by silent signal both readers closed the books sounding out an almost silent, "WOW". Looking at each other the pair smiled. Arlene was first to put her thought into words.

"This is like an autobiography."

"I was just thinking the same. It's not like one, it is one." Tom commented.

"There are a few incidents, so far that were not in the journals." observed Arlene.

"And I'm sure there will be many others." was Tom's smiling answer. "Even if only a hand full of people read this book it will make it easier for me when we have our meeting."

"Perhaps the meeting will not be necessary."

"I wish that were true but I believe the specific point will have to be emphasized strongly. Strongly, yet without vindictiveness. A soft presentation of the truth rather than a hard driven vengefulness."

Without hesitation Arlene replied.

"If anyone can do such a thing, I believe it will be you." Her eyes showed her sincerity in what she verbalized. "I'm sure reading this is very emotional for you, so why don't you take a break while I fix us some lunch. We can read again after that.

Tom nodded his agreement as he put the book aside.

A delightful warm luncheon was just ending when Eileen returned.

"What an exciting day I had. The library committee was talking about another novel they just received by William McClain. He has written four or five before this and they were all best sellers. I can't wait to read this. The library only had three copies which were already checked out so I splurged and bought one for myself.."

Arlene glanced at Tom confusion showing in her eyes. Tom quickly put his finger to his lips indicating quiet, his eyes explained I'll tell you later. Arlene relaxed somewhat but was still puzzled. Eileen continued spilling out the details of her day dropping in a positive note regarding the new book, every now and then. She was very upbeat and neither Tom nor Arlene wanted to burst her bubble. After ranting on for another six or seven minutes she finally came to an end of her morning.

"And how have my two lovebirds been getting along ? Did you have a nice morning ?"

Arlene answered with out hesitation.

"Everything has been going along just fine this morning but we are going to Tom's right after we do these lunch dishes. I'm going to help him with some housecleaning." she fibbed.

Tom in the meantime went to the living room, collected the two novels and brought them to his truck. When he returned he found Arlene and her Aunt caught up in a friendly argument about who would do the cleanup

"Okay ladies, that's enough, I have the solution to your dilemma."

Both women smiled, looking over to Tom.

"I have a few questions for Eileen and while we have our little talk, you Arlene can do the dishes. I promise , next time I will take care of that while you two relax."

Arlene turned to clearing the table while Tom and Eileen settled themselves in the living room.

"Okay, Tommy love, what's your question ?"

Tom slowly explained his earlier talk with Sam McCort in reference to the town meeting and feeding the group.

Smiling, almost laughing, Eileen answered.

"So now we're into feeding the masses, are we ? Why that's no problem Tommy love. Use the coliseum. They are set up for just such a thing. Much more room than town hall or the high school and have catering facilities right there."

Tom, puzzled by her answer, dumbly asked, "What coliseum ?"

"Sorry love, I forgot you have not been here for a while. There's a new North East Coliseum about twelve or thirteen miles outside of town to the Northeast. It can seat about three thousand people more or less at the main arena, you know for sporting events, concerts and the like."

"But surely I don't need that much space ?"

"Not to worry love they have other function rooms also accompanied by catering service. Some of my club groups have used them, you know quilt shows and art exhibits and the like. And to answer your next question, No, they are surprisingly not that expensive."

Tom was again bewildered at this woman's knowledge of the workings of this town. He was actually glad she was on his side. Feeling that this was the perfect answer he gave Eileen a big thank you hug.

"Careful love, you'll get the young lass jealous." quipped Eileen.

"I heard that. What are you two up to now." Arlene yelled from the kitchen.

"Nothing serious hon, I just could not resist hugging your charming Aunt." Tom answered while winking at Eileen.

~ ~ ~

Arlene could not hold her curiosity any longer on the drive to the cabin.

"Didn't you tell my Aunt about Bert's writing gift ?"

"Obviously I didn't, but it was strictly an oversight. I got so involved in Bert's journal and thoughts of clearing his name it just slipped my mind."

"Then why didn't you say something today ?"

"Because now knowing what the book is about I would prefer her unbiased critique. The same with my Aunt Martha."

Smiling again Arlene replied with.

"Always thinking ahead. You're right though, it should be interesting to see her reaction when she finds out."

"I personally think it perhaps will be representative of the general public's opinion, and that will be of great help for my town presentation venture."

"That would be great, darling. I truly hope all works well for you. For us."

The afternoon at the cabin was a subdued quietude save for the occasional page turning as the young couple buried themselves in reading. Old Bert had a way with words that hammered his message home without being vengeful or attacking. *This should definitely get some people thinking.* Tom thought. No words were spoken directly though there were periodic muttering's of shock, disgust and unbelieving.

Bert had managed well to put his life into a novel without identification or similarities of Tylerville characters yet his point was made time and time again.

Minutes later Arlene also put aside the book. With a half smile but with tears she voiced aloud, "WOW". Tom replied almost incoherently.

"I know what you mean."

"Oh my, look at the time. How about some dinner before I go ?" She asked, neither one wanting to discuss their reactions to the book. Like two children they walked hand in hand to the kitchen.

~ ~ ~

"Can we finish reading tomorrow, please." pleaded Arlene before getting out of the truck at Eileen's. I purposely left the book at the cabin. Pick me up at your convenience." She paused for a second. "Unless you have something else to do tomorrow."

"Reading for tomorrow will be fine. I'll pick you up around ten. There's something I want to check out, then we can go to the cabin, have lunch and read.

"You're so good to me. I guess that's why I love you so much."

They kissed good night and as Tom was driving home all his thoughts were on Arlene. Once home he chose not to read more of Bert's novel, rather, he spent some time on quick calculations on the cost of having this town meeting. He even gave this up after a short time acknowledging he did not presently have enough information to make a proper decision. He turned instead to one of the war journals to take his mind away from the present. This proved to be a good decision, his mind was swept into the story allowing the needed relaxation to take over. So much so that he found himself falling asleep. Silently saying good night to Arlene he fell into bed enveloped in a restful sleep.

~ ~ ~

With renewed spirit and energy Tom drove to Arlene again singing along with the radio. Arlene, as expected, was waiting on the front steps. He smiled observing she looked like a young teen awaiting her first real boy friend to arrive. She jumped into the truck, kissed him on the cheek and commanded, "Let's go."

Tom looked at her, a question in his eyes.

"To the coliseum of course." She smiled.

"I see you have been talking to Eileen." Tom stated.

"No keeping secrets from you." she replied as she snuggled closer to him. "The coliseum sounded like just the right answer." she continued.

"I hope so. We'll find out soon enough."

The short time the couple spent at the coliseum was most rewarding. Final arrangements were not concluded just yet but things looked like it would be a go. Tom could hear Sam laughing already knowing he would after hearing the results of his talk with Eileen.

Tom felt the fifteen to twenty minute drive from town would not discourage too many folks from attending and knowing they were going to be fed for free.

As he navigated his way back to his home he cheerfully asked Arlene.

"Are you still up for a reading day ?"

"You bet I am. I feel we can finish the book today."

"Tell you what, If we finish reading today I'll treat you to dinner tonight.

"You're on big guy, but I'm not dressed to go out."

"No problem, I know a quiet little Mexican place that you will just adore."

"I'm game, as long as you don't mind the way I look."

"You are, as always, beautiful, no matter how you dress."

Arlene glowed with his words and at the same time felt a flush cross her face.

Read they did once comfortably settled at the house. Arlene stretched out on the couch while Tom chose his favorite rocker on the porch along with a tall glass of lemonade. The autumn wind through the tree tops was the appropriate music for the story.

At about three thirty Tom turned the last page but remained on the porch running a review of the book through his mind. This was one of the most insightful and poignant stories he had ever read. Bert managed to capture every one of Tom's innermost concerns and put them into words he was unable to do himself. Tom thought of his dear friend carrying that burden for all those years, yet at the same time not holding a grudge against the town who knowing or unknowingly persecuted him. He himself took strength from this, resolving to continue his crusade to clear and rebuild Bert's reputation. This novel, as hurtful as it was at times gave him a renewed dedication to succeed in his self assigned task and to do it with a smile and a happy heart knowing he was in the right.

Tom reentered the house only to find Arlene, clutching the closed book, sound asleep. He stared at her peaceful beauty for a time realizing how lucky he was to have her love. Not disturbing her he went about some quiet chores and returned to the porch, enjoying the sounds of quiet.

Sometime after four Arlene joined Tom on the porch sporting an embarrassed expression and apologizing. He assured her there was no need and was happy that she could feel that comfortable. This proved to him that theirs was a true love connection. She sat in his lap her head on his shoulder, neither saying a word.

Time being unmentioned, Tom finally whispered.

"I don't know about you young lady but I'm hungry. We never did have lunch."

"You're right and the thought of the Mexican food has got me intrigued.

The drive home to Eileen's was anticlimactic for the day. Arleen enjoyed dinner though she did admit not being accustomed to such spicy food. They kept their discussion of Bert's book to a minimum each still digesting its full impact.

Tom turned down the invitation to stay at Eileen's for the night with out any argument from Arlene. Back at the cabin in short order Tom slowly gazed at the surroundings, which was all Bert, smiled at the portrait of his friend and being content, went to bed.

Chapter 30

The nine thirty telephone call startled Tom out of his extended peaceful sleep. It was Fred from the Youth Corps asking for a meeting with Tom.

"By all means Fred, I said I would always be there for you men. This afternoon after school would be perfect. I'll meet you at the Country Luncheonette, say about three thirty."

Tom was trying to sound as if he had been up for hours. He checked the clock again as he hung up the phone.

"I haven't slept like that since I can't remember when." He said out loud. "I guess I was content for a change. A happy mind means a happy body. Let's hope when this is all over I will be able to sleep like this all the time."

He called Arlene to tell her of his meeting with the guys and that he would see her tonight. She insisted on dinner at her place, and Tom readily agreed.

~ ~ ~

"The young gentlemen are waiting for you in the back booth." said Brenda and with a smile added; "Please try to keep the noise down sir, we do have other customers."

Tom returned the smile.

"I don't guarantee anything but I will try my best to control myself."

The back booth was occupied by three teens, Fred, Ace and Josh.

"Hey Mr. T." was the collective greeting.

Tom enjoyed the warm greeting knowing he was truly welcomed.

"Good to see you. How's school going ?"

"Great Mr. T., especially math and science or physics, if you will. You were right in what you told us, Tom, and we are all doing better." Fred answered.

"Even me." chimed in Ace proudly. I got a ninety plus on my last math test, thanks to you."

"No thanks to me Ace, you're the one who took the test."

"But you're the one who taught me how, sir. I've never had an "A" in my life, and so far I've two this term."

"I'm proud of you Ace, keep on plugging."

"You bet I will, now that I see what study can do. Dirk is doing better also."

Tom was truly pleased for both Ace and Dirk, and of course the other boys as well.

"How can I help you guys ? I assume that's why you called this meeting. But before we get into anything why don't you guys put in your orders, my treat."

Josh smiled his answer.

"Not this time Mr. T. We already put in our orders and coffee for you, our treat."

"Well thanks guys. Okay now what can I do for you."

Fred took the lead.

"The local Rotary group contacted us. They heard what we were doing and asked if we would be interested in some winter work for them."

"That's great men. It's a good sign that you have been recognized and accepted. I'm both proud and happy for you."

"And we owe that to you Tom." Fred furthered.

Tom, trying to ignore Fred's comment continued.

"The Rotary's interest in you is a good deal and a step in the right direction, so what do you need me for ?"

"Apparently for years they have been helping the elderly with snow shoveling so they are not house bound."

"Again," Tom acknowledged, "Sounds like a perfect fit and a good deal."

"Well, a lot of their members are getting older themselves and the physical efforts are becoming too much. They asked if we would be interested in doing the snow removal for the winter, and they are willing to pay us. They said they have a contingency winter fund for just such a thing."

"Sounds better all the time, where do I come in ?"

"Well- - -." hesitated Ace. "We have also been active along those lines and have acquired a list of our own. When you combine these two lists, that is a lot of shoveling."

Tom smiled knowing where they were going with this. Anxiety could be seen in the young mens eyes which was answered or rather interrupted by Brenda bringing their orders. This obviously gave them time to collect their courage to ask what Tom already knew was the request. Before Fred could continue Tom spoke up.

"The answer is yes."

The three teens looked at each other totally confused.

"Snow blowers. That's what you were wondering about, correct ? Do you think three will be enough ?"

The youths smiles grew wider as they looked at Tom in disbelief. Josh found his voice making it clear.

"This is not a gift Tom. We want and will pay for them. Over time of course. We're too young to get a loan at the bank but we want to be self sustaining. You have already extended yourself on our behalf, but this is something we want to accomplish on our own. We just need the up front money."

"I will repeat what I just said? Will three do ? I also agree that this is something you should do on your own. Consider it an interest free loan. I'm sure we can come to mutual terms as far as how long the loan should be."

The boys were all in a tongue tied silence. But their eyes showed their joy.

"We don't know how to thank you Mr. T.   Whatever you want from us just ask." spouted Ace.

"No need to get carried away guys, you have my full faith and trust."

Tom raised his coffee cup up as a toast.

"Here's to a successful business agreement."

The three boys raised their soda glasses and happily agreed.

~ ~ ~

Tom felt good about the arrangement with the Youth Corps and even better that they were getting recognition. This is something he would definitely pass on to Judge McCallister.

Before he returned to Arlene he stopped at the Tylerville Book Shoppe. Trying to play innocent and be as inconspicuous as possible he was thumbing through the magazine rack. Lucky for him it was not far from the "This Month's Special" stand featuring the latest novel by "William

McClain." There were four or five books there. During Tom's short time there two copies were purchased. He chose a magazine and commented to the sales person in a purely ignorant fashion, about the new book.

"Yes, that book is selling like crazy, but then again the man is a great writer. We had thirty copies shipped in the original order. Looks like we're going to have to order a few more."

Tom had to work at holding back a huge grin. Once outside his smile burst forth. He almost felt like shouting and jumping. He was trying to keep a sense of decorum while he walked to his truck. Driving out of town he was singing and shouting to no one but himself, out of pure happiness. He could not contain his joy.

~ ~ ~

Tom tapped on his horn as the truck entered the driveway. He couldn't wait to tell Arlene. She met him on the porch with a questioning smile. He jumped a few steps rushing to her, picked her up and swung her around a few times. By this time she was laughing insisting he put her down.

"What's gotten into you ? You're acting like a madman."

"The book, the book my sweet. It's selling like crazy."

He almost shouted in her ear. Her elation showed in her smile as she jumped into his arms again kissing him this time.

"I'm so happy for you Tom. This is wonderful."

"You bet it is. I'm counting on it to make it easier for me at my meeting with the town folk."

"My aunt is home so you better tone it down unless you're going to let her in on your secret.

"No, not just yet. I still want to see her unbiased reaction."

Tom recovered himself as best he could before entering the house.

Ah, Tommy love, where have you been all day. You shouldn't be leaving this pretty lass alone all day, you know. She may just find another new love." Eileen kidded.

"Then that would leave more time for you and I." Tom joked in answer.

"Don't I have anything to say about my love life ?" pouted Arlene.

A dual "NO" was her answer.

"I know it's early but how would you two ladies like to go out for dinner ?" Tom voiced.

"Tommy love, that couldn't have come at abetter time. I am a bit tired and have not prepared a thing, that is if the lass here will approve of you going with two women."

"Given the circumstances and the fact I can't trust you two alone, I'll go along as a chaperone." replied Arlene.

The three met in a big hug.

Dinner was over early enough for Tom and Arlene to share a loving stroll before Tom departed alone for his log cabin. Still riding a high from the afternoon Tom parked himself in the porch rocker and let his mind run amuck. It was a perfect night, almost a full moon backlighting the trees with a relatively warm temperature. He fetched a cold beer from the house returning to the rocker to further enjoy the night. The silent symphony of the night replaced the more active music of the day, either of which Tom relished and savored immensely. It always amazed him how the simple things of nature could turn a day from bad to good, or from good to total peace, almost spiritual.

"Listen to yourself." he said aloud, "Trying to sound like a poet, just appreciate what you feel."

He rested there quietly for quite a spell before retiring. Just before reentering the house he looked at the moon, lifted his bottle in toast saying softly, "Semper Fi" Bert."

~ ~ ~

Tom sang quietly along with the radio as he prepared breakfast. Starting on his second cup of strong black coffee, his mind was already made up of the things he wanted to accomplish this day. He knew Arlene always wanted to help and be part of his days, but this was something he knew he had to do alone. He would see her later this afternoon.

First on his list was to see Sam. He called early and left a message hoping Sam would have some time today. Shortly after nine Sam McCort returned his call and would be free to meet at eleven. In the meantime he went through the paper work from Chase Manhattan. He would call either or both Richard Zankle &/or Howard Martin after conversing with Sam. His next call would be to the publisher of Bert's novels.

As Tom scanned the records of the New York bank listing the business names who received financial help from Bert's foundation something caught his eye. The local Flooring and Tile store had floundered a few times because of the up and down economy. There were a few significant dollar injections followed by some stabilizing smaller amounts of financial aid in succeeding years. The business owners name was Charles Thompson. A huge grin broke across Tom's face as he voiced out loud, "Gotcha." It was this sort of info that he needed to make his points at the mass meeting. But Tom also knew it had to be done graciously without vindictiveness. His words would have to be chosen carefully, written ahead of time and reviewed by a few people he could trust so that his presentation was a positive thing.

Tom's thoughts drifted for a moment. "Sometimes I think it was easier back in Afghanistan." He smiled to himself.

Putting his record reviewing aside Tom went on to complete his personal hygiene and dressing so as not to be late for his meeting with the attorney.

Tom entered Sam McCort's office exactly on time, as was his trained habit. Sam was always pleased to see Tom. He never once considered his visits an inconvenience or burdensome. As expected, Sam smiled, almost laughing, when he heard the results if Tom's chat with Eileen referencing a place to hold the meeting.

"I should have known better. Come to think of it, I should start using both Eileen and Martha myself as a go to information center on my trial cases."

Tom briefed Sam on his appointment with the coliseum people, then led right into the foundation business. Sam was most familiar with the basics having been with Bert right from the beginning. The minute details of the who's and whys remained a bit unknown, he left that research to the Chase Manhattan people, although he did provide some word of mouth background on the approved groups and businesses.

Tom opened his folder of the foundation donations. Sam immediately, with a grin, noticed the various donations to Charles Thompson.

"I'm sure these entries made you sit up and notice." Sam commented.

"You bet it did and as you can be rest assured I am going to use that information." Tom replied quickly.

Sam's antennae were instantly alerted which Tom could see in his eyes. In a soothing voice Tom answered before Sam could say anything.

"Relax Sam. I have mentioned previously I am going to do this without vengeance. I am not a vindictive person." With a big smile he added; "I presently have three women and a group of teens watching my every move, keeping me calm and pointing out the errors of a revengeful attitude. By the way Bert already did all of that for me."

Now Sam's furrowed brow asked for further explanation.

"I guess you haven't read Bert's last book yet ?"

"You're right I'm sorry to say. I have been very busy of late and just too tired at night to do anything."

"I need no apologies from you. Believe me I totally understand.

Let me fill you in briefly. The book is almost autobiographical of his life here in Tylerville with out it being recognizable as Tylerville. The only thing it doesn't cover is the foundation. Bert attained such a level of language and understanding with his words that even the worst perpetrator of the misdeeds he suffered I'm sure would not recognize himself, yet at the same time I'm sure could feel empathy for and with Bert or in this case the hero of the book. This story is going to make my town meeting a success. I can feel it."

Sam sat back, pleased with what he just heard. Tom noticed Sam relaxing somewhat and therefore continued.

"I just wish Bert could be here to enjoy the fruits of his own words and labors. It's not fair that he can not take a part in his own redemption."

Smiling as a true friend Sam commented.

"I'm sure he's watching your every move and giving you the courage to finish the job he started."

Tom was almost embarrassed by Sam's insightful reply. Recognizing he was right there definitely was another dimensional, or spiritual realm if you will, assistance to his efforts giving him the strength and will to not be deterred. He was no longer tilting at windmills. This was now down to the final show and he must maintain the sophistication, presence of mind and charitable outlook that Bert himself set as example. Tom's presentation of himself at this mass meeting had to be impeccable. He knew humility must rule the day not antagonism.

Tom's mind continued non stop even though he stopped physically speaking. Sam could sympathize with what he was going through yet remained silent. This was something only Tom could work out for himself. And of course with Bert's help even if it was in spirit only. The inner peace one searched for must be achieved alone. Outside influence can sometimes confuse or sidetrack what must really take place.

At last shedding the conscience of his mind Tom returned to the real world apologizing to Sam.

"No apologies necessary my friend. I do agree though that the answer to your presentation dilemma lies in the words of Bert himself. Write yourself a guideline based on this present novel."

"A great idea, thanks. I was going to prepare a paper ahead of time but using some of Bert's words will be better in making my point. In all the time I knew and spent with Bert I was never aware of his mastery with words. Thanks Sam, you always know the right thing to say to keep me grounded."

The attorney just nodded and smiled.

"Right now I feel I'm on top of things, thanks to all the help I get. I will definitely want your input on my final wordings before the real thing."

"I'm always here for you Tom, as I was for Bert. You also might want to consider Judge McCallister as a go to man. Trust me Tom, He is on your side all the way."

Tom readily accepted the advice though with a slight flush.

As Tom was ready to leave he jokingly stated.

"I'm on such a high right now I feel like I could fly all the way home."

"Watch out for low flying helicopters." smiled Sam in return.

~ ~ ~

Back in his truck and knowing he still had calls to make Tom decided on seeing Arlene first. His mind free from business for the moment he concentrated on the love of his life. Arlene, as always was overjoyed at his arrival and convinced him to stay for lunch before they headed for the log paradise.

Eileen was still spouting the merits of the new book by William McClain.

"In fact, Tommy love, we're having a special book club meeting to review and discuss his latest gem. Perhaps you two young ones would care to attend. Have you seen the book yet? Tell you what, Martha is coming over tonight. She and I are sort of hosting the special review at the library and are going to do some planning tonight. Join us and see what you think of the book, then you can decide about the library get together."

Arlene's eyes went instantly to Tom inquiringly. Surprised but pleased her smile grew as Tom answered.

"That sounds like a great idea. I would love to hear what you two ladies think about the book. How about you Arlene ? Did you have anything special planned for tonight ?"

"Not at all, I think it's a great idea. I've already prepared a special Irish meal for tonight and there's more than enough for four people."

"Oh good !" interrupted Eileen. I'll go call Martha right now."

Alone with Tom, Arlene inquired.

"Why the change of mind ?"

"I was trying to think ahead." Tom replied smiling. "This library gathering could be a wonderful lead in to the town meeting. Sort of pre publicity."

"Won't that present problems ? If people know the whole topic before hand they may not want to come to your town meeting. Food or no food." posed Arlene.

Tom became pensive. "Maybe you're right. I guess the four of us can work this out tonight."

"I think that's a much better idea my love. We can get our aunts true feel for the book and then plan accordingly."

Tom, now showing a loving smile softly replied.

"I guess that's why I need you with me.

Arlene moved to Tom, kissed his cheek saying,

"And don't you forget that."

Eileen reentered the room.

"Cut that out you two. Martha is on her way. Tommy love, why don't you take a quick run to the store and pick up a nice bottle of wine ?"

Replying with a huge grin, "I guess I'm staying over tonight."

Which prompted an "Oh goody" from Arlene followed with "But no wine."

An inquisitive expression showed from Tom and Eileen. With her glowing Irish eyes Arlene happily answered.

"This recipe would blend itself far better with good old Guinness Stout."

"Stout it is." grinned Tom already heading for the door.

"And you'll still be staying over tonight." Arlene called after him.

~ ~ ~

Dinner was superb. Tom couldn't really say enough about it. Arlene called it beef in stout with dumplings. She was also right about the Guinness as the correct beverage. Eileen and Martha joined in praising the sweet Irish lass.

"Tis a good thing you'll be getting, Tommy love. Don't lose this pretty young thing. Of course you will end up being overweight with her feeding you like this." Eileen said in jest.

Dinner over and with all four joining in clean up saw them finally settled in the living room, glasses of stout still in evidence. Eileen remaining excited about the book started off the conversation.

"You have got to read this book, Tommy. It's almost like Bert's story, but much more involved than I knew about him."

Arlene and Tom, trying to hold back their smiles acted very interested. Martha interjected her opinion.

"You know Eileen there could have been many instances in Bert's affairs that we were not aware of. Knowing the man like we did, he may have been trying to shield us from the same treatment he was receiving."

"But ole Bert, God rest his soul, passed on months ago. How could this be his book ?"

"Perhaps he wrote it before he passed. A book isn't something you write overnight." replied Martha.

Tom laughed internally as he compared this on going dialogue to a tennis match. Back and forth, back and forth.

"I've never known Bert to be a writer. I've never seen him writing."

Laughing her return Martha stated.

"You've never seen him go shopping either but he certainly wasn't starving."

Tom, quietly raised his hand to signal stop.

"Ladies, if I may before you have an all out "Donnybrook".

Everyone was now laughing.

"Maybe I can shed some light on the subject. Do either of you recall Bert's mothers maiden name ?"

Blank stares registered on the two women Tom did not interrupt their thinking. A few moments passed when Eileen at last muttered quietly.

"Twas a grand strong Irish name I remember."

"I believe you're right." joined Martha. "McNiel or something like that."

"McClain" both women shouted at the same time

"But what's that got to do with the book we're talking about ?" asked Martha..

While Martha was questioning Tom Eileen was staring down at the book in her lap, then burst out loud.

"Saints preserve us, a "nom de plume"

Martha instantly looked at the book she was holding.

"You're right my dear and his fathers name was William."

Both surprised women turned to Tom, mouths partially opened.

"You knew ?" they asked in unison

"Yes, but I only found out about a month and a half ago. This was a total surprise to me also."

Yet in a shocked state Eileen queried.

"Those other five books he wrote also ?"

"Yes Mam, that he did."

Over the initial shock the two aunts listened to Tom as he brought them up to date on all of Bert's many secrets and business. He cautiously outlined everything; his letters, notes, journals, accounts and even the foundation. At the end of the explanation he extracted a promise from each that this information had to remain secret, especially the financial foundation. This should always remain hush-hush. Peoples financial status should remain private.

"**W**e understand completely Tom and you have our word."

Tom did feel better now and the group quietly went on to discuss the book and the effect it would have on the town as a whole. Tom did, however, beg off from attending the library group the next day. He would leave that to Martha and Eileen to handle and see what feelings they could glean about the story contents.

The night ended with positive thoughts along with good feelings about restoring Bert's reputation.

Tom and Arlene did manage some alone time as they went for a night time stroll before retiring.

~ ~ ~

The blinking red light drew Tom's attention as he entered the cabin. Arlene made for the kitchen with the shopping bags from the market while Tom listened to the message.

***H**i Mr. T. This is Fred. I hate to bother you at home but we were wondering if we could get to see you this afternoon. The barn just outside of town that we're presently working on would be great. That is if not too inconvenient.   This may sound like a funny request but could you bring Miss Arlene along. We have our reasons.*

Not realizing Arlene was behind him, Tom heard her sweet voice.

"**S**ee, I do have a fan club." Glowing she added; "Can I go, please Daddy, can I go with you ?"

"**W**ell okay, but first make sure all your homework is done."

Arlene jumped up and down like a ten year old.

"**O**h goody, goody, goody. Just for that I'll make you lunch."

Making sure she heard and saw him, Tom turned to the portrait asking.

"**I**s it always like this ?" With a smile of course.

She continued along, with a smile.

"**C**areful there Bud, I'll un paint that portrait."

They hugged on the way back to the kitchen.

Chapter 31

As the barn loomed into sight Arlene commented she could only see four people and one of them looks like a girl who was carrying a long piece of wood. Tom slowed down and confirmed Arlene's observation.

"I guess that's why they wanted to see us."

"I think this is great if it's what we think it is." said a happy Arlene. Eyes sparkling again.

Tom could never get used to all the wonderful changes of her outer and inner beauty. He smiled inwardly, glowing as much himself.

Ace was the first one to meet and greet Arlene and Tom. The first words Tom uttered surprised those within hearing range.

"It's about time you men learned what real life was all about."

Word was passed of Tom and Arlene's arrival. And soon eight boys and two girls were gathering before the pair. Not waiting on formality Arlene, hand extended, approached both girls.

"Hi, I'm Arlene." she smiled

The two teenaged girls grinning from ear to ear accepted her hand, each giving their name.

"I'm Kathy and I'm Lisa."

Arlene then presented them to Tom with a repeat of hand shake and names.

Fred assumed his quasi leadership roll.

"I'm glad you could make it Mr. T."

"I think it's now obvious why you called us. The answer is yes. I, or we think it's a great idea."

Smiles and grins spread around to all present.

"But I didn't even say why we asked you here yet."

"You're right Fred. I apologize for assuming. The floor is yours."

Fred, now trying to look and sound official explained their situation.

"These two young ladies heard about our group and what we were attempting to do and were bold enough to ask to join us. None of the guys saw a problem with this so we agreed. The now ten of us had a meeting and set up our own rules of behavior."

Josh interjected; "We think it's an okay thing, but we wanted both your and Arlene's approval."

Tom somewhat taken aback by the teens forthright level of maturity, paused a moment before speaking.

"I'm sure this is a first for these young ones, including the girls. This new development will definitely be mentioned to the judge." This thought occupied the pause.

Smiling his warmest and friendliest smile Tom looked over the youth group whom he considered all friends now.

"Well, as usual guys you're one up on me. You don't really need my approval but the answer is yes. This is a wonderful addition to the Youth Corps."

"We kinda knew you would approve but we wanted your advice on handling the mix of both boy and girl." continued Josh.

Tom instantly corrected. "You mean handling the mix of men and women."

All ears perked up on hearing this, particularly the two young girls.

"Actually I'm glad you asked me for my two cents. I am going to give you my two cents. Or rather I should say we will give you our four cents."

Tom said this looking directly at Arlene who smiled and nodded. The group gathered closer and tried to make themselves more comfortable. Tom waited for the resettling then began.

"From what I have seen so far you don't need my input. In fact, perhaps some more established places of business could learn from what you're trying to do. First of all, remember this founding moment. Not just now, but months and years from now and why you're doing what you are doing. This shows a maturity on your part for both the men and women present. Equality in all areas is the key. I don't mean in just the equality between the sexes. I mean the equality of the individual. You have already shown this in the way you work. It should be no different with the women you chose to join you. Or in this case the women who have chosen to join you. You men have already learned that each of you is better at something than the others. These young women I'm sure possess the same qualities. Just because these two women look better in mud and dirt than you do doesn't make them any more special than any of you. They will bring their own leadership abilities into play when called for. Accept that for what it is as you have accepted each others leadership in certain given areas. As soon as you create jealousy between each other you will defeat yourselves. That goes for both men and women. Jealousy has no preferred sex. It will ruin anybody. It does not discriminate. I have seen you guys work together for the good of the whole. I do not expect any of that to change with the addition of a few women. Are we all in agreement ?"

A resounding "YES" was sounded. Tom then turned to Arlene his eyes asking if she wanted to add anything. Smiling ear to ear she stood, much to his surprise.

"I also think this is a wonderful thing you are starting and yes I do have something to say to just the young women."

The guys looking disappointed started to stand as Arlene continued.

"But I want these gentlemen to hear also. All of you combined are starting a good movement. You're setting an example for others your age, and for that matter , older and younger groups. Feel proud in what you are about to embark on. Continue to make decisions as a group and avoid individual jealousy. Now to get to the girls specifically. Refrain from using your feminine wiles to get your way. That does not make for a cooperative venture. True, you may be lacking in some physical prowess but that's where cooperation comes in. These young men may be lacking in some fashion design abilities but, again that's where cooperation comes in. Together you all can work wonders. Just look at yourselves and what you have already started. We are all equal when it comes to what we can do. Yet together we can do even more. The stars and beyond are yours. Together you can get them."

By now Arlene was totally red faced. She could not remember when she felt this passionate about something. The applause she heard just made her even more embarrassed to the point that she stood behind Tom to avoid looking at the teens. When things calmed down Ace, in his not so shy manner spoke out.

"Mr. T., do you think Bert would approve of us and what we're doing ?"

Tom felt a tear grow in his eye as he answered.

"Bert would definitely approve of all you have accomplished and especially this."

Looking at Kathy and Lisa Tom smiled a welcome aboard.

"Now don't you people think you have goofed off enough today ? Don't you have any work to do ?"

Of course this brought laughter all around including Arlene.

"Let them celebrate their milestone of success, you old grouch." she whispered to Tom

After a few moments the two young women approached Tom and

Arlene politely excusing themselves but asking Tom.

"Could we hear the Bert stories also ?"

A little surprised, Tom stuttered for a brief moment. Arlene chose to field the question.

"You're part of the group now, so everyone gets to hear Bert stories."

The girls were thrilled by the answer and sort of drew Arlene aside.

"Is it true you're from Ireland ?" quizzed Kathy.

Arlene felt special being asked this.

"Aye, tis true lass." she purposely threw in the accent phrase. She wanted to make the girls welcome. For the next ten minutes or so the three women were occupied with Ireland. Tom finally called an end to the meeting and all parted for the day.

~ ~ ~

In the truck driving back to the cabin Tom reached one hand over to touch Arlene's hand.

"I'm very proud of you, my sweet. What you said today and how you said it was wonderful. It couldn't have been more perfect. It seems to me if I recall correctly not too very long ago you said you didn't want anything to do with speech-a-fying. Back there you sounded like a pro."

Embarrassed but smiling at Tom's praise, Arlene tried to make light of it.

"It was just something that I felt should be said, and to both guys and girls."

"And very elegantly said it was." Tom replied.

"What shall we do about dinner ?" Arlene quickly threw out in order to change the topic.

Tom recognized this and did not pursue it any further.

"I don't even know what's left at the house. We'll decide when we get there."

Dinner turned out to be a quick burger on the grill and a perfect walk in the woods.

"After today I feel so content and satisfied." stated Tom. The success of the boys and now girls makes it all worth while."

"They need to be recognized for what they are doing." posed Arlene.

"You're right and I intend to talk to Judge McCallister about that very thing.

"I agree with letting the judge know, but I was thinking along the lines of something more public."

"You mean like the library ladies and their little luncheon."

"Yes, that was nice but I still think something even more public, but what, I don't know."

Tom was quiet for a while thinking that Arlene was correct. Some sort of public acclaim would be appropriate.

" Maybe we should consult with the Rotary on that. They did recognize the guys for the winter cleanup jobs."

"I guess we could." Arlene replied not very convincingly. "Let's just give this some more thought."

"You're right I know. We could always ask the experts." Tom stated referencing their two aunts. Arlene grinned at this cuddling closer to Tom as they continued their evening nature stroll.

With mutual silent agreement the subject was dropped. Enjoying each others company was all there was right now.

The drive back home after dropping Arlene at Eileen's caught Tom briefly thinking of their wedding. Soon after the town meeting came to mind. Here or in Ireland was the bigger disturbing thought. He knew though that would be up to Arlene and their respective aunts. Tom dismissed the wedding as he entered the house. As he threw his keys on the table he noticed the message light.

"Tom, Judge McCallister here. I had a brief conversation with Sam McCort this afternoon and based on that I would like to see you when you're free. I was hoping tomorrow about ten would be nice. No need to return this call unless you can not make it. Hope to see you then." End of message.

"I wonder what they spoke about ? Oh well, I'll find out tomorrow."

The fact that the judge called did not seem to bother Tom in any way. He picked up one of Bert's Korea journals and headed for bed.

Chapter 32

Just after breakfast Tom called Arlene to let her know about his appointment with the judge and a few other things he wanted to take care of. She was disappointed of course but looked forward to seeing him for dinner with the aunts.

~ ~ ~

"Come inTom, make yourself comfortable. Care for some coffee ?"

"No thanks Judge, I'm sort of coffee'd out this morning."

"Glad you could make it. I had a long chat with Sam yesterday. He was filling me in on something I was not aware of."

"Am I now in trouble for something ?" Tom asked trying to hide his nervousness.

McCallister grinned as he answered.

"On the contrary Tom, in fact I would like to help in any way I can."

"I assume you mean the town meeting."

"Exactly, which is why I asked you here. I would like you to fill me in with more detail than Sam gave me. If that's okay with you ?"

"Thank you sir. Of course it's okay"

"Perhaps you should start from the beginning. I'm short on all of the history of Tylerville, I was only assigned to this district court nine years ago."

"Sure thing, but before I go into that, let me update you on the Youth Corps."

"Oh, is something wrong ?"

"No sir, just the opposite. They, of their own choosing have expanded their enterprise to now include women, or girls their own age of course."

The judge looked at Tom with a serious and concerned expression.

"Do you think that's wise, given today's youth and attitudes ?"

Smiling, Tom answered.

"I appreciate your concern sir. But personally I think this is a good thing, especially for Tylerville. Arlene and I met with them yesterday. They asked our approval. Both Arlene and I spoke at length to them about equality and discrimination. I firmly believe sir that this is a good thing. They are very proud of this move and are setting an example for others, including adults. They honestly believe this can work. They want it to work to show this town how well youth can operate for the good of all. Believe me they are not your typical teens that everyone looks down on. Which brings me to your topic of interest."

"Mine ?" said the judge. "I wanted to discuss Bert Morrow with you."

"Exactly sir, bear with me and I can show you how both topics are related."

McCallister threw his hands up smiling as he sat back in his chair.

"As usual Staff Sergeant you have me at a disadvantage. Please go on with your story."

Tom was also smiling now. He explained to the judge all that had transpired with the boys since the court hearing. His introduction of Bert to them through the journals and their reaction. Unlike the adults they felt empathy for Bert. They all seemed to take to heart his plight particularly in his younger years that they themselves could relate to. They listened to me also talk of Bert and his dramatic influence on myself. How he tamed my wildness helping my Aunt Martha raise me to be a man who does not judge without reason. Who looks for the truth no matter what the result. I am also proud of these young men for seeing who they have become in such a short time. I believe Bert is responsible for that."

"You sell yourself short Tom. Your influence has changed these boys."

"That may be true sir but my influence came from Bert. In my humble opinion he was a man among men."

Tom then finished his narrative describing the novel Bert wrote and the foundation he started to anonymously help the people of Tylerville."

"Sam did mention these things, in fact he loaned me this latest novel."

"You will enjoy that sir especially when you consider that it is autobiographical."

Silence filled the room for a few seconds as the judge digested all that Tom had said.

"I do urge you to read it sir. Perhaps then you will understand more of where I'm coming from. My only goal is to clear Bert's name and reinstate the dignity that was blatantly stolen from him. But I do want to do it without hurting anyone, guilty or not guilty. Enough harm has already been wrought by ignorance."

Tom paused again realizing he was monopolizing the whole conversation. With obvious humility in his voice Tom continued.

"Forgive me judge. It appears I got a little carried away. Now what was it you wanted to see me about ?"

Tom inhaled deeply and sat back in his chair. Byron McCallister smiled and accepted the opening to speak.

"My original intent was to learn more of the town meeting, why you were calling it, and what your intention was. Actually, truth be known, I was concerned that you were going to be out for revenge. I know better now and want to help in any way I can. I don't want to see you get yourself into trouble, legal or otherwise."

Tom suddenly felt a bit awkward at hearing the judge's words realizing the man genuinely cared and wanted to help. An abrupt thought popped into his head of a Major in Afghanistan who looked after him in the same way. Tom considered himself a very lucky man to have friends like this. Interrupting this thought process the judge inquired.

"Now getting back to the dinner party meeting. What made you decide on a town wide meeting ?"

"Stubbornness I guess. I came home from Afghanistan too late to see Bert again. After meeting with attorney McCort and reading the many notes Bert left for me, then journals of his not so good life, it all got to me I guess. The injustice of it all. My Aunt Martha and old Bert raised me differently than what Bert endured. When I thought back on my upbringing I realized how wronged Bert was. I felt an urge down deep inside to make it all right again. Thinking about it these last few months, particularly my success with the teens, made me want to address everybody all at once instead of one at a time. Bert's memorial service was successful which just spurred me on. Meeting with the whole town just seemed logical."

"Your Marine training sure didn't hurt your decision either." McCallister replied with a smile. "Okay, Tom, you have convinced me of your honest intentions. I will admit I had some doubt before you spoke. As I mentioned I just wanted you not to get into trouble. Please keep me in the loop with Sam. Trust me we are both on your side."

~ ~ ~

Tom actually felt good because of the meeting with Judge McCallister. *"One more person to keep me on the straight and narrow."* he thought. The meeting took longer than expected so Tom decided to forego the New York City phone calls and went straight to Arlene. After her usual jump into his arms she inquired about the meeting to which Tom willingly filled her in. They also discussed and set a meeting date for three weeks ahead. It was determined that Eileen and Martha could follow through with getting the word out while Tom put a notice in the local paper

The next few weeks were uneventful save for a few meetings with the Youth Corps and of course more journal readings, girls included. One surprise did come for the guys and new girls of the Youth Corps. They were interviewed by the local newspaper at the barn job site. Apparently Judge McCallister posed the idea to the paper. The article was well received by the townspeople. Naturally the guys were thrilled. This meant the potential for new business and the public recognition Arlene was desiring could be easily achieved.

Chapter 33

The big day finally arrived. Tom was anxious but not nervous. He knew he was prepared except for the unknown. He also knew he would adapt to anything that came his way.

The publishing company committed to be there. The Chase Manhattan people also promised. He had his notes prepared and had them pretty much memorized. Sam was there for support and last, but far from least, he had Arlene. Even if the day was not successful he considered his life still complete with Arlene.

"I'm ready." he said to himself "Let's do it."

~ ~ ~

Tom arrived at the coliseum greeted by a more than half full parking lot and it was still early. He and Arlene entered the building by a side entrance and stayed out of sight till the appointed time. Then and only then did he alone approach the podium and switched on the microphone.

"Good afternoon and thank you for attending. I hope not to bore you too much but this is something that means a lot to me personally."

Tom looked over the audience but chose not to see individuals. He breathed deeply and started.

"Since I returned from my deployment in Afghanistan a lot of you have come to know me. It took a while but most of you have accepted me and my contribution to Tylerville. For this I am most grateful. But the real reason for today is to right a wrong that occurred many decades ago.

Tom could see the crowd was interested but questioning.

"A wrong that should not have happened, but did happen because of prejudice and rumors. Rumors that need not have started because they were not based on truth but supposed lies. They weren't even lies. Just made up stories based on not one thread of truth, started by one or two ignorant people who thought nothing of destroying another man's life that did not happen to fit with theirs at the time. That man was Bert Morrow. He was my friend and my father figure.

Bert Morrow's name, knowingly or unknowingly became a dirty word. These made up stories spread as most untrue rumors do. Save for a few who really knew Bert as the real man he was, not one person even tried to get to know the man. They believed the rumors rather then seek the truth. That was decades ago, yet the rumors and hate lives on.

I'm here today to hopefully change that. I want to show you and explain to you who Bert Morrow really was. He was an honest and proud man. Stubborn he admittedly was, but for a reason. Tylerville was his home. He was raised here. His mother was buried here. He wanted to be part of the town and contribute what ever he could to the town. But, and here's where the trouble began, because of a few misplaced malicious lies the man suffered a life of loneliness and total disrespect.

Did he give up. "NO" He became inwardly stronger. He was not going to allow hate to destroy him. He was ostracized by his own kind.

As you found out many weeks ago, the man was a war hero, yet no one in Tylerville even knew he was in the Korean War. Not just a war hero but a Medal of Honor winner. That alone should tell something of the kind of man he was.

The many years of ill-gotten lies were passed down without thought of the fact that others were being hurt by this negativism. I for one am living proof of that fact. I was born and raised here in Tylerville. Most of my proper upbringing was through the efforts of Bert Morrow who helped my aunt keep me on the straight and narrow. Most of you did not even know my name before a few months ago. I came to the forefront of this community because of the hate for Bert Morrow. When he passed away he left me his home and property and other things I am extremely proud to have. Unfortunately my connection to Bert also made me a prime target for harassment. Here again, no one sought to find the truth about a person. I must have been guilty by association. Some teens decided to redesign my garden when I was not home. Because that was always done to Bert because of the passed down lies that became the truth. You all know the results of that. These same teens I am now proud to call my friends. Why ? Because like Bert, I would not give in but reached out to know my silent gardeners. Truth was sought by both of us. We grew to know each other which was quite easy once you establish what the truth really is.

I am the product of old Bert. You know him as the ne'er do well, the no good, the trouble maker. Your prime example of one who never amounted to anything. I am the product of your hateful rumors and lies about a man you chose not to try to know.

I apologize for being long winded and I also apologize for sounding as if I wanted revenge. That's the last thing I want to be remembered for."

Tom paused looking at the crowd. He appeared to have their attention.

"You grew to know me and accept me and for that I am ever grateful. Now I want you to know Bert Morrow and accept him. Accept him as the friend to Tylerville he always was. If you will allow me your patience just a short while longer I want to share with you my friend Bert Morrow. To show you his unwavering love for the people of Tylerville."

There appeared to be no objection and interest was being peaked.

"Bert kept many journals during his life, the main theme being to record the ridicule he was the object of with out truth to substantiate the lies. I am willing to share these stories with you but now is not the time or place. Besides his personal journals Bert Morrow was an accomplished author. I know for a fact most of you have read his books, particularly the most recent. **"The True Cost of Ignorance and False Judgement"** by William McClain."

Tom lingered a moment to let that news sink in. Low mummers could be heard stirring through the crowd.

"Yes he wrote under a pseudonym. As you yourselves will attest to they were all best sellers. Mr. Alan McKeever is with us here today representing the publishing house of Bert's books. He will answer any inquiries you may have regarding the books. I also have with me today two gentlemen from Chase Manhattan Bank of New York City. A Mr. Richard Zancle and a Mr. Howard Martin. They also are willing to answer any questions you may have regarding what I am about to say. As most of you are aware, and as I previously mentioned all of Bert's novels were on the best seller list for extended periods of time."

Again Tom let there be a hesitation.

"Bert Morrow was a wealthy man."

Reading the facial expressions, Tom smiled internally.

"He could have let this be known but he did not want to be suddenly respected because he had money. All he wanted was to be respected because of the person that he was. It showed his deep compassion for the people of what he considered his home and gave him the idea to use this sudden found wealth to benefit them. A nameless foundation was set up through the Chase Manhattan Bank of New York City, For almost two decades now various businesses and Fraternal charitable organizations have benefitted from this foundation and will continue to do so for many years to come. Some businesses received interest free loans with extended pay back periods. Charitable organizations received anonymous donations, large and small. I will not name these establishments because a person's financial status is his or her own business. Let's just suffice it to say this was Bert's unknown generosity. Why ? Because this was his home and this was the only way he could help his community. It made him feel good in spite of his treatment due to the ignorance of a few. The ignorance of a few that tainted the many."

Tom took a long drink of water, mainly to pause and calm himself down. He looked over to Arlene who smiled and winked at him through tear filled eyes. He returned his attention back to the silent audience.

"All I ask of you today is to reflect on Bert Morrow's plight. Put yourself in his shoes over the last seven decades and ask yourself where is the justification for such ostracism. Think of the future and the future generations. Do you want to have this ignorance to continue based on absolutely nothing. Bert Morrow was a good, loving and decent man. He deserved more from this town. It is my fondest desire to see the end of this ill treatment of Bert Morrow today. No one cared to get to know Bert while he was alive, perhaps we can do it now that he has passed. I believe this town owes him that much. That's all he ever asked for.

Thank you for your patience and for the compassion I hope you will show my friend Bert. I know that would make Bert very happy."

Now with a genuine and loving smile Tom finished with.

"Enjoy your day and this great food. Thank you for allowing me your time."

He turned away from the microphone to where Arlene and the aunts were sitting. With his back to the audience Tom did not see Judge McCallister approach the podium. Suddenly hearing the unexpected voice startled him a bit. He turned his head toward the podium as Arlene and the aunts smothered him in hugs, teary eyed that they were.

Before any final discussions are made by this group I would like to add a few thoughts to what Mr. Thatcher just revealed.

Here the judge hesitated while everyone settled again.

"You all know me and most of you are aware of Tom Thatcher's compassionate generosity when it came to punishing the teens who destroyed his gardens and by their own admission were going to also tear apart his house. Bert's house. They did not know Bert, only his reputation passed down by older generations. Their unexplained hatred for Bert had no basis in fact. It was maliciously passed down from generation to generation. Tom Thatcher had his day in my court. Instead of prosecuting these teens for their scornful deed, he actually defended them and offered an alternative to social punishment. A program called Restorative Justice was founded for this town because of him. It gave these errant young men a way to change their behavior before their future was doomed. As it turned out they took to this program with a changed frame of mind. And unlike generations before them they sought the truth of Bert Morrow and the truth they found through a man not too much their senior.

"Just as an aside, I personally did research into the old court documents of court cases involving the supposedly guilty Bert Morrow, both school records and district court records. The very things the hurtful rumors were saying about Mr. Morrow had no basis in fact. He was totally innocent of every and all charges. He spent seven months in prison as an innocent man because of those hateful gossip mongers. For this alone we owe the man an apology. We can't give it to Bert, but we can offer it to Tom Thatcher who has worked so valiantly to clear the name of a man he loves as a father."

"Now back to this generation of youth. Rather than listen to me tell their story I thought it best you hear it direct from them."

Tom and Arlene stared open mouthed at the podium not believing what they just heard from Judge McCallister.

"Gentlemen, if you please." said the judge his arm outstretched welcoming the teens. The seven original participants in the Restorative Justice Program walked to the podium. They were all well groomed and looked impeccably dressed in suits and ties.

Tom, still in a state of unbelievable shock sat down with Arlene, pleased and upset at the same time. Judge McCallister remained just off center of the podium with his back to Tom.

Fred, as calm as could be was first to the microphone giving his name. He outlined in detail his and the others experience with Bert, admitting they never met the man. He and his friends were only acting on hand me down rumors and lies. It was the thing to do, pick on old Bert. He drifted into getting arrested while attempting to demolish Bert's gardens. Each young man followed suit continuing the story up to the present time. They spoke fondly of getting to know the real Bert through the stories presented by Tom who shared the journal anecdotes with them. How they learned other things that were now part of their everyday lives. Respect for others being first and foremost. The teens admissions held the audience spellbound.

The last to speak was Jonathon. Ace, in his own inimitable way was far from a public speaker. But on this day he impressed even Tom and Arlene. Lacking an advanced vocabulary he nevertheless put across his points succinctly and with a clarity that even surprised himself. He admitted with genuine humility all that he learned from Bert, indirectly through Tom in the treatment of others. He then continued to add other things he grasped through examples by Tom. He confessed how much better he was doing in school because of Tom and indirectly Bert.

Ace calmly and proudly ended his time at the podium with

"I am glad I got to know this guy Bert. He changed my whole life. I'm sorry I missed out on knowing him in person. This man will always have my respect. Thank you for listening to our story."

Ace returned to the group and they all quietly backed away and out of the spotlight. McCallister returned to the podium his court room seriousness showing on his face.

"Genuine honesty is hard to come by" was all he said then left the stage.

Silence filled the room until a lone clap was heard from the back. Slowly it caught on till the room was shaking with applause which lasted for many minutes. Tom was visibly shaking with emotion. Tears fell freely down his cheeks. He allowed himself to be enfolded in Arlene's arms. Eileen leaned close to him.

"Tis a good man you are Tommy love."

~ ~ ~ ~

It was more than an hour of people seeking out Tom to apologize individually for themselves and for generations past. Eventually the people left the coliseum. The boys and Judge McCallister were nowhere to be found. Tom was hurt and disappointed that he could not thank them in person. Arlene never left his side as they were the last two to exit. They silently walked to the parking lot. As Tom drove away from the coliseum he quietly said.

"I think I want to go straight home now, do you mind ?"

"Not at all my darling, I know this was a big day for you and I'm sure you need to rest ." Arlene whispered.

Chapter 34

The drive was quiet with Tom reflecting back on what he said at the meeting. Was it too much ? Not enough ? Was it too much of an attack ? Was it too soft an approach ? He smiled at the biggest surprise - Judge McCallister and the guys. He never expected that sort of backing.

Turning into his drive he found five vehicles already there. He pulled in as far as he could then he and Arlene walked the balance of the way. Awkward surprise showed on both faces as they stared in disbelief at the gathering around the picnic table. The Judge and his wife, Sam McCort and his wife, Eileen and Martha and the whole of the Youth Corps including the two new girls.

Byron McCallister was first to speak. Moving to and addressing Tom with an outstretched hand.

"My congratulations Tom, I believe you have won the day."

Yet again Tom's emotions took over allowing tears to flow.

"I don't know sir, I really could not judge the outcome, but I do sincerely want to thank you for your support."

Turning to the teens he smiled and with a shaky voice mouthed -

"Thank You. I don't know how I'll ever repay you for your loyalty."

"You already have Mr. T. By believing in us when no one else did." confirmed Fred.

Ace stepped up. "We have one more thing the Youth Corps needs your approval on. Yours and Miss Arlene's."

"And what's that Jonathon ?"

"Well sir we held a meeting and came up with a unanimous decision. We are changing the name of our group from the Tylerville Youth Corps to - -"

Here he paused for a few seconds.

""The Bert Morrow Youth Corps." And our ranks are open to any and all teens without discrimination. Do we have your approval ?"

Aware of Tom's choked up state Arlene approached Ace taking his face in both hands and saying.

"Of course you have his approval. And I know you have Bert's approval also.

Then she kissed him on the mouth leaving him red faced. She proceeded to all the teens and kissed them thanking each one individually.

The End
&
A New Beginning

Also by Author

<u>Simple Short Stories</u>
(To tingle the imagination)

<u>Simple Short Stories II</u>
(To further tingle the imagination)

<u>The Dead Living Mummy</u>
(An epic story of a lost city
that ended with a lost mind)

<u>The Innocent Murder</u>
(The tranquility of an English Manor
upset by a sudden death)

<u>The Ancient Ones</u>
(Another adventure with Eric Dexter
of The Dead Living Mummy)

<u>The Librarian Checked Out</u>
(A murder Mystery)

<u>The Other Planet Earth</u>
(Travel Between Worlds)

~ ~ ~ ~

<u>Children's Stories</u>
(Eight adventures with Squiggy the Squirrel)

1- The Garden Mystery
2- The Christmas Garland Mystery
3- The New Land
4- New Friends
5- Squiggy and the Bear
6- Squiggy and the Storm
7- The Next Generation
8- Squiggy's Maine Vacation